Her uncle may not have been the greatest magician who had ever held the highly honored position of Wizard of Dark Street—some even criticized his magical abilities as downright mediocre—but he was surely the greatest uncle and guardian a girl like Oona could have hoped for. And besides, he had, after all, agreed to let her out of her magical obligations so that she might better pursue her true interest in detective work. What more could she have asked from him? So Oona had agreed, no more snooping around deadly criminals . . . if she could help it.

OTHER EGMONT USA BOOKS YOU MAY ENJOY

Guinea Dog
by Patrick Jennings

Popular Clone: The Clone Chronicles #1
by M.E. Castle

The CyberSkunk Files #1: The Rendering
by Joel Naftali

The Paradise Trap
by Catherine Jinks

The Wizard of Dark Street

AN OONA CRATE MYSTERY

SHAWN THOMAS ODYSSEY

EGMONT
USA
NEW YORK

EGMONT

We bring stories to life

First published by Egmont USA, 2011
This paperback edition published by Egmont USA, 2012
443 Park Avenue South, Suite 806
New York, NY 10016

1 3 5 7 9 8 6 4 2

www.egmontusa.com
www.thewizardofdarkstreet.com

THE LIBRARY OF CONGRESS HAS CATALOGED
THE HARDCOVER EDITION AS FOLLOWS:
Odyssey, Shawn Thomas.
The Wizard of Dark Street : an Oona Crate mystery / Shawn Thomas Odyssey.
p. cm.
Summary: In 1877, in an enchantment shop on the last of the Faerie roads
linking New York City to the Land of the Fey, just after twelve-year-old
Oona opts to relinquish her apprenticeship to her uncle, the Wizard,
and become a detective, her uncle is stabbed, testing her skills.
ISBN 978-1-60684-143-3 (hardcover) — ISBN 978-1-60684-277-5 (electronic book)
[1. Wizards—Fiction. 2. Magic—Fiction. 3. Apprentices—Fiction. 4. Uncles—
Fiction. 5. Orphans—Fiction. 6. Mystery and detective stories.] I. Title.
PZ7.O258Wiz 2011
[Fic]—dc22
2011002496

Paperback ISBN 978-1-60684-386-4

Printed in the United States of America

For Anne, Barbara, and Shari.
The magic is real.

←——————→

Be sure to check out Shawn Thomas Odyssey's
mysterious performances and curiously concocted
music videos, all created specifically for this book,
at www.thewizardofdarkstreet.com.

On the fourth of November, 1876,

the Wizard of Dark Street placed the following advertisement in the classified section of the *New York Times*:

WANTED: ONE WIZARD'S APPRENTICE.

Must be punctual, literate, courageous, clever, imaginative, adventurous, mysterious, open-minded, openhearted, intuitive, and above all else must be trusted with some of the most secret and powerful knowledge in this world or any other.

No experience necessary.

Please send résumé to:

Pendulum House, Number 19

Dark Street, on the Drift

New York, New York (Little London Town)

Within three days of the advertisement's publication, the New York City post office received a grand total of 3,492 letters addressed to Pendulum House, Number 19. To the postmaster's great displeasure and utter vexation, no Dark Street could be found on any of the regular route maps, city plans, or postal grids. Nor could anyone recall ever having heard of a Little London Town located anywhere within New York City. The letters were stamped ADDRESS UNKNOWN and returned to their original senders.

Six Months Later

CHAPTER ONE

Oona and Deacon

(Monday, May 14, 1877)

"Magic is a fickle thing," said twelve-year-old Oona Crate. "I prefer things that work."

Deacon stood upon her shoulder, silent and foreboding. Black as midnight and glossy as ink, the magnificent enchanted raven ruffled his feathers as the two of them peered curiously through the window of The Dark Street Enchantment Shop, the storefront where Oona's uncle sold his latest bits of magical wonder. Behind the shop's cobwebby windows could be found all manner of mysterious things: charmed feather dusters that giggled when dusting, and sponges that gargled a tune. Ever-burning lamps and never-melting ice—two of the Wizard's best sellers—lined the shelves, ready for purchase and gift wrapping. But Oona had little interest in entering the shop today. Nor did anyone else, it would seem.

The storekeeper, Mr. Alpert, a grizzled old man with an enormous overbite and glasses as large and round as tea saucers, sat idly at the front counter, his magnified eyelids drooping as if he might doze off at any moment. From the look of the empty store, one might begin to think that magic was about as exciting as watching fruit dry on a windowsill. Not very exciting at all. And quite honestly, the store itself looked in dire need of a good paint job.

Next door, however, a handsome, newly painted storefront stood squarely between the enchantment shop and the shoemaker's shop on the other side. With its doors open wide, the shop in the middle was a bustle of activity. A large sign over the shiny front window advertised: MR. WILBER'S WORLD OF MODERN WONDERS. Shoppers and lookie-loos alike jostled to get out of one another's way as they pressed through the doors of Mr. Wilber's fantastic shop, which sold everything from the latest in modern toothbrushes and bicycles to photographic equipment and spectacular newfangled waffle irons. Nearly any technologically advanced gadget to have come out in the present year of 1877 could be found at Mr. Wilber's World of Modern Wonders.

Mr. Wilber, a gawky toothpick of a man with a flat

face and highly pronounced Adam's apple, never looked bored, such as Mr. Alpert so often did, and Oona supposed that this was because Mr. Wilber was far too busy trying to keep up on the demands of his technology-craving customers.

Oona sighed. The day was bright and the air clean. The smell of spring leaves and dusty cobblestones permeated every shadowy corner of the street. Gazing at her reflection in the enchantment shop window, Oona straightened the lace-trimmed bonnet on her head before running her fingers through the front of her hair. The hair had grown little, if at all, since the incident with the guillotine the previous night, and she couldn't keep from readjusting her headpiece to flatten her hair down—a near impossible proposition.

"You've got to be more careful!" That had been her uncle's advice on the subject of her nearly getting her head chopped off. His words had been direct, and his tone uncharacteristically stern. "I will only agree to this detective business of yours if you promise not to go getting yourself into such terrible trouble. I mean it, Oona! Igregious Goodfellow is a scoundrel, a thief, and a homicidal maniac all rolled into one. You're incredibly lucky that it was only your hair that got caught in that horrible man's guillotine. You should never have followed him to his secret hideout. The moment you discovered he was the Horton Family Jewelry Store thief, you should have left matters to the police."

Oona had rolled her eyes at that. Surely her uncle knew better than to place his faith in the police. For nearly three years, ever since Head Inspector White had taken over the top position, the Dark Street Police Department had become an utter joke in the eyes of both law-abiding citizens and criminals alike. It was no secret that crime on the street was at an all-time high.

"You are lucky that you managed to slip out of those ropes before that madman released the blade," her uncle had continued in a stern voice, "and that Deacon got to the police as quickly as he did, or . . . or . . ." The Wizard sighed, shaking his head. "You are still a child, Oona. And you are not your father."

Those words had hurt. Oona had needed to bite her tongue to keep from telling the Wizard that *he* was not her father either, and that her father was dead, buried six feet under the ground in the Dark Street Cemetery. But why bring that up? It would only have upset him.

Her uncle may not have been the greatest magician who had ever held the highly honored position of Wizard of Dark Street—some even criticized his magical abilities as downright mediocre—but he was surely the greatest uncle and guardian a girl like Oona could have hoped for. And besides, he had, after all, agreed to let her out of her magical obligations so that she might better pursue her true interest in detective work. What more could she have asked from him? So Oona had agreed, no more snooping around deadly criminals . . . if she could help it.

Presently, she turned her gaze north, and before her lay all of Dark Street, the last of the thirteen Faerie roads, connecting the World of Man to the fabled Land of Faerie. A broad cobblestone avenue more than thirteen miles long, the street stretched out in a continuous line, a world unto itself, unbroken by cross streets or intersections. The buildings rose up from the edges of the sidewalks like crooked teeth crammed into a mouth too small to fit. They listed and leaned against one another for support, giving the impression that if one of the buildings should ever fall down, then all of the others would quickly follow, toppling one by one like dominoes.

She considered the street for a moment, this ancient world between worlds, with its enormous Glass Gates at one end and the equally vast Iron Gates at the other. And yet of these two gateways, only the Iron Gates ever opened, and then only once a night, upon the stroke of midnight, when the massive doors would swing inward on hinges as big as houses, opening for a single minute upon the sprawling, ambitious city of New York. For the amount of time it took a second hand to travel around the face of a clock, the Iron Gates remained open to any who should choose to venture across their enchanted threshold. Few ever did. Few ever even noticed.

In a city such as New York, even at midnight, the people were too busy getting from one place to another to observe anything out of the ordinary. And those who did see the street suddenly appear out of nowhere might simply pretend that it was not there at all. They might turn their faces, and when they looked again, the street would be gone, and they would tell themselves that it had been a trick of the light. Nothing more. The children of New York would surely have been more apt to see the street than adults, but of course, at midnight most good little children were tucked safely away into their beds, dreaming of stranger places still.

But if an outsider *had* ventured through the gates, what he or she would have found was a place not so different than the city from which they had just come. A place filled with everyday people going about their everyday lives—lives of simple pleasures and skullduggery alike. They might first notice how the majority of residents on the street carried on their conversations in various British accents, instead of American ones, and how some of the inhabitants referred to the street as Little London Town. A visitor might then observe how, no matter the season in New York, freezing cold or blisteringly hot, the temperature on Dark Street would be breezy and mild, just cool enough for a jacket or shawl. Or it might be pouring rain on the street, yet New York would be dry as a bone. And the peculiarities would not stop there, for upon closer examination the outsider would find that, here, the shadows appeared slightly darker, so that they might think twice before stepping on them, for fear of falling in. They would discover a world where the blue of the sky in daytime appeared almost purple, and by night the stars shone bright enough to read by. It was a place as ancient as the wind, where candlestick trees replaced light posts, and street clocks told jokes as well as time.

Yet to the sensitive tourist, even more striking than the discovery of new and enchanted things, there was the subtle sense of magic lost—a street that had forgotten more magic than drops of rain had fallen to the earth. It was an ancient road, from time before time. Since before the construction of the Iron and Glass Gates, before the building of Pendulum House, and the naming of the first Wizard, and even before the great Magicians of Old fought their terrible war against the armies of the mighty Queen of Faerie, Dark Street existed. In one form or another it had always been there, a bridge between the fantastic and the ordinary, between magic and reason, between the Land of the Fay and the city that never sleeps.

Oona returned her attention to the enchantment shop window and stared for a moment at her reflection in the wobbly glass. Large green eyes with thick, curling lashes blinked as they took in the heart shape of her face, and the full-skirted, gray dress that cinched in around her waist. Really, her uncle had been right. What had she been thinking to believe that she, a slight four-foot-three-inch-tall girl, could ever have hoped to apprehend a dastardly lunatic like Igregious Goodfellow, the Horton Family Jewelry Store thief? At twelve years old she was still a child in the eyes of Dark Street society, and yet her birthday was only three months away. Thirteen was a special age for a girl on Dark Street. It was the age when she became a lady proper, the age at which many girls entered the Academy of Fine Young Ladies. It was a prospect that Oona had no interest in. She preferred to continue her independent studies with Deacon. The raven was, in her eyes, the best teacher on Dark Street.

As it nearly always did, the thought of her birthday sent a shock of guilt through her, bringing with it a wave of sadness that seemed to make the daylight dim slightly, and turn the soft breeze to a chill. The image of her mother's wondrous face drifted through her mind like a distant ghost—those great green eyes so similar to Oona's own, with a bright, radiant smile like a gleam of sunlight—and another image, this one of Oona's baby sister, too small and too young even to walk, clapping her tiny hands in her mother's arms. The image was burned into Oona's memory like a cruel scar: the mother and the baby beneath an enormous fig tree, its leaves rustling in the breeze as the magic lights danced around them, swirling faster, and faster, and then . . .

Oona quickly shoved the thought away. She swallowed a lump in her throat and thrust her finger in the air. "I prefer science, Deacon! Not spells, and wands, and magic rings. Give me facts. Give me logic. Give me the most incomprehensible riddle . . . the most complicated problem. That is what I love."

Her tone was markedly serious, and her London Town accent both highly educated and refined.

Deacon dug his talons into her shoulder, ruffling his thick black feathers as the two of them began to stroll up Dark Street in the direction of Pendulum House. Horse-drawn carriages clattered and clacked up and down the broad avenue, and the sidewalks bustled with pedestrians, all of them hurrying this way or that, hardly taking notice of the girl with the chopped hair and the raven on her shoulder. Surely they had all seen her before. She was the Wizard's niece after all. His apprentice. More than that, however, she was the so-called Natural Magician: a freak of nature so rare that in every hundred years only one might be born.

"You are very special, Oona," the Wizard had explained to her nearly five years ago on her first day as his new apprentice. Several months past her eighth birthday, she'd listened eagerly to the gray-bearded man she so revered, her father's older brother. "I myself am what is called a *Learned* Magician. Like nearly all the magicians who have ever lived, I have had to learn magic through decades of hard scholarship and training. Someone like myself must *force* magic to do my will. But a *Natural* Magician such as you, Oona, is a human being born with the extraordinary magical powers of a faerie. No one quite knows why. Indeed, some believe that Natural Magicians have active faerie blood in their veins, but so far as I know, that is but a rumor. And yet, unlike faeries, who are born with the instincts and know-how to control their spectacular magic, Natural Magicians must *learn* to handle their powers. They must be taught. You must be trained."

And Oona had trained. For nearly two years the Wizard had schooled her. She lived with him in the great Pendulum House, assisting him, absorbing all she could, honing her skills so that one day she might become the next great Wizard, which was the title given to the head of all magical activity on Dark Street, and the protector of the World of Man.

"What good is being the head of magical activity," Oona had once asked the Wizard, "when no one on

Dark Street does any magic? There aren't any magicians anymore, Uncle, except for you and me. I read in the *Encyclopedia Arcanna* that Learned Magicians used to number in the thousands, both on Dark Street and in the World of Man."

The Wizard nodded. "Yes, but that was nearly five hundred years ago. After the end of the Great Faerie War—after Oswald the Great closed the Glass Gates, cutting Dark Street off from Faerie—the magic began to weaken. People eventually lost interest in the old ways, and, as it is said, the world moved on. You are correct, Oona, that there is less interest in magic than there ever has been before. Some would even call magic impractical. But there are still those out there who might find some bit of spell work in a book and attempt to use it. There are still innumerable magical objects out there, many of them faerie-made bits of mischief left over from five hundred years ago. It is the Wizard's job to handle such occurrences when they arise, and of course to protect the World of Man, should the Glass Gates ever be broken and the Land of Faerie once again be opened. It is an important job we do, keeping magic alive. Do you believe that?"

On that day, which now seemed like a lifetime ago, Oona had nodded that she did believe. But that would all change. It would change a year and a half later, the very day she'd turned ten years old, when the sudden and hard truth that magic could not be trusted proved itself to Oona once and for all.

←——————→

Presently, Oona paused to examine one of the famed Dark Street candlestick trees. An oddity like no other, the trees lined the shopping district of the boulevard like living lampposts, their flames flickering faintly against the bright light of day. Between two of the branches, a plump little spider worked tirelessly in the late-morning breeze. Oona reached into one of her dress pockets. Though she may not have possessed the most fashionable sort of dresses, Oona found the multitude of pockets sewn into the folds of her skirts to be quite handy. They allowed her to carry around all sorts of useful objects: a needle stuck in a bit of cork, a small ball of string, red phosphorus matches, a bit of metal wire she'd used to pick the lock on Igregious Goodfellow's hideout, paper and pencil, and many other functional things that never failed to come in handy.

She removed a small magnifying glass and used it to study the web. The spider worked away, seemingly unaware of Oona's huge eye leaning in close to observe. The strangeness of a tree that sprouted candles instead of fruit did little to capture Oona's interest, yet the complex pattern and dazzling intricacy of the spider's web drew her curiosity in like iron shavings to a magnet; each strand of the web was a trap, yet also a clue; each clue connected to another, all of them spiraling into the center, where the core of the mystery resided.

It's beautiful, Oona thought. *Meticulous and reliable.*

At last she pulled away from the web and looked at the magnifying glass itself. She held it up, watching the sun glint off the gold rim. The well-worn handle was lacquered oak, and the two-and-a-half-inch-wide glass was flawless. This had been her father's very own magnifying glass, and sometimes when she looked through it she could imagine that she was seeing through his eyes. It was possibly the dearest possession she owned.

She pocketed the glass and started up the street once more, tossing her hand in a dismissive gesture. "So, Deacon, it would seem that the day I have been waiting for has finally arrived. Tonight is the Choosing." At just the mention of it, Oona could feel her heartbeat quicken and her palms go wet, though whether from nerves or excitement she could not have said. Rubbing her sticky hands together, she said: "Tonight my uncle chooses my replacement."

Deacon bristled on her shoulder. "Hmm" was his only reply.

Oona gave him a sideways glance. "I take it you are not pleased. Tell me, Deacon. Why should I be the least bit upset about giving up my position as Uncle Alexander's apprentice?"

Deacon made a cawing sound as if this was all he intended to add to the conversation, but finally he spoke.

"Perhaps you should be upset because you've trained for the position since you were eight years old, the youngest apprentice ever." His tone of voice was that of someone who undoubtedly has had the same conversation countless times before. "Perhaps because—despite your outright refusal to perform any magic whatsoever—you are the most competent and informed talent to have held the position in over a hundred years. Or perhaps because your uncle is so desperate to find someone to replace you that six months ago he placed an advertisement in the *New York Times*. It's simply unheard of."

"But don't you see, Deacon?" Oona said. "This is the perfect opportunity for me to start my dream."

"I take it you are speaking of The Dark Street Detective Agency?"

"It does have a nice ring to it, don't you think?"

Deacon cocked his head to one side. "It is rather plain, if you ask me, but it is your dream, not mine. And I must confess, I don't understand how finding lost puppies could possibly be any more exciting than performing complicated magic."

"But that's just the thing!" Oona said so loudly

that several pedestrians glanced in her direction before continuing on their way. "At least in finding lost puppies there is a point to be accomplished," she said. "A sequence of events happens, and I am able to follow those events through a series of clues. That, Deacon, is true purpose! What use is there in floating teacups and silly love potions?"

"There is more to magic than that, and you know it," Deacon said. "What about the great Magicians of Old?"

Oona shook her head. "Ancient history."

"But I myself am a product of magic," Deacon insisted. "Your uncle created me as a present for your eleventh birthday, and there is nothing silly about me."

Oona raised a playful eyebrow at him. "I sometimes wonder why my uncle created a *raven* encyclopedia for me, rather than an owl. Owls are such noble creatures . . . if only in appearance. Or perhaps a magpie, which could better understand the emotions of a girl. Or even . . . a rook."

"A rook?" Deacon bristled, ruffling his feathers indignantly. "A rook couldn't hold half a haiku in its pea-size brain," he continued, "let alone the entire *Encyclopedia Arcanna*, *The Complete Oxford English Dictionary*, and *The Dark Street Who's Who: 36 B.C. to Present*. There is no other bird in all the world more intelligent than a raven. You are simply taking your present frustrations out on me."

Oona nodded. It was true. Deacon was a wealth of information. The *Encyclopedia Arcanna* was perhaps the most comprehensive set of texts to be found on nearly all things magical, and the dictionary came in quite handy, especially when she was writing angry letters to the Dark Street Council about the stupidity of the police department. But it was the *Who's Who* that Oona found to be the most fascinating book in Deacon's memory, because the *Who's Who* was a set of reference books that briefly described the lives of nearly every inhabitant of Dark Street, alive or dead. It was truly handy to have around. And in spite of her baited words, Oona was quite certain that Deacon had become far more to her than just some novelty pet—a bird that could talk. He was unique, there was no denying that, as there were no other talking birds like him to be found anywhere in all of the world, so far as Oona knew, but he was more than just that. By all accounts, he was a true friend, and after nearly two years of his company, she could not imagine life without him.

The two of them walked on in silence for several minutes before coming to a stop in front of an empty lot. The buildings on this part of the street were so crooked and crowded together—with shops below and apartment houses above—that this sudden empty space between the buildings seemed almost startling to behold. In the center of the vacant lot stood a barren mound of dirt. Flanked by a theater on one side and an apothecary on the other, the unsightly hill rose up several feet from the sidewalk, where a leafless, gnarled-looking tree grew at its top like a twisted claw. A twelve-foot wall of crumbly stones cut across the back of the lot, and Oona felt a shiver run down her arms.

"Take this, for instance," she said. "Witch Hill. It is a complete mystery waiting to be solved. How many witches live inside? What do they do in there? Do they work magic, or are they simply called witches because people fear them? No one knows. Why is it that when one of the witches comes out, it is always one of the girls, and never a full-grown witch? And of course, the most pressing question: Why do they not plant a more appealing tree atop of their home, such as an apple tree or a nice willow?"

"According to the *Encyclopedia Arcanna*," Deacon said, "the original witches of Witch Hill were once highly active magicians on Dark Street. They were called the Sisterhood of the Witch, but that was hundreds of years ago, and when the Glass Gates were shut, they all moved underground. The following generations all stayed there. The entrance to the hill appears to be enchanted, so that when one of them does come out, no one can see where she came from."

"Yes, yes, I know all of this," Oona said, and then

began to sing the lyrics to a traditional Dark Street children's rhyme.

The witches moved beneath the hill
And to this day they live there still
What they do, you'll never know
You'll never see them once they've grown
For only girls are seen up top
Upon the street and in the shops
A mystery that is worth unearthing
How the witches keep a-birthing
All alone, a woman's clan
Without the benefit of man

Oona paused a moment before adding: "I tell you, Deacon, sometimes I believe that this street is so full of mysteries that I should like to—"

But a sudden fit of shouting cut her short. Oona whirled around, searching for whoever was making such an awful racket. Peering across the street, her eyes widened as they took in the scene. She shook her head at first, not understanding, and then, like the unveiling of some strange new work of art, the mystery spread out before her, opening its darkened doors and inviting her in.

←——————→

The first thing she noticed was an enormous top hat taking up most of the sidewalk across the street. It stood nearly seven feet tall and sat at the base of the vast granite steps in front of the Museum of Magical History. The hat appeared to be carved out of stone, and Oona guessed it to be part of some effort to draw people inside the museum. Immense as it was, the museum was a seldom-visited place, and it could be safely said that if modern-day magic could not capture the public's interest, then certainly the history of magic was even less likely to do so.

The steps to the museum were usually as empty as a poor man's belly, and yet today, a tall, gaunt-looking man with a waxed mustache stood on the topmost step. Stranger still, the man appeared to be having some sort of argument with someone, except that there was no one nearby for him to be arguing with. The fingers of his left hand clenched tightly around a folded red umbrella, while his free hand waved wildly in the air. Oona could hear the peculiar man shouting something, but she couldn't make out the words.

The man slowly began to descend the steps, pointing at some invisible person with the tip of the red umbrella. He was halfway down the stone staircase when Oona asked: "Who is that madman, Deacon?"

Deacon peered across the street. "According to the Dark Street *Who's Who*, his name is Hector Grimsbee. He was an actor, a member of the Dark Street Theater until just last year when a scandal got him kicked out. It had something to do with a sandbag and a director's head. The *Who's Who* also mentions that he has been blind since birth."

"Blind since birth?" Oona asked. Her heart lurched as she watched the man make his way back up several of the stone stairs, his arms continuing to flail in all directions. "That's quite dangerous. And who is he arguing with?"

"I haven't a clue, though perhaps—" But a sharp cry cut Deacon short. A woman's shriek.

Oona's head jerked around. She saw no one in obvious distress: only a scattering of pedestrians, many of whom, like her, were looking around to discover who had screamed. Perhaps it had not been a woman's scream after all, she considered, and then wondered if the sound had perchance come from Hector Grimsbee, and she simply hadn't realized it. But when she turned back to the museum, the blind man was suddenly gone. She scanned the sidewalk in both directions, but Grimsbee was nowhere to be seen.

"Did you see that?" Oona asked.

"What?" asked Deacon.

"The blind man on the steps. He just disappeared."

"Nonsense," Deacon said. "There are no records of a person being able to simply disappear. At least not in recent times. Such arcane magic as invisibility and human teleportation vanished with the last of the Magicians of Old nearly five hundred years ago."

"Then where is he?" Oona asked. "I only looked away for a few seconds."

"He must have gone in the museum," Deacon reasoned.

Oona hesitated to agree. It seemed unlikely that the blind man could have moved so fast, but after a moment's consideration, she nodded. "That seems to be the only logical explanation."

A second shout, this one a clear cry for help, pulled her attention to the dress shop next door. The shop was squashed between a handbag store to the left and the museum on the right. A sign above the window read: MADAME IREE'S BOUTIQUE FOR FINE LADIES.

A girl of Oona's own age, or perhaps a little older, stood in the center of the arched doorway. Her golden hair fell down the sides of her cheeks in curling locks. She wore a tightly corseted dress with red and gold stripes, and she was dazzling to behold. Though Oona had never met the girl before, she recognized her to be Isadora Iree, the daughter of Madame Iree, the most famous dressmaker on all of Dark Street.

"Help!" Isadora shouted. "Police! Madame Iree's has been robbed! The dresses are all gone! Help!"

Oona's heart skipped a beat, and her eyes widened with excitement. "A case, Deacon!"

And then just as quickly, her mouth turned to a frown. Head Inspector White was striding purposefully up the sidewalk, his black coattails billowing out behind him, his pale white face like a reflector in the sunlight.

"Young lady!" the inspector shouted. "I am the police. Now stop shouting 'help,' or I'll have to cite you for unnecessary repetition."

Oona's hands flew to her hips. "There is no such law," she said, though not loud enough to be heard from across the street.

Deacon, who knew Oona all to well, said: "Perhaps we should let the police handle this . . . alone. Remember what you promised your uncle."

Oona's forehead wrinkled above her nose. "What I told Uncle Alexander, Deacon, is that I would keep away from deadly criminals. How many deadly criminals do you think steal dresses?"

"Any criminal can be deadly," Deacon said.

Oona paused. There was certainly truth to Deacon's words. Hadn't her own father been killed while attempting to apprehend a pair of thieves? And *he* had been the Head Inspector of the Dark Street Police Department— Inspector White's very own predecessor. Torn between keeping her promise to her uncle and making sure Inspector White didn't bungle the case, an idea popped into her head like a mischievous sprite.

She grinned as she stepped from the curb to cross the street. "I believe I will keep my promise, Deacon. It's just that . . . Well, there is the little matter of the masquerade."

Deacon shook his head, clearly confused at the sudden change of subject. "The Dark Street Annual Midnight Masquerade?" he replied. "You are referring to the dance held at Oswald Park?"

She swerved to step around several potholes in the street. "You have deduced correctly, Deacon."

"I don't understand," Deacon said. "The ball is tomorrow night, and you've never expressed any interest in attending . . . not this year or any other."

Oona shook her head. "You see, Deacon, you know nothing of the problems of a girl. Nothing at all. I've already quite made up my mind. I *will* be attending the masquerade."

"And when did you come to that decision?" Deacon asked, though he sounded as if he already knew the answer.

"Why . . . just now," she replied innocently, and then added: "But there is one tiny problem."

"And that is?" Deacon asked dryly.

Oona sighed. "It seems I have absolutely nothing to wear!"

With that, Oona strode through the arched doorway into Madame Iree's Boutique for Fine Ladies.

CHAPTER TWO

The Missing Dresses

Four well-dressed ladies huddled close together in the front room of Madame Iree's Boutique for Fine Ladies. They stood near the sign in the window that read: OPEN BY APPOINTMENT ONLY.

A single dress stood in the window. It was a small dress, clearly made for the likes of someone smaller than Oona, but all the same, the moment she entered the shop, the dress drew in her gaze. The fabric seemed to shine with a light all its own, and if Oona had been asked to describe the color, she would not have been able to choose. One moment it appeared a shimmery blue, the next a dazzling shade of green, and for an instant Oona found herself wishing that the dress weren't so small, otherwise she should very much like to have it.

Deacon adjusted his position on her shoulder, and she pulled her gaze away from the dress, back to the shop.

Madame Iree was a tall, matronly woman with a prodigious bosom. She wore the most opulent, jewel-studded dress Oona had ever seen, and she stood apart from the other ladies, looking as if she might faint at any moment. On her head she wore a hat that sprouted so many exotic feathers, it looked like it might take flight at any moment. Her picturesque face was lined with concern, and Isadora stood at her mother's side, patting her hand, trying to console her.

Oona took in the shop. For years it had been a fancy of hers to venture into Madame Iree's and try on some of the most beautiful dresses on all of Dark Street. But Madame Iree was extremely selective of her clientele. The shop was not at all what Oona had expected. The front room was set up for tea service, with two cloth-covered tables surrounded by chairs near the front window. A glass case containing various accessories stood near one red-and-gold-striped wall, and an open doorway at the far end of the room led into another room at the back. The air smelled of lavender potpourri.

"What has happened?" Oona asked.

Inspector White's impossibly white face poked out of

the doorway at the back of the store and was quickly followed by his lanky body. "I'll be asking the questions!" he said as he stepped through the threshold, nearly tripping over his own feet in the process. He swept his suspicious gaze around the room. "What sort of illegal activity has been going on in here?"

"We were having tea," said Isadora. "I already explained that to you, Inspector, before you went back there to see the showroom."

"Tea?" said the inspector. "And do you expect me to believe that?"

"Well . . . yes," said Isadora, pointing toward the empty cups on the tables.

"Hmm," the inspector intoned. "I thought this was a dress shop, not a tea shop."

Madame Iree looked all at once highly irritated on top of being distraught. "We sometimes have tea here. But that is not the point. Inspector, someone has stolen my dresses!"

The inspector noticed Oona standing near the front entrance. His eyes narrowed. "What are you doing here, Miss Crate? I've told you before to stay out of police affairs."

Oona swallowed hard, but the lie was already upon her lips. "I was shopping for a dress for the masquerade tomorrow night."

And making sure you don't bungle this case, she thought to herself.

"You?" said Isadora Iree. She released her mother's hand and cast a long look over Oona. The girl did not appear impressed. Oona cleared her throat nervously as Isadora's disapproving eyes came to a stop at the top of her head. Oona adjusted her bonnet in an attempt to flatten down the front of her chopped hair. Isadora smirked. "I'm afraid you cannot shop here. Not unless you are a student or an alumna of the Academy of Fine Young Ladies." She considered Oona for another moment, her pretty little nose squinching up as if Oona were giving off an undesirable smell. "Which I'm guessing you are not. I mean, just look at that hair."

Several of the older ladies tutted their agreement, and Oona could feel her face flush with embarrassment. Before she could find a suitable reply, however, Isadora added: "In case you didn't know, the word *alumna* means a female who has graduated from the academy."

Oona frowned. She knew what the word *alumna* meant, and she also knew that Madame Iree sold dresses exclusively to the academy and its lifelong members. It was for this reason that Oona had never entered the shop before today. Presently, she looked around at the other ladies' faces and began to wonder if she actually wanted to offer her help at all. Noses raised, they stared at her with an air of both surprise and contempt, as if she had soiled their beloved store by simply stepping inside. She was nearly ready to turn right around and leave them all to the idiocy of Inspector White—*Who cares about their stupid dresses, anyway?* she thought—when Deacon spoke from her shoulder.

"When did the theft occur?" he asked.

"It is strange enough that your bird can talk, Miss Crate," said the inspector, "but I will not have him asking ridiculous questions at my crime scene. Is that under- stood?" He turned back to Madame Iree. "Now . . . when did it happen?"

"Sometime in the last hour," said Madame Iree. "We were all out here in the front room having tea." She pointed toward the door at the back of the store. "The door to the showroom was locked shut, as it always is when I am not showing a dress. And then around two o'clock, Isadora wanted to show the ladies the gown she would be wearing tomorrow night to the Midnight Masquerade. But when I unlocked the showroom door, I found . . . I found . . ."

She gestured weakly toward the door. "The dresses are all gone. They were all in there an hour ago when I locked the door, but now . . . oh, dear . . . now the only dress left is the one in the window."

The ladies all turned to admire the dress in the

window, and for a long moment the room was silent, as if the dress had somehow hypnotized them. Madame Iree breathed a deep sigh. "At least that one was spared."

"It truly is a masterpiece, Mother," said Isadora. "I wish it weren't so small, or I should like to wear it to the masquerade."

"I told you, Isadora," said Madame Iree, quite irritably, "the glinting cloth I used to construct the dress was the last remnant of a six-hundred-year-old faerie-enchanted fabric. It was one of a kind, and there was only enough cloth to make a dress for a younger girl. Certainly younger than anyone at the academy." Madame Iree sighed. "That is why I placed it in the window. It is no more than a showpiece, I'm afraid. Oh, what I would give for a bit of turlock root, so that I might grow younger and wear the dress, even for an hour." The four older ladies gave a collective sigh, as if this idea were quite appealing to them as well.

"Turlock root is a mystical root known for its powers of reversing the aging process," Deacon said, apparently unable to keep from dispensing his vast knowledge of the magical world. "But it grows only in the Land of Faerie."

Oona was sorely tempted to point out to him that there was turlock root growing in the inner garden at Pendulum House, along with countless other mystical plants native solely to the Land of Faerie. But then again, the Wizard's house was the only structure outside of Faerie that had been built upon imported Faerie soil. Some of the plants were quite powerful, and highly dangerous, which was why the inner garden was kept secret from anyone other than the Wizard and his apprentice.

"Did I not tell you to keep that bird quiet?" Inspector White nearly shouted.

Madame Iree slapped an open palm to her chest. "All my precious dresses, gone!"

The four ladies fell in around the dressmaker like a flock of chickens consoling a mother hen.

The inspector snapped his fingers, a look of sudden realization flashing across his face. He turned dramatically on his heel and made his way back into the showroom. While everyone else was distracted with consoling Madame Iree, Oona seized the moment. She quickly crossed through the front of the shop and stopped in the doorway to the next room.

Several ever-burning lamps hung against the walls, illuminating the showroom in a ghostly light, while a beautiful crystal chandelier hung unlit from the center of the ceiling. At present, the room was nothing more than a gathering place for naked mannequins. It was a strange and almost eerie sight, as if the space were a showroom for invisible dresses.

The floor was polished wood, gleaming and flawless,

and in the center of the room, a single white candle lay conspicuously tipped over on its side. A long mirror hung against the wall to the right, and Oona could see the back of the inspector's black jacket in the reflection, his split coattails moving in sync with his lanky legs as he moved about the room. In front of the mirror stood a raised platform where the customers could stand and admire themselves as Madame Iree made alterations. The inspector stepped onto the platform and stared fixedly at his own ghostly reflection.

Oona ignored him. She was looking at the single candle on the floor. It seemed a curious thing, quite out of place, and yet it was no real mystery where it had come from. Her gaze rose to the crystal chandelier, which hung from the high wood-paneled ceiling. She counted seven unlit candles, and one empty candleholder. Clearly the candle had fallen . . . but why? She was about to propose the question to the inspector, but at the moment, Inspector White appeared quite occupied with his own reflection.

Oona could only shake her head as she watched him attempt to straighten his tie. When this did not satisfy him, he proceeded to adjust the way his well-fitted jacket hung from his shoulders. He frowned, unable to get the desired effect he was looking for. Finally, he went so far as to straighten the entire mirror on the wall. At last he grinned, quite pleased with what he saw.

He turned from the mirror and struck a pose as if someone were about to take his photograph. But seeing that Oona and Deacon were the only ones watching, his mouth flattened into an irritated line. He moved to the center of the room and stood directly over the candle on the floor, spreading his arms wide. "I see no evidence of a break-in. There are no windows, and the only way someone could have gotten in is through that door." He pointed to where Oona and Deacon stood half silhouetted in the doorway. "Perhaps *you* are the thief, Miss Crate."

Oona took in a sharp breath at the accusation.

"Don't be ridiculous," said a voice from behind her. Oona turned to find Isadora Iree staring down the sides of her nose at her. Isadora stood a good inch taller, and her expression was disapproving. "I know who you are. You're the Wizard's niece. And I heard that you're so stupid and incompetent that he fired you, and now he's looking for a new apprentice."

Oona could feel her temper beginning to rise. She had heard similarly false rumors going about town, and she had told herself to ignore them. *She* knew they were not true, and yet it irked her to have this infuriating girl throwing the rumor in her face.

Isadora looked over Oona's shoulder at the inspector. "You see, she doesn't even deny it. She's too stupid to have stolen the dresses. I mean, look at what she's wearing.

Such drab, gray colors in the springtime. She wouldn't know what to do with high fashion if it fell in her lap."

A new voice cut into the conversation, this one thick with an Irish accent. "And you wouldn't know what to do with common courtesy if it hit you in the head, Isadora."

Isadora whirled around. A boy had just entered the shop. He wore a raggedy black cloak about his shoulders and a tattered, cockeyed top hat on his head. He was a fine-looking boy whom Oona had seen out on the street from time to time, but only from a distance. His name, she knew, was Adler Iree, and he was Isadora's twin brother.

"Adler!" said Madame Iree, her bracelets clicking and clattering as she waved away the cluster of consoling ladies. "What are you doing in the boutique?"

Adler sauntered into the ladies' dress shop as if it were the most natural place in the world for him to be. In the crook of one arm he carried a large book, which he promptly set on the tea table and then plopped himself down in one of the chairs. From this angle, Oona had a perfect view of the boy's face. It was handsome enough, with high cheekbones like his sister's, and the two of them shared the same bright blue eyes and dark eyelashes. But while Isadora's features were clearly more soft and feminine, it was the strange tattoos on Adler's face that, more than anything else, told the two of them apart.

An intricate pattern of symbols laced together across

his cheeks and around his eyes: a mysterious assortment of squiggles and stars and lines, some of which resembled ancient runes and Egyptian hieroglyphs. They varied in color from purple and blue to shimmery lines of gold and silver. A pair of tiny scarlet-colored crescent moons had been inked in at the corners of his eyes. The tattoos were an unmistakable sign that Adler Iree was a member of the Magicians Legal Alliance, the guild for the practitioners of magical law. Adler Iree was studying to be a lawyer. Upon the completion of every new course of study, the guild of lawyers bestowed a new symbol upon the faces of its members. Adler's tattoos were, as of yet, still sparse. The faces of some of the most esteemed members of the Magicians Legal Alliance appeared almost to shimmer, showing none of their original skin color at all.

"Adler, I asked you a question," Madame Iree told her son. "You know how I feel about having boys and men in the shop."

Adler raised an eyebrow and pointed toward the doorway to the showroom. For an instant, Oona thought he was pointing at her. Her heart quickened, and her cheeks flushed. Her breath caught in her throat, and she suddenly remembered the very sad state of her hair. But an instant later Oona realized that the boy was not pointing at *her* but at the inspector, who stood just behind her.

She found herself feeling both disappointed and relieved at the same time.

"That's a man there," the boy said, his finger leveled at the inspector. Adler's thick Irish brogue, so very different from his mother's and sister's cultured English accents, only added to the boy's mysterious qualities. Adler leaned forward in his seat, blinking at the inspector. "At least, I'm thinkin' so. You are a man, aren't you, Inspector?"

Before the inspector could reply, Madame Iree let loose a heavy sigh, and said: "Inspector White is here, Adler, because someone stole all of the dresses out of the showroom."

Adler nodded. "I know, Mother. The news is all over the street. That's why I came, to make sure you were all right."

"Oh, I see," said Madame Iree, who once again looked as if she might faint. Her flock of ladies rushed in again to give her support, but she shooed them away. "Those dresses were all custom made for the Midnight Masquerade tomorrow night. Twelve dresses in all, and they were all for students at the academy. The girls will all be so disappointed, because they will have nothing to wear to the event. It is all just horribly, horribly wrong!"

The inspector pushed his way past Oona and stopped before Madame Iree. "I see no possible way anyone could have broken into that showroom while all of you were out here. You, Madame, must have misplaced the dresses."

"Misplaced?" said Madame Iree, her welling tears all at once replaced with rage. "I'll misplace you, you useless fool!" She shoved her nose as close to the inspector's ghostly face as her immense bosom would allow. "Get out of my shop, you walking catastrophe in inspector's clothing! Get out before I knock you out!"

The inspector began slowly to back away through the front door, but Madame Iree continued to stalk him, looking as though she might bite him on the nose.

"You . . . You wouldn't dare harm an officer, Madame," the inspector stammered.

Madame Iree considered him for a moment, and then whirled around. "Everyone out! And that includes you, Adler and Isadora. And your little friend as well."

Isadora scowled at Oona. "She's not my friend."

"The feeling is mutual," Oona replied, before attempting: "Ah . . . Madame Iree. Might I have a look around? I might be able to find some clue as to—"

"Out!" Madame Iree cried, stomping her foot so hard that her hat toppled off her head.

Oona's mouth clamped shut, and she and Isadora headed toward the exit. As the two of them passed the tea table, doing their best not to look at each other, Adler

Iree stood. Taking his enormous book once again under his arm, he cocked his head to one side and gave Oona a quick wink before stopping at the doorway and extending his hand.

"Ladies first," he said.

Oona's cheeks flushed red. All thoughts of trying to persuade Madame Iree to let her examine the shop were gone, and she once again remembered the dreadful condition of her hair. Madame Iree slammed the door behind them. The flock of older ladies dispersed in a chattering knot in one direction, and the inspector sauntered off across the street in the other, leaving Oona, Deacon, Isadora, and Adler alone in front of the store. Halfway across the street, the inspector tripped on a cobblestone and fell flat on his face. He quickly pushed himself back up, peering at the elbow of his jacket, and then glared over his shoulder with an accusatory expression on his pale face. Oona was certain that he was about to blame her or someone else for tripping him, but instead he abruptly marched off down the street in the opposite direction he had been going.

Adler laughed. "Dark Street's finest!"

"Indeed," said Oona, unable to keep the corners of her mouth from creeping upward.

"You think you can do better?" said Isadora, the gold stripes of her dress glinting in the sun.

"Better than Inspector White?" Oona asked. "I should say so. Anyone could solve a crime better than Inspector White."

Isadora looked unconvinced. Deacon rustled his feathers uneasily as she leaned in close, hands on her hips. "Prove it," she said. "You get those dresses back before tomorrow night, and I suppose that would prove you're smarter than . . . well, than you look. My own masquerade dress was in that showroom. It is very pretty, and very extravagant, and *you're* going to get it back for me."

There was more than a hint of dare in her voice, and Oona was about to tell Isadora that she couldn't care less how fantastic Isadora's dress was, and that she could find it herself, thank you very much. . . . Only what came out of Oona's mouth was: "You're on."

Isadora grinned. "That's good, because I want to look my best tomorrow night when I attend my first dance as the Wizard's new apprentice."

She turned and sauntered away down the street, giving a catty little backward wave over her shoulder as she went.

Oona felt a sudden tightening in her chest. "*She's* applying for the position of Wizard's apprentice?"

Adler Iree gave her a wry smile, the scarlet moons at the corners of his eyes crinkling up as he did so. "Oh, to be sure," he said in that thick Irish accent of his. "We both are."

Oona's astonishment showed clearly on her face. Just

why she was so surprised to hear this news, she did not know, but for some reason coming face-to-face with her would-be replacements suddenly made her decision to give it all up very real indeed. Adler bowed slightly before saying: "I suppose I'll see you this evening, at the Choosing," and then turned to follow his sister down the street, leaving Oona with a strange mix of emotions. Intrigue and apprehension, nervousness and sadness all swelled in her at once.

"Perhaps we should be returning to Pendulum House," Deacon suggested. "Your uncle did say that you would need to be present for the Choosing. Shall we hail a carriage?"

"I suppose so," Oona said, though absently. Her mind was all over the place: the Choosing, the missing dresses, her promise to avoid danger, the candle on the floor of the showroom, Isadora Iree's challenge, Adler Iree and his wry smile. All of it danced through her head in a confused jumble. What she needed was . . .

$$\longrightarrow$$

"A walk," Oona said.

"What?" asked Deacon.

"I will walk home, Deacon. I'll need to clear my head if I'm going to solve this case."

"But it's nearly three miles to Pendulum House," Deacon pointed out.

The nearest clock was on the other side of the street, in front of the Dark Street Theater. The hands of the clock were too small to read from where she stood, so Oona stepped into the street. She was halfway across, attempting to re-create the layout of the showroom in her mind, when Deacon shouted: "Look out!"

Oona flinched as a horse and carriage came perilously close to hitting her. It swerved at the last moment, the horse whinnying its displeasure as one of the wheels struck a pothole and the entire carriage came to an abrupt halt in front of her.

"Oh, blast it, now look what you done!" cried the driver. He snapped at the reins, but the horse could not move forward. Finally, the driver jumped down and spat on the cobbles. He was a short man, dressed in the blue-and-white uniform of a cabdriver. "Why don't you watch where you're goin', miss? Look what you did. Gone and made me swerve right into that bloody pothole! And I pride myself on knowing how to *avoid* potholes, I do." The driver turned to the open carriage window, and said: "Sorry about this, sir, but that girl there made me swerve. Otherwise, I'd surely have missed those missing cobbles. I know this street like the back of my hand, I do. Now if you'll just sit tight, I'll have us out in a jiffy."

The driver scowled at Oona, and she could hear him mumbling something about losing his tip as he pulled a plank of wood from the driver's seat and attempted to lever the front wheel out.

Oona was about to apologize when she realized that the passenger in the carriage was staring at her. He was a boy, perhaps thirteen years old, with a chubby round face. His neatly cut brown hair was parted down the middle, and a set of small spectacles rested upon his nose. He stared out the carriage window with eyes as round as full moons. And then it occurred to Oona that the boy was not looking at *her* but at the museum behind her, as if he saw something there that amazed him. Oona turned to see what the boy was looking at, but she saw nothing out of the ordinary: only the enormous sculpture of the top hat and the empty steps leading to the museum. The sight of the steps reminded Oona of the blind man she'd seen standing there, just before Isadora had come rushing out of the shop.

The man who seemed to have disappeared, she thought.

When Oona turned back around, the boy in the carriage was looking at her.

"Hello," she said.

"Oh," the boy said, looking quite startled that Oona should have spoken to him. "Hello," was all he had time to say before the carriage lurched forward and the driver climbed back onto his driver's seat and snapped the reins.

As abruptly as the carriage had stopped, it began to roll again, making its way up the street in the direction of Pendulum House, kicking up bits of dust behind it that swirled and danced in the afternoon breeze.

She finished crossing the street and started up the sidewalk toward the street clock. "Who was that boy?" she asked.

"I haven't the slightest idea," Deacon replied.

"You mean there's no information in the *Who's Who*?" Oona asked, more than a little surprised.

"None at all," Deacon replied. "Whoever he is, he must not be from Dark Street."

"Someone from New York then?" Oona asked. It was not unprecedented that people from the outside world ventured onto Dark Street. Most of them happened upon the street by accident, but it was still unusual. While it was true that Dark Street received most of its food and products from the outside world, it was much more common for the merchants of Dark Street to venture out to get their supplies than for outsiders to bring them in.

Oona stopped at the foot of the old ironwork street clock in front of the Dark Street Theater. A sign over the box office read:

THIS FRIDAY ONLY

OPEN-CALL AUDITIONS FOR *OSWALD DESCENDS*

Oona tutted. *Oswald Descends*, a play named after Oswald the Great, the most powerful of the Magicians of Old, told the story of the crucial role he played in the Great Faerie War nearly five hundred years ago. The play was put on at least once a year without fail. Oona found such old-fashioned stories of magic and history quite boring, although she had to admit that the final scene in the play—when Oswald descends the steps of Faerie, locked in battle with the terrible Queen of Faerie—was always quite spectacular. Unfortunately, you needed to sit through the entire play for one bit of excitement at the very end.

The clock read 2:36. Since the Choosing was set for seven o'clock, this left her more than enough time to reach Pendulum House on foot. Satisfied, Oona turned to go, but just then, two metallic-sounding voices emanated from deep inside the iron clockwork, half startling her.

"Knock, knock," said the first voice.

"Who's there?" asked the second.

"Kent."

"Kent who?"

"Kent remember my name, I'm so bloody drunk. Now open up!"

Oona rolled her eyes. Nowhere else but on Dark Street did the street clocks tell not only time but jokes as well . . . and quite bad ones at that.

Her shadow stretched out behind her as she strolled up the street, wondering how she might solve the case of the missing dresses with so little information. Especially when she was unable to examine the crime scene itself.

Her pace quickened as she passed in front of Oswald Park—the mile-long recreational area named after the great magician—though not solely because of the young hooligans in shady hats near the front gate. Oona had Deacon with her, and the menacing-looking raven would make most anyone think twice about approaching her. The real reason she quickened her pace was because it was at Oswald Park that she had conjured her last spell. It was there that the magic had flown out of her control.

The iron bars separating the park from the street slid quickly past as she attempted to hold her eyes dead ahead. But the pull was too strong. She stopped a little ways past the entrance, pressing her face to the fence and peering through the bars at an open, grass-covered space near the center of the park.

It wasn't always an open space, Oona thought grimly. *Not too long ago there was a great tree there. A huge fig tree where people could sit under its branches and lean against its trunk.*

"Hey, girlie," said a voice, and Oona turned to see one of the shadowy, hat-wearing young men approaching her. His voice was rough from smoke. "You got a light, girlie?"

Deacon puffed up his chest, his head rising to his full menacing height. "Back away, sir!" he half cawed.

The hoodlum quickly backed away, turning to his companions, who were all having a good laugh. Oona watched him go. In the distance she caught sight of the very top of the Black Tower. The ominous-looking tower was the tallest structure on Dark Street, and it could be seen from miles away. Also known as the Goblin Tower, the solid black, windowless structure was a relic of the past: a prison built to hold powerful faeries during the war. It was said that the Magicians of Old had placed goblins inside as keepers of the prison, and that they lived there still, to this day. Oona didn't know if she believed that, but it was true that people were so fearful of the tower that no one wished to live too close to it, and so that was where they had built the cemetery. The tower rose up out of the center of the graveyard like some enormous black tombstone.

It was there, beneath its shadow, that Oona had watched them first bury her father . . . and then not long after, her mother and baby sister had joined him in the Crate family plot. Oona had not been back since.

Currently, she returned her gaze to the place where the tree had once grown near the center of the park, and a sudden wave of grief and guilt washed over her. Decorations were being put up in preparation for the masquerade the following night. Lanterns were being hung in trees, and tables were being set up around the pond. Streaming bits of shiny fabric dangled from branches, giving the park a whimsical appearance, but going to the masquerade all at once seemed like a bad idea.

How dare I think of having fun in that place, she thought. *They were killed there. And it's all my fault.*

The thought was cruel and biting, but Oona heard the truth in it. And then she thought: *It's the magic that killed them. The Lights of Wonder did it . . . Lux lucis admiratio . . . it's the magic's fault.* And she felt the truth in this as well. She turned away from the park with a sudden urge to run, feeling more certain than she had in weeks that she was making the right decision to give up her apprentice-ship. She couldn't wait to sign the papers and have the whole business over with, to be done with magic and all of its ridiculous instability.

She simply couldn't wait for the Choosing to be fin-ished.

CHAPTER THREE

The Faerie Servant

Pendulum House sat squarely in the middle of Dark Street, where the broad avenue split apart in a wide circle around the extensive grounds. An old, rusty ironwork fence surrounded the yard, and the house seemed as ancient and foreboding as the powerful magic held within its walls. Yet the style of the house was that of a modern Victorian manor. It stood four stories tall, its numerous interlocking sections and slanted roofs giving the impression that it was several homes pieced together by some eccentric, yet brilliant architect.

Sticking out of the second floor, like a bizarre sea wreck, was the prow of a ship. The carved image of a wide-eyed mermaid had been mounted on the front, where she stared out at the drifting crowds of Dark Street, looking both beautiful and disastrously out of place. A crooked and rather unsafe-looking tower protruded from the uppermost story of the manor, at the very top of which an ironwork weathervane slowly rocked in the breeze.

Oona's bedroom resided on the third floor, her window overlooking the tangled mess of the front gardens, which clearly had not been tended in a very long time. Twisting snakelike vines and tall, prickly weeds crisscrossed through the sparse trees, all of which were in need of a good pruning.

Yet sitting in her room, in front of her dressing table mirror, Oona was not concerned with the deplorable condition of the front yard; instead, she was applying all of her skills to the taming of her hair. She ran a hairbrush across the top of her head, feeling the situation was simply hopeless. Deacon stood atop a nearby bedpost.

Oona dropped the brush on the tabletop. "How on earth did someone break into that showroom, Deacon? Inspector White was correct when he pointed out that there were no windows to climb in or out of."

She closed her eyes, once again attempting to re-create the crime scene in her mind—the naked mannequins, the crystal chandelier, the platform.

"The candle on the floor," she said, opening her eyes

and staring at her reflection. Large green eyes stared back, the skin above her small nose dimpling.

"The candle?" Deacon said. "What about it?"

"Something . . . but what?" She let out a little groan. "Oh, it is useless, Deacon. I need to examine that showroom closer! Perhaps tomorrow Madame Iree will let me in."

"Perhaps," Deacon said doubtfully.

Oona gave him a shrewd look before turning her attention to her dressing table. An assortment of glass vials and laboratory beakers littered the tabletop, along with her discarded hairbrush. She picked up a yellowed folder containing a thick stack of edge-worn paper. Printed on the cover, in her late father's blocky handwriting, was the name RED MARTIN.

Oona thumbed the file open to the middle before musing aloud: "You know, I wouldn't be surprised if Red Martin was behind this crime."

Deacon shuddered at the mention of the name, and Oona couldn't help thinking to herself how it was not a very original name. The history books were full of one ambitious scoundrel or another who would start calling himself Red Martin in order to strike fear into the hearts of the people of Dark Street. Some people even believed that they were all the same person, and that Red Martin was hundreds of years old. But that, of course, was only silly gossip, and Oona put little stock in such rumors. She preferred hard facts.

"The current Red Martin is the worst criminal of them all, as far as I'm concerned," she said. "So bad that he never shows his face in public."

"But why would he have anything to do with this particular crime?" Deacon asked. "You said it yourself. Why would a deadly criminal want to steal a bunch of dresses?"

Oona nodded thoughtfully. "Only because, according to my father's files, Red Martin is the driving force behind nearly *every* crime on the street. Three-quarters of the unlawful activities on Dark Street can be traced directly to Red Martin's Nightshade Corporation. Somehow he always manages to keep his own hands clean. He is as greedy as they get."

"Indeed," said Deacon. "But where is the proof?"

"You mean proof that he is a villainous crook?" Oona closed the file and tossed it on the bed. "There is enough evidence in that file to prove that most of the criminals my father ever captured had at least some connection to Red Martin's Nightshade Corporation. But the man himself is an enigma. A shroud of mystery. In his ten years as head inspector, my father never once came face-to-face with the man. Red Martin hides up there in that money-making temple of his, the Nightshade Hotel and Casino.

Some people even question his existence at all. Others say he's as old as the Glass Gates. There is also a rumor that he has plans to build an even bigger, more grand casino than the one at the Nightshade Hotel."

Deacon scoffed. "Where would he build it? Dark Street is already so packed with buildings."

Oona considered this. "There is Witch Hill."

"But the hill is too small," said Deacon. "It's no bigger than a storefront, really."

Oona nodded. "True. If Red Martin is planning on building an even larger casino than the one he already has, then he would need a much larger spot of land."

"The question is, why would he need a larger casino at all?" Deacon asked. "I would not believe that there are enough gamblers on Dark Street to *support* two casinos."

Oona had scarcely begun to consider the question when there came a knock at her bedroom door.

"Who is it?" Oona called.

"It is I." The voice drifted through the door, its tone sly and cool, like a whisper from the back of the throat. "The applicants are arriving, and your uncle wishes to see you."

Oona rolled her eyes. "Tell him I'll be down shortly." She paused, an idea reoccurring to her. "Samuligan, are you still there?"

"I am."

"Please come in. I have a question."

The door fell open and the click of boots echoed about the room. Samuligan's gaunt body and long hooked nose gave the impression that he might be half bird. A knee-length, black coat hung ill-fitting from bony limbs, and his thin, dark eyes peered out from beneath a broad-brimmed cowboy hat.

Deacon cawed loudly before flying from the bedpost to the top of the mirror, where he peered uneasily at the bizarre-looking, pointy-eared figure.

"How may I be of service?" Samuligan asked. He hooked his long thumbs into his belt.

Oona stood, nervously smoothing out her dress. She had been considering whether or not to ask a certain favor since the previous night, and it was only now, with the memory of Isadora Iree's cruel japes and Adler's handsome stare still so fresh in her mind, that she decided to go through with the request, regardless of how completely at odds it was with her feelings toward magic. She said: "Well . . . it's my hair, you see, Samuligan."

Samuligan smiled. It was a horrible smile, filled with too many teeth. "Or rather," he said, "it is your hair that I do not see."

Oona nodded, her cheeks slightly flushed. "Well, that's just the problem. It got sort of . . . chopped off. An unfortunate incident with a scary man and a guillotine."

"Yes, I know," Samuligan said dryly. "And you did not think to use magic to escape?"

"Of course I did," Oona replied. "But that's as far as I got . . . *thinking* about it. Anyway, as you can imagine, it's a little unseemly for a young lady to go about looking like"—she pointed to the top of her head—"well, like this. And I was wondering . . . if . . ." She trailed off.

"If I could grow it back for you?" Samuligan finished for her.

Deacon cawed at Oona. "You hypocrite!" He flew around her head before landing on the dressing table. "One moment you are bashing magic, and the next you're asking your uncle's faerie servant to grow your hair back for you."

Oona turned to Deacon, eyebrows raised. "There's a distinct difference between Faerie Magic and human magic, Deacon. Two very different methods. You know that."

Deacon made a throat-clearing sound: a sound that meant he was about to impart some extended bit of encyclopedic knowledge. "There are *four* types of magic, actually. First there is *Faerie Magic*, which is any magic performed by a faerie. Then there is *Natural Magic*. A human such as yourself, born with faerielike powers, but without the faerie's natural-born instincts to control it, uses *Natural Magic*, and it is considered the rarest form. *Learned Magic*, also known as 'forced magic,' is performed by Learned Magicians, such as your uncle, and must be acquired through decades of dedication and scholarship—mental exercises, potion making, et cetera, et cetera. And lastly, there is *Pedestrian Magic*, perhaps the most dangerous of them all, which is any magic conjured by a nonmagician through use of an enchanted object."

Oona rolled her eyes. "Thank you for that little lesson, Deacon, but as I was saying, human magic—Natural or Learned—is temperamental at best. Faerie Magic, on the other hand, can at least be *trusted* to work."

"Trusted?" Deacon said. He flew into the air and circled Samuligan, eyeing him skeptically. "That remains to be seen."

Samuligan's grin only widened.

Oona smiled, looking at the faerie servant. Samuligan the Fay: how extraordinary he was. So absolutely different from anyone she had ever met. For five hundred years he had served the occupants of Pendulum House, ever since the great Magicians of Old had enchanted him into a lifetime of servitude. Being that faeries were immortal, that was a long time, to say the least. If he held any resentment with regard to his fate, Samuligan never showed it. Her uncle had once told her that Samuligan had been a powerful general in the Faerie Royal Army during the Great Faerie War, fighting under the banners of the Queen of Faerie against the likes of Oswald the Great. And looking at him now, as he stood near the doorway in his attire of boots, and coat, and cowboy hat—a fashion that Samuligan assured her had originated in Faerie hundreds of years before it became the fashion of the American West—Oona could undoubtedly see how this tall, shadowy figure would indeed inspire fear in the hearts of his enemies.

The faerie did not frighten *her*, however. Not like he did nearly every other inhabitant on Dark Street. Yet Oona felt that she could never be entirely sure how he would react to any one particular situation.

Once she had witnessed Samuligan howl with laughter when a beautiful woman stumbled while crossing the street, and yet on another occasion, a similar situation occurred when a young lady, dressed all in white, had been splattered from head to toe by a passing carriage. Samuligan had rushed to the distraught young lady's aid as if it were the most important thing in the world. He took hold of her dress in his unnaturally long fingers and began to utter something in a low grumble of a voice. Oona had thought perhaps he was going to tear the young lady's dress in two. But he did nothing of the sort: indeed, the mud that had bespeckled the dress abruptly winked out of existence, not a spot to be found.

Samuligan had then stepped away from the young

lady, gifting her with his best attempt at a gentlemanly smile. In response, the young lady merely whimpered before running away as fast as her feet could carry her.

In short, Samuligan was an enigma, which was surely due to the fact that he was the only faerie Oona had ever met—indeed, the only faerie any living human had met. And as far as Oona knew, the faerie servant was the only creature of his kind this side of the Glass Gates, which made him all the more curious.

"Don't mind Deacon," Oona told Samuligan. He tipped his hat back on his head, carefully eyeing the flying bird as it circled him. "He's always suspicious of tall, dark figures," she said.

Samuligan's hand shot out without the slightest hesitation—brilliant, keen. He snatched Deacon out of the air with a snakelike deftness and smiled as the bird twitched in his gangly fingers. "As well he should be," Samuligan said.

"Free me this instant," Deacon squawked.

Oona watched the two of them, shaking her head. The funny thing was that she had always harbored a sneaking suspicion that it had truly been Samuligan, and not her uncle after all, who had enchanted Deacon with the gift of speech and invested in him such vast quantities of reference materials. Even almost two years ago, when she had received the bird as an eleventh birthday present,

Oona had been aware of what a highly impressive magical achievement Deacon was, and though she loved her uncle very much, she didn't think he was truly capable of such a powerful creation. At least not on his own. Surely Samuligan had had a hand in it. She would never have told Deacon of her suspicions, however. Not with the bird's presently justifiable mistrust of the faerie servant.

"Now, Samuligan, that's not funny," she chided. "Let Deacon go."

Samuligan nodded, but instead of simply releasing the bird, the faerie servant glanced toward Oona's dressing table and nodded. Simultaneously, he stamped his foot and said: "Switch!"

Half a second later he no longer held the bird, but instead his fingers were wrapped around the handle of Oona's hairbrush. Deacon appeared just as suddenly on the spot where the brush had been on the table. His legs wobbled and his head jerked around, as if trying to understand what had just happened.

"I've never seen that trick before," Oona said, quite impressed, while at the same time feeling a twinge of guilt at having had enjoyed the magic.

Samuligan ran his thumb over the bristles of the brush. "I just made it up," he said.

"I never!" Deacon said. "What utter savagery!"

Samuligan reached into his pocket and produced a

dead mouse. He tossed it upward and Deacon dove for it, snatching it out of the air as deftly as Samuligan had snatched Deacon himself. The faerie rubbed his fingers together. "Savage indeed," he said.

Deacon landed on the floor, biting the mouse in two and devouring it with unrestrained vigor.

"Oh, I wish you hadn't given him that," Oona told Samuligan. "I don't like it when he takes his meals in here."

"I apologize," Samuligan replied. "Now about your hair."

He ran the brush across the top of Oona's head.

She took in a sharp breath, her eyes falling shut as she rose onto her tiptoes. She could feel it. The charge. The energy. The magic. The shock of it sent her tumbling back into her chair. It was like an old friend, or an enemy. She could not have said which was more accurate. The image of hundreds of sparkling lights swirling around an enormous fig tree filled her vision like a terrible dream. She wanted to cry out, to tell Samuligan to stop . . . that she had made a mistake . . . but before she could do so, the image dropped away. The magic withdrew, and that oh-so-familiar feeling of fear and wonderment dissolved away almost completely—*almost*, but not quite.

She became acutely aware of the soft carpet under her feet, and the wood beneath the carpet. She looked into

Samuligan's long face. Her midnight-black hair cascaded down her shoulders, full, and straight, and shining as if it had been freshly washed. She ran her fingers through the familiar strands and nodded.

"Thank you," she said, her voice trembling.

"Your uncle awaits you in his study," Samuligan said before handing her the brush and then striding out of the room, the dark folds of his coat billowing behind him like a curtain of night.

Deacon peered up at Oona, the bloody remains of the dead mouse now nothing but a thin stain on the carpet. The mouse's tail hung limp from his dull, black beak like a dead worm.

"Really, Deacon. Bones and all!" Oona said. "You must learn to control yourself."

He flew to her shoulder. She winced as the tail slapped against her newly grown hair and then disappeared down Deacon's gullet. She stood, and the two of them followed the faerie servant to the bottom floor, where she found her uncle waiting for her in his study, along with the lawyer.

CHAPTER FOUR

The Wizard and the Lawyer

I must admit," said the Wizard. "I did expect somewhat of a larger response from New York."

His long beard hung from his face as gray as a winter storm. He leaned forward in his chair, picking up the single résumé on his desk. He frowned, deepening the lines about his eyes. With the hood of his dark purple robe thrown back over his shoulders, the Wizard's bald head glinted in the ever-burning magical lamplight. A large nose and generous mouth gave him a gentle appearance, while his green eyes seemed somehow older than his sixty years. He studied the résumé. The paper was creased in the middle and charred black around the edges.

"I warned you," said the lawyer, Mr. Ravensmith.

"Times are not what they once were. There is no more interest in magic these days than there is in cave painting. It has now been over six months since your original post in the *New York Times,* and if you ask for my counsel, the advertisement was wrongly worded."

Oona stood beside her uncle, who sat slumped forward in a high-backed, wooden Wizard's seat, his elbows resting on the ornately carved desk. The desk—an ancient relic, purportedly carved from the bones of a dragon—gave the appearance of slowly breathing in and out, as if the dragon from which it had been carved were merely sleeping, its breath as faint as a mouse's footsteps.

Her uncle's study was a solitary place, filled with shelves of books. A stone fireplace was set into the corner of the room, in front of which sat a cozy chair and side table. A lone tea saucer floated aimlessly above the table, moving in figure eights, as if in search of its missing cup. It was a testament to the eccentric magic that the Magicians of Old had long ago placed into the house itself. The house was, in many ways, like a living thing, filled with peculiar pockets of energy that manifested in often strange ways. The first lesson that any new apprentice learned was that, should the Glass Gates ever fall, it was the current Wizard's responsibility to access the magic stored in the walls of Pendulum House in order to protect the World of Man from faerie attack.

Deacon stood wraithlike upon Oona's shoulder, and Samuligan had disappeared into the shadows of the grandfather clock near the door. The room smelled of incense, and books, and dust.

The gentleman seated across from the Wizard wore the finest of modern clothing. His beautifully tailored jacket showed off his broad, well-built figure, and his hair was groomed in the cleanest, most stylishly neat fashion. Mr. Ravensmith's most striking characteristic, however, was his face. Much like young Adler Iree, the lawyer's face was covered in tattoos of odd shapes and symbols of varying colors, except that Mr. Ravensmith's tattoos numbered far more than Adler's. So plentiful were Ravensmith's markings that the skin around his cheeks and eyes appeared to be a mask of solid silver and gold, with intricate veins of purple and blue crisscrossing like cracks in weatherworn paint.

Ravensmith brushed away a nearly invisible bit of dust from the sleeve of his black jacket. "The advertisement should have mentioned a large sum of money. That would have gotten their attention."

"Money?" said the Wizard.

"Or, at the very least," Mr. Ravensmith went on, "you might have specified the proper method for the applicants to send in their résumés. No doubt, anyone interested in the position tried to use their American postal service instead of properly addressing their letters and then setting them on fire."

"Well, if they couldn't figure that out," the Wizard said stubbornly, "then they don't deserve the position. And look here." He waved the résumé with the blackened edges in front of him. "At least someone from New York figured it out. And as far as money is concerned, I think you are quite wrong, Mr. Ravensmith. If someone is more interested in money than in learning magic for its own sake, then I won't have them."

Mr. Ravensmith raised his thick eyebrows before clearing his throat. "Speaking of money . . . and with all due respect, it is something I am loath to bring up, but my secretary, Mr. Quick, has informed me that we have yet to receive any payments from you, whatsoever, for services rendered in the past two years."

Mr. Ravensmith pulled a thick envelope from his inside pocket and gave it a little shake, as if ringing a bell. "Mr. Quick was so good as to tally up all one hundred and sixteen invoices."

The Wizard said nothing, only sat there, elbows pressing in on the slowly breathing desk. Deacon shifted restlessly on Oona's shoulder.

"And that, I'm afraid, is just the beginning," Mr. Ravensmith went on. "While it's true that you have sold quite a lot of your ever-burning lamps, and that your never-melting ice was a great success in the past, the problem remains that no one ever needs to come back and buy more. The lamps stop working the instant they are removed from Dark Street, and the ice immediately begins to melt the moment it crosses through the Iron Gates, so there is no chance of selling them in New York. Your enchantment store has done nothing but lose money for three years straight. Your house staff has dwindled to one servant because of lack of funds, and those who have left are demanding their severance pay. Your love for throwing frivolous parties has pushed you into considerable debt. The list goes on and on, Alexander."

Mr. Ravensmith paused to once again brush some bit of dust from his jacket. The room remained decidedly silent. The lawyer shifted uneasily in his chair before continuing, his voice losing all sense of formality and dropping into exasperation. "Do you know, Alexander, that Miss Colbert, your former cleaning maid, came to me not six months ago complaining of her sudden dismissal from your service? She was threatening to sue. I was forced to take her on as a maid myself, if only to appease her. It is lucky for you that I can always use another cleaning lady, so I hired her on the spot. And to tell the truth, her superior talent for cleaning both my office and my home leaves me completely baffled as to why she was let go in the first place. Perhaps if you gave up these outlandish parties you keep throwing, then you might be able to hire her back."

Mr. Ravensmith ran a finger along the arm of his chair, creating a trail in the dust. The tattoos on his face squinched up, and he sat forward in his seat, as if in imminent danger of sullying his jacket.

Oona frowned. It had been Oona herself who had discovered the maid stealing silver from the Pendulum House kitchen, and Oona believed that her uncle had been extraordinarily lenient by simply relieving the maid of her duties and not reporting the incident to the police.

Mr. Ravensmith might want to lock up his silverware, Oona thought.

"I fear, Alexander," Mr. Ravensmith added in an eerily hushed tone, "that your . . . creditor . . . has become somewhat impatient."

Oona glanced suspiciously at her uncle, but remained quiet. She had known he was having financial troubles, but to what extent, she was unsure. Her uncle disliked the subject of money, she knew, and had never shared such information with her.

As if to prove his dislike for the subject, the Wizard ignored Mr. Ravensmith's envelope, focusing instead on the résumé.

"Well," he said after a long moment, "this applicant will have to do. Samuligan, where is he now?"

Samuligan spoke from the shadows. "As Mr. Ravensmith has instructed, he is in the parlor. With the others."

"The others, yes," the Wizard said, opening a drawer in the desk and removing four more sheets of paper. Similarly burned around the edges, he placed those résumés on top of the first, looking more disappointed than ever. "Four applicants from Dark Street, and one from the World of Man. That is all. There was once a time when . . . when . . . Ah, but let's not dwell upon the past."

He turned to Oona, a sadness in his face that she found difficult to look at. He appeared reluctant to speak. "You will need to sign away your rights as my apprentice, Oona. This is very serious now, and if you are certain that this detective business is what you want, I won't stand in your way. So long as you are careful."

Oona nodded, afraid that if she spoke, her voice would betray her mixed feelings.

The Wizard turned to the grandfather clock. "Samuligan, please accompany Mr. Ravensmith to the parlor."

"It shall be done, sir." The faerie servant stepped from the shadow of the clock, his tall, razor-thin body poised to attention.

"Mr. Ravensmith," the Wizard said. "Please have each of the applicants sign the appropriate eligibility contract.

Miss Crate will be along in a moment to sign her own relinquishing document as well, but I wish to speak with her alone."

Mr. Ravensmith sighed, agitatedly returning the unpaid invoice to his pocket. He stood, brushed the dust from his coattails, and followed Samuligan to the door.

"I can wait outside, if you wish, sir," Deacon offered, but after a moment's consideration the Wizard shook his head, indicating that that would be unnecessary. He waived a hand to Samuligan, who closed the door, leaving the Wizard alone with Deacon and Oona.

"Lawyers!" said the Wizard. He leaned back in his chair and, in a softer tone, said: "You have backbone, my dear. A spirit I can only admire. It is a spirit that would serve this seat well. The things you could do." He nodded to no one in particular and added: "I envy you. As an apprentice I, too, had other interests. Other aspirations. I might have gone on to become one of the great badminton players of our time. But that is neither here nor there. I stayed. There were others who were even better suited for the position than I was, but I stayed because it was what was expected of me."

Oona felt a dull ache growing in her chest. She bit the

71

inside of her cheek, trying not to let her emotions show. She felt sad for him, this old man who had sacrificed himself for the honored magical position. Dutifully. In a way, she felt she was letting him down, he who had raised her as his own. Educated her. Protected her.

"I don't blame you for abandoning your post," the Wizard continued. "Nor do I blame you for your dislike of magic. How could I? What happened to your mother and sister that day in the park was very sad. Very, very sad, and unfortunate. I loved them deeply as well. We both miss them very much, but you can't continue to blame yourself, Oona. It was an accident. I am as much responsible for what happened as anyone else. I was responsible for you. For honing your extraordinary powers."

He gazed at her as if expecting a reply. But what reply was there to give? She was silent. The dragon-bone desk breathed steadily in the background, and the floating tea saucer over the fireside table continued its endless pattern of crazy eights.

"I must warn you, Oona," the Wizard continued, "some people may be able to simply walk away from this position and leave the magic behind. But not you. You are a *Natural* Magician. The magic is in you. And while you continue to live with me, though I will have a new apprentice, I believe I still have the responsibility of helping you control those powers."

The thought was a sobering one. Oona had of course known that leaving her position as apprentice would not rid her of the magic, but only of her obligation to practice it. Still, the idea that she would need to keep it under control for the rest of her life was an unpleasant thought, to say the least.

She glanced nervously at Deacon, but the bird remained respectfully silent.

"The reason I bring these things up now," the Wizard said, "is because if your disinterest in magic spawns solely from what happened in the park, then I urge you to reconsider giving up the apprenticeship. If, on the other hand, it is something more than that . . . for instance, your heart calling you in another direction, then I urge you to follow this new direction. Think on that before you sign the papers. That is all I ask."

Oona swallowed hard. "I will." She felt like a little girl again, small, and fragile, and confused.

"Now please, Oona, leave me alone for a moment. I will meet the applicants only after they have signed the documents. In the meantime, I need to drink." He cleared his throat, and corrected himself: "I mean think."

Oona pushed open the study door, exited the room, and turned back. The Wizard sat drumming his long, wrinkled fingers on the desk, introspective, not looking at her. The door had just begun to close when her uncle abruptly stood and moved to the bookcase behind the desk. He made a sudden motion with his hand. The gesture was quick and precise, but with his back to her, such as it was, Oona was unable to make out what the movement had been. To her surprise, a shelf swung outward in front of the Wizard, revealing a hidden compartment behind the books. The study door had closed almost completely when Oona stopped it with her foot, leaving only a crack through which to see. Inside the hidden compartment she could make out what looked like the curling edges of several flat sheets of paper, on top of which sat a mysterious black ball. A bottle of scotch whiskey and a glass sat beside the papers, and farther back in the compartment, she thought she glimpsed the dark outline of a large book. The Wizard poured a drink, closed the shelf, and returned to the desk.

Oona let the door fall slowly shut behind her.

The Wizard's disappointment in her decision could not have been more obvious, and she suddenly found it very hard to bear. She knew that he felt nearly as guilty about her mother's and sister's deaths as she did. It was soon after the accident in the park when he had begun his drinking. Oona also suspected it would have been around that time that he had begun to let the servants go, and allow the gardens to fall into disrepair.

Halfway across the antechamber Oona stopped and

peered sidelong at Deacon. An idea occurred to her that she thought just might raise her spirits.

"What do you say we get a good look at the applicants before going into the parlor?" she said, rubbing her hands excitedly.

"An excellent idea," Deacon replied. "And how do you propose we accomplish it?"

"The broom closet."

"I beg pardon?"

"Why, through Oswald's portrait, Deacon. I'm sure I've mentioned it."

Deacon slowly nodded his head. "Ah, yes. Now I remember. That is rather convenient, would you not say?"

Oona gave him a wink.

"Indeed, Deacon," she said. "Nothing like a bit of spying to put one in the right mood."

CHAPTER FIVE

Through the Eyes of the Magician

The broom closet, located inside the front entryway to the house, was small. The pine-branch broom that usually sat in the closet was nowhere to be seen, and Oona had a sneaking suspicion that their old cleaning maid, Miss Colbert, had made off with it when she'd been fired. Miss Colbert had made off with quite a few things, Oona was fairly certain. Currently, however, Oona was pleased that the broom was absent because it allowed more room for her to squeeze inside the tiny closet.

The knob on the door had fought stubbornly against Oona's initial turn, and only by squeezing down and heaving with all of her strength had she managed to unlatch it.

Now staring at the filthy inside, she began to have second thoughts about going in. After a moment's consideration, however, she decided that getting a good look at her would-be replacements, without their having the ability to see her, was worth getting a little dirty. She squeezed awkwardly into the tight space, Deacon perched like a gargoyle on her shoulder. The door clicked shut behind her, leaving the two of them in complete darkness.

"Oops," Oona said. "I hadn't meant for that to happen."

"Rather a tight fit," Deacon said.

"Yes, sorry," Oona said. "And get your beak out of my ear."

Her foot pressed against something hard in the darkness: a low footstool that she now stepped up onto.

"Where are the spy holes you spoke of?" Deacon asked.

Oona fumbled in the dark. "Ah, here," she said, and slid a small part of the wall away. Two holes appeared in the wall, spilling light onto Oona's grinning face.

"And here, Deacon. I believe the other is . . ." She found the second concealed panel and slid it open, revealing two more holes to the left.

Deacon peered through. "And you say that I am looking through the eyes of the lizard?" he mused.

"Precisely," Oona said. "And I am looking through

the eyes of Oswald the Great." She placed her own eyes against the first set of holes and peered into the next room.

The grand parlor at Pendulum House was tall and wide. It was without question the most comfortable room in the house and had been furnished as a place for entertaining guests. It seemed to Oona that not a week would pass when the Wizard wasn't hosting some party or another, using the room to celebrate the full moon, or the new moon, or the existence of the moon altogether. He had thrown parties to show off a new robe, or an old one that he'd had tailored, or simply because it was Wednesday. On such evenings, plates of hors d'oeuvres floated several inches above the tabletops, along with bobbing wineglasses and hovering teacups. While many agreed that the Wizard was a second-rate magician at best, it was also said that he was a fabulous host, and that if you wished to see his best magic, then you simply needed to get invited to a party at Pendulum House.

Though the room had no windows to speak of, that did not affect the lighting, since the entire ceiling was lined with countless glowing balls of light. The walls were decorated with enormous portraits of past Wizards and historical figures, as well as intricate tapestries depicting mystical creatures—sprites and goblins, elves and gnomes. Though the creatures appeared frozen in place, like in a photograph or a portrait, if a houseguest should happen to look away from the tapestry and then back again, the creatures would appear to have shifted positions—as if, while the observer had been distracted, the creatures were having a party themselves.

The most peculiar aspect of the parlor was the enormous pendulum that swung in a perfect arc through the center of the room. This, of course, was the very pendulum for which Pendulum House took its name. It rocked back and forth, slowly swinging through the parlor, dividing the room into two separate gathering areas. A sofa had been cut in half to make way for the seven-foot pendulum bob as it swept through its middle.

The portrait that Oona stood behind was that of Oswald the Great and his faithful lizard, Lulu, who sat on the magician's shoulder, the two of them looking remarkably dignified and brave.

A long, cushioned bench had been placed in front of the fireplace, parallel to the swing of the pendulum. On it sat four applicants for the Wizard's apprentice. Oona recognized Isadora and her brother, Adler Iree, instantly, but there were two other applicants she had never seen before. The first was a girl dressed in a black witch's costume, complete with pointy black hat, who looked younger than Oona, perhaps nine or ten years old. Oona was shocked to see her there.

"Is that a witch?" Oona asked.

"It certainly is," said Deacon, sounding equally surprised.

Oona considered the oddity for a moment. "You don't see many of them outside of Witch Hill. And even then, only the girls."

"You speak truly," Deacon agreed. "I don't believe any of them have ever applied for the position of apprentice before."

"What does the *Who's Who* have to say about her?" Oona asked.

"Nothing," Deacon said. "There are no entries for any of the witches, old or young. It is a testament to how very reclusive they are."

"Hmm," Oona replied, and then turned her attention to the second stranger on the bench: a rather plump young man, perhaps thirteen years old, dressed in a fine suit. He wore small round spectacles, and his hair was parted straight down the middle. Oona blinked in surprise, realizing that she had seen the boy before.

"The stout young man, at the far end of the bench," Deacon said. "He's the one we saw in the carriage earlier today. That must be the New Yorker."

"An excellent observation, Deacon," Oona replied. She couldn't have said why, but it bothered her to think that a total stranger to Dark Street might take over the apprenticeship. She couldn't help but wonder about how the boy had known to light his letter on fire in order to send it to the Wizard.

She watched the boy for a long moment, curious as to how he had found his way to Dark Street, though in truth her curiosity was not all *that* strong, since it was Adler Iree, who sat beside the boy from New York, whom she could not stop looking at and wondering about. He wore the same ratty old top hat on his head, and the same shabby cloak draped across his shoulders. Presently, he was bending over a large book in his lap. From this angle, it was difficult to make out the tattoos on his face, but she *could* see the cute way his brow furrowed as he concentrated on his reading.

On the other side of Adler, his sister, Isadora, sat perfectly still, her posture perfectly straight. Her perfectly manicured hands rested in her perfectly composed lap. The beautiful girl searched the room, studying the others with her deep blue eyes, which were huge and stunning and, most unmistakably, perfectly wicked.

"But wait," Oona said. "Uncle Alexander spoke of *five* applicants. One from New York and four from Dark Street. Someone is missing."

As she spoke, Mr. Ravensmith and Samuligan entered the parlor carrying a narrow wooden table. They set the table in front of the applicants, and the lawyer pulled a large paper scroll from his pocket.

"Come, Deacon," Oona said, sliding shut the two hidden panels. "I'll sign the papers and be done with it."

But when Oona swiveled her hand round for the doorknob, she found it was stuck tight.

"What is the problem?" Deacon asked.

"The door. It seems to be . . . somewhat . . . stuck."

"Somewhat?" Deacon questioned.

Oona tried once again to twist, only to have her sweaty palm slip from the awkward grip.

"Oh, all right. *Completely* stuck. Must you be so literal, Deacon?"

Oona felt the bird bristle against the side of her face. "Perhaps if you could manage to turn around," he suggested, "you could get a better grip."

This was easier said than done, considering the fullness of her skirt. After what might have been several long minutes, she managed to get herself fully turned around and facing the door. The closet was full of dust, and she could feel bits of spiderweb clinging to her face.

She twisted the doorknob. Nothing happened. The latch had jammed. She twisted again. Again, nothing.

Deacon clacked his beak before saying: "Perhaps if you attempted . . . well, you know, some . . ."

He trailed off, and Oona suddenly realized what he was getting at.

"No magic!" she shouted, and heaved at the door with

everything she had, teeth clenched, fingers squeezing, shoulder shoving. The door snapped open, and the two of them went flying.

Oona landed hard on her side and slid several feet across the entryway floor. Behind her, the closet door slammed open against the nearby coatrack with such force that the rack toppled over, crashing painfully against her side.

"Oh, oh, are you all right?" Deacon asked, landing safely beside her. "Should I get some help? I could find—"

"No, Deacon," Oona told him. She shoved the coatrack aside and pushed herself into an upright position. "It's my pride that is the most injured. No need to damage it any more by drawing attention."

She rose to her feet, brushing several ghostly clouds of dust from her skirt, and then propped the coatrack back into its upright position. That's when she noticed a beautiful shawl lying on the floor. The shawl was made of the same red-and-gold material as Isadora Iree's dress. Oona admired it for a moment before hanging it back on the rack, and then calmly closed the broom closet door. She straightened the top of her dress, which was sooted with a fine layer of dust and cobwebs.

"Remind me to have Samuligan oil that latch," she said.

Deacon returned to her shoulder, chuckling. "Or

perhaps I should remind *you* never to go in that closet again."

Oona grinned. "Oh, Deacon. Where's your sense of adventure?"

She turned her back on the closet, and the two of them made their way to the parlor.

CHAPTER SIX

Lamont Learns the Basics

M y name is Mr. Ravensmith," said the lawyer. "Now, if you would all be so kind as to sign your names to this contract, you will become eligible for the position of apprentice to the Wizard of Dark Street, blah, blah, blah, and heretofore throughout the universe, blah, blah, blah, and until the end of said selection process be bound by the agreement laid out before you, and so on and so on."

Oona entered the parlor and stood beside the door, Deacon on her shoulder. Isadora Iree glanced in Oona's direction and snickered. Looking down at her own dress, it wasn't until that moment, standing in the bright glow of the parlor's magic lamplight, that Oona saw precisely how filthy she was. She ran a hand through her newly grown hair and brought it away filled with cobwebs. Adler Iree chanced to look her way at precisely the same moment, and she flushed with embarrassment.

Presently, the well-dressed, chubby New York boy spoke up. "What precisely does the document say?" he inquired.

"And you would be?" asked Mr. Ravensmith.

"Lamont John-Michael Arlington Fitch the Third," the boy said. He stared at the document on the table. The contract was so long that it had been rolled into a thick scroll, with only the bottom portion showing, where the applicants were to sign their names.

"I'll tell you what it says," said Isadora Iree. "It says if you do not sign it, you won't get the job." She snatched the fountain pen from Mr. Ravensmith's well-groomed fingers and scribbled her name so large that it took up three lines.

"Next," said Mr. Ravensmith. His gaze fell back to the New York boy.

"My father is the head of the Palmroy Manhattan Bank," Lamont said. "He told me never to sign something before reading it."

"Your father is a wise man," said Mr. Ravensmith. "Do you read music, Mr. Fitch?"

"Music?" said Lamont. "Why, no."

"Well, then," said Mr. Ravensmith, "how are you going to read the document before you?"

Lamont gaped down at the contract as Mr. Ravensmith partially unrolled the immense document. Oona was fairly certain that she knew what was causing the boy's vexed expression. There would be no actual words on the contract, but instead only a very complex musical score. Clearly, the boy did not know that magical contracts were always written in musical notation.

"I don't understand," said Lamont. "What kind of contract is this?"

"A legal and binding one, young man," said Mr. Ravensmith. "Now, if you would be so good as to sign . . . there, just below Miss Iree."

Lamont blinked at the lawyer. He glanced once toward the other occupants on the bench, who appeared to find nothing strange in musical documents, and then shrugged. When he had finished signing, Lamont set the pen on the table and squared it, lining it up perfectly with the edge of the paper. "I have one more question," he said.

Mr. Ravensmith grimaced. "If you must, but make it quick. Time is money, Mr. Fitch. Your father must have taught you that, at the very least."

"What precisely is Dark Street?" Lamont asked.

Mr. Ravensmith slapped his own forehead. "Goodness! If you don't know that, then I can't possibly see—"

But Mr. Ravensmith stopped speaking when Samuligan placed his gaunt hand on the lawyer's shoulder. "Now, now, Mr. Ravensmith. Let us be fair."

The lawyer bowed slightly and stepped away, brushing his fingers at the place where the faerie servant had touched his jacket.

Samuligan moved forward, his cowboy hat shading his eyes. He smiled at Lamont, an expression that made the boy shrink back in his chair. "Mr. Fitch. The question you ask is a complicated one, for sure. But for you, the basics will have to do, so listen up. Dark Street is the last of the thirteen Faerie roads. It is not like any other road you have known. It exists in the space between two worlds—a place known as the Drift. It is called the Drift because in this *in-between* place, nothing stands still, but instead remains in nearly constant flux. The street acts much like the hour hand on a clock, rotating through the Drift in a great circle. Do you follow me so far?"

Lamont John-Michael Arlington Fitch III nodded his round head, though to Oona it appeared that the boy was more frightened of annoying Samuligan than truly understanding.

"Very good," said Samuligan. "Now, at the north end of the street stand the Iron Gates. This is important to know, because at precisely twelve o'clock midnight, every night, the Iron Gates open upon New York City, where they remain open for exactly one minute before closing, and once again beginning the rotation. The pendulum that swings through this room is the instrument that keeps the street moving in perfect time.

"Also worthy of note is the fact that the Iron Gates are far older than the city of New York. There was once a time when, at midnight, the gates opened upon Paris. Before that it was Prague, and before that, Oxford, all the way back to five hundred years ago, when the Magicians of Old first set the street into motion as a protective measure against faerie attack."

At the mention of attack, Lamont's eyebrows shot up in alarm.

Samuligan strode the length of the room, pointing at the portrait of Oswald the Great and his lizard, Lulu. Oswald was beardless and hatless. He looked to be a man in his mid-forties, yet appeared both young and old at the same time; as wise as any sage, and wild as the wind. His long, straight hair fell just past his shoulders, black as a raven's wing. With his famous magic wand in hand, and dressed in his dark green magician's robes, he stood before an enormous open gateway made of glass, beyond which a great stone stairway ascended endlessly into the clouds.

"Which brings us to the opposite end of Dark Street," Samuligan continued. "The south end. That is where you will find the Glass Gates, which do not open, and which have remained locked shut ever since this man, Oswald, the greatest of the Magicians of Old, closed them nearly five hundred years ago. As you can see in this painting, those gates lead to a set of enormous steps, which in turn lead to what some refer to as the Other-lands, or the Land of the Fay, but which most people simply call Faerie—a place where every grain of sand, and every breath of air, is filled with magic. It was through the generosity of the mighty Queen of the Fay that the Magicians of Old learned their first spells, and it was there, in Faerie, that they became greedy and stole the secret knowledge that the queen would have kept hidden. The magicians were very clever, indeed, but when the queen learned of their treachery, so began the terrible thirteen-year Great Faerie War. Many and more perished, magicians and faeries alike. I should know. I was there. But that is a tale for another day. All you really need to know is that the place where you now rest your ample bottom is Pendulum House. It is the magical anchor to which the street holds its course. It is also the home of the Wizard, whose sole job is to protect the World of Man should the Glass Gates ever fall. Does that answer your question?"

The chubby New York boy looked as though he might ask yet another, but upon second consideration he simply nodded.

"And now if we are quite done with the history lesson," said Mr. Ravensmith in an exasperated tone, "I implore the rest of you to please sign below Miss Iree and Mr. Fitch before we are asked to explain why the sky is dark at night." He thrust the fountain pen into Adler Iree's hand, watched as the boy signed his loopy scrawl, then snatched the pen back and handed it to the witch. She signed the paper with a shaky hand.

"Well, then," Mr. Ravensmith said, "it appears we are missing one applicant. But that is to be expected. People are always backing out at the last minute. Magic isn't as popular as it used to be." He turned to Oona. "That leaves only you, Miss Crate." He extracted a second scroll from his inside jacket pocket, this one nearly double the size of the first. He set it on the table with a heavy thump. "If you would sign here at the bottom of this document, thereby forfeiting all rights and privileges to said apprenticeship, wizardship, benefits, and properties, blah, blah, blah, et cetera and et cetera."

Oona's heart skipped a beat as the lawyer extended the pen and motioned her toward the table.

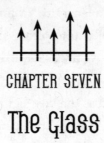

CHAPTER SEVEN

The Glass

What a ghastly sight I must seem, Oona thought. She brushed a string of cobweb from her sleeve and made her way across the parlor to the table.

The smell of ashes from the fireplace filled the air, and she stifled a sneeze before receiving the pen from Mr. Ravensmith, a bit clumsily, but she managed to keep from fumbling it to the floor. The realization of what she was about to disown came into full focus. One of these four strangers was going to become her replacement. She read the signatures affixed to the first document and assessed them one by one.

The young witch's handwriting was so absurdly

small that Oona was forced to dig her magnifying glass out of her pocket in order to read the minuscule letters. Sanora Crone. She was a toothpick of a girl with a sweet face, but she looked as though she might be frightened of her own shadow.

Next there was Isadora Iree of the Academy of Fine Young Ladies, Adler Iree from the Magicians Legal Alliance, and lastly, the New Yorker, Lamont John-Michael Arlington Fitch III, a round-faced boy whom she knew absolutely nothing about.

What had Uncle Alexander been thinking to advertise such a position in the New York Times? she wondered.

Mr. Ravensmith gave her dusty appearance a disdainful look before indicating the line at the bottom of the second document. "Sign right there."

Oona set the magnifying glass on the table, looked at the pen in her other hand, and hesitated.

"You don't have to do it," Deacon whispered in her ear. "You can talk to your uncle, and he will be happy to have you stay. I'm sure of it."

Oona licked her lips, which suddenly felt dry and chapped. Her heart began to beat faster, and her palms felt slick.

She leaned over the table, pressing the tip of the pen to the bottom of the scroll. Everyone leaned forward with her, and suddenly her fingers felt all tingly, as if she had placed her hand too close to a fire. Her hand pulled away from the paper.

How very curious, she thought, amazed that her heart was racing. Was this the magic inside of her attempting to thwart her decision? She did not know. This was what she wanted after all, wasn't it?

Of course it is, she told herself. *There's no backing out now.*

"Having trouble?" said a voice, and Oona looked up. Everyone turned. It was Isadora Iree. "Can't you sign your name?"

"I beg pardon?" asked Oona.

"I asked a simple question," said Isadora, a kind of sneaky malice in her eyes. "If you are unable to sign your name, then all you need to do is make an X. Do you know what an X is? It goes like this." She drew an invisible X in the air with her finger before adding: "I hope you are better at finding my mother's dresses than you are at dressing. By the way, you might consider taking a bath and having your clothes laundered every once in a while. Looks like you just crawled out of a coffin. What is that on your head, anyway? A wig?"

Oona stiffened, her temper beginning to rise. "It is nothing of the sort!"

Deacon whispered in her ear. "Easy now."

Isadora smirked, disbelieving. "Well, your hair must grow very fast, then. Is that why it's so filthy?"

"Bloody hell, Isadora," said Adler in his thick Irish accent. "Don't be such a witch."

Isadora gasped, as if Adler had just called her the worst name possible, and yet it was Sanora Crone, the young witch, who appeared the most hurt by the insult. She flinched in her seat.

Isadora snatched up the magnifying glass that Oona had left on the table and held it up threateningly, as if about to smash it against Adler's head.

"You take that back," she demanded.

"I won't," said Adler.

Oona took in a sharp breath at seeing her father's magnifying glass in Isadora's hand. The glass was very delicate and was by no means meant to be used as a weapon.

"You give that back!" Oona shouted.

Isadora looked at what she was holding and either realized that it was, after all, a rather ineffective tool to threaten someone with, or she simply grew bored of the little scene, but either way the effect was the same. She rolled her eyes at Oona and said: "Catch."

Time seemed to slow down as Isadora tossed the magnifying glass in Oona's direction. Whether on purpose or not Oona was unable to tell, but the toss had a bit too much strength behind it, and the glass sailed over Oona's head. It flipped end over end like a baton and slammed against the corner of a side table. The sound of shattering glass filled Oona's ears, and her mouth formed a perfect O as she watched the lens explode into a hundred pieces and fall to the floor.

For the briefest of moments, the room went deathly silent, and then Oona felt something snap inside of her.

"Reconcilio!"

The word seemed to come from deep within her; a place she had hoped would stay hidden forever. But the anger had somehow pulled it out of her. The shattered bits of glass began to fly off the ground in little arcs, as if time had been reversed. The shards came together, forming a swirl within the gold-plated metal ring. A flash of brilliant white light filled the room, along with a cracking sound that echoed off the giant pendulum, making it ring like a bell. It was a complex sound that might have been the bowing of a thousand violins. Lamont John-Michael Arlington Fitch III shouted in surprise, and the young witch screamed. And then the ringing sound abruptly stopped.

The magnifying glass lay whole and unblemished on the carpet, its lens flawless and glistening once more.

Oona snatched it up from the ground, but her mouth had gone terribly dry. A sharp stab of guilt pierced her heart like a dart, and she stuffed the instrument into her pocket like a little girl afraid of getting caught with something she was not supposed to have. She blinked several times, shaking her head in disbelief, not because the magic had fixed the glass so perfectly, but because she had used magic at all. She had not meant to. It had just . . . come out. On its own. The realization frightened her, and, with a quick glance at the others, it seemed that she was not alone in her surprise. Adler Iree's were the first set of eyes that she saw. They were wide with astonishment. The expressions on the faces of the other three applicants were, likewise, filled with amazement.

Oona wanted suddenly to plead with them to not say a word about what she had just done, especially not to the Wizard. He would not be angry. She was not afraid of that. Indeed, he would likely be interested to hear all about it, but all the same, she did not want him to know.

Again she looked to Adler, who continued to stare at her, his large blue eyes glued to her in a look of perpetual wonder.

It was Isadora who broke the silence. "When I'm apprentice, will I learn to do that?"

Oona turned on her, eyes slitted, suddenly seething at the careless way the girl had treated her father's magnifying glass.

Mr. Ravensmith cleared his throat. "Miss Crate, your signature please."

Oona turned her fiery gaze upon the lawyer, about to give him a piece of her mind, but then, realizing that she had nothing to say, she pressed the pen to the bottom of the rolled-up document, wanting nothing more than to have done with it all. Again her hand began to tingle, as if some inner part of her were fighting against her actions, but this time she gritted her teeth, hastily signed her name, and then dropped the pen to the table as if it were a hot ember.

Mr. Ravensmith signed his own name as witness to both contracts. As he finished, the parlor door opened and the Wizard strode into the room, his purple robes billowing out behind him. He glanced at the lawyer.

Mr. Ravensmith bowed slightly. "Everything is in order, sir."

CHAPTER EIGHT

The Faerie Catcher
and the Faerie Death

I will take my leave of you," Mr. Ravensmith told the Wizard. "I do have an actual *paying* client awaiting me."

Oona stood apart from the applicants, all of whom had stood up from the bench upon the Wizard's entrance, and were now on their feet in a line behind the table. Oona watched the proceedings, feeling slightly dazed. She was still reeling from what she had done, trying to understand what had happened, and why she had used the magic. Something deep inside of her had stirred. And it hadn't been just anger. She had been quite angry and afraid the night before in Igregious Goodfellow's hideout. No magic had come spilling out then. No. Whatever the reason behind her spontaneous act, it had something to do with the thought of losing her father's magnifying glass.

The Wizard glanced in the lawyer's direction, but before he could give the lawyer leave to go, the door to the parlor banged open, startling everyone.

"Sorry I'm late!" cried a voice, as a tall, gangly man stepped into the room. He spoke in a loud, theatrical voice that Oona found both overbearing and highly irksome. She did a double take, realizing that the latecomer was none other than Hector Grimsbee, the blind man whom she had seen disappear from the steps in front of the museum. He was no longer carrying his red umbrella, and Oona noticed that, for some reason, his clothing appeared quite disheveled. He looked as if he had been in some sort of scuffle. The top of his head was wrapped in a thick white bandage, and an oily bloodstain could be seen seeping through the raggedy cloth at his forehead.

"And you would be?" asked Mr. Ravensmith.

"Hector Grimsbee," said the mustached man. "I am an applicant for the position of Wizard's apprentice."

Oona gaped at him. Though there was no age limit for applicants, the man appeared to be at least forty years old, which in Oona's opinion was far too old to be applying for the position of apprentice. Grimsbee turned his head, sniffing in her direction, and Oona saw that the man's eyes were completely white, devoid of any pupils at all. Like two bottomless pools of milk, they appeared to look right at her. Oona stepped back as Grimsbee grinned, tweezing the end of his bullhorn mustache between his fingers.

"You are late," said the Wizard, sounding very displeased.

"And you need to sign the contract to be eligible for the position," Mr. Ravensmith said, sighing. "It's on the table." He took hold of Grimsbee's arm, as if to guide the blind man to the table, but Grimsbee jerked his arm away.

"I do not need assistance. I can *smell* my way." His nostrils swelled, nearly doubling in size, so that they resembled nothing less than two enormous tunnels in the center of his face. He stepped forward, moving quite confidently around an unoccupied chair, stepping over a footstool in the process, and then proceeded to march directly toward the enormous swinging pendulum. Everyone gasped, but before anyone could say anything, Grimsbee abruptly changed directions and walked to the table with the contracts on it. Leaning down, he sniffed inquisitively at the large book that Adler Iree had left on the tabletop, and then promptly followed his nose to the two rolled-up contracts. He straightened. "There are two documents here, each with very distinctive smells. Which do I sign?"

Mr. Ravensmith moved quickly to his side, appearing

quite astounded at Grimsbee's extraordinary sense of smell. The lawyer slid the proper contract in front of the blind man and handed him the fountain pen. Grimsbee signed his name . . . and then pocketed the pen. With a twist of his mustache, Grimsbee fixed the lawyer with his sightless eyes, as if daring Mr. Ravensmith to ask for the pen back. Mr. Ravensmith, who seemed all at once quite anxious to get as far away from Grimsbee as possible, only said: "I believe my work is done here." He brushed nervously at the sleeve of his jacket and turned to the Wizard. "With your leave, sir."

"Of course," said the Wizard, and the lawyer hurried out of the room, closing the door behind him. The Wizard looked Grimsbee over. "Haven't I seen you somewhere before?"

Grimsbee cleared his throat, and, utilizing the full volume of his theatrical voice, said: "Most likely you saw me upon the grand stage at the Dark Street Theater, and were wowed by my incredible thespian skills."

He gave a little bow.

The Wizard snapped his fingers. "Oh, yes, that's it. You are an actor. There was an artist's sketch of your face in the *Dark Street Tribune* about a year ago. I believe you were accused of dropping a sandbag on a director's head."

Grimsbee's face flushed red. "That was never proven."

"I see," the Wizard said. He peered suspiciously at the bloody bandage around Grimsbee's head, but made no mention of it. "Well, please, Mr. Grimsbee. Take your place next to the others."

Grimsbee sniffed the air and took his place beside Sanora Crone. He turned his ghoulish face down toward the young witch. "You smell awful."

Sanora looked ready to cry, and Oona had a good mind to tell the blind man to keep his horrible mouth shut, but before she could do so, Isadora pointed at Grimsbee and said: "Hey, I know you. You live in one of the apartments above my mother's dress shop."

Grimsbee nodded, tweezing his mustache between his fingers before adding, rather defensively: "I live on the third floor, right above Mr. and Mrs. Bop. What's it to you?"

"I was only saying . . ." Isadora trailed off, clearly disliking the blind man's haunting stare.

The Wizard clapped his hands together, catching everyone's attention.

"Here is how the Choosing will go." He walked to the center of the room and stood just in front of the pendulum, watching it swing back and forth several times before turning to face the applicants. "I am now going to ask each of you to—"

But the Wizard suddenly staggered, his eyes round

with surprise. He took in a sharp breath and then buckled forward, dropping to the floor. Oona gasped.

Someone shouted: "What's wrong with him?"

Someone else screamed.

Samuligan darted forward, dropping down beside the fallen Wizard, the sound of his bony knees echoing against the floor. Oona rushed to his side, a thousand frantic thoughts racing through her head. What was the matter with her uncle? A stroke? A heart attack?

But even as Oona prepared for the worst, she quickly found that her mind was in no way equipped to understand the sight before her. Her breath hitched in her throat as she peered over Samuligan's shoulder at her uncle's body, only to discover that there was no body there at all, just the Wizard's empty robes sprawled out flat, like a deflated balloon on the floor.

She stared in disbelief. A long metal dagger protruded from the empty robes, sticking straight through the fabric and pinning it to the floor. The hilt twinkled in the sconce light, the double-edged blade protruding from the very place where her uncle's chest should have been.

Deacon let out a sharp cry.

"What has happened?" asked Hector Grimsbee, though oddly enough, his blank eyes appeared to be looking directly at the spot where the empty robes lay. "Who screamed?"

"What has happened to him?" Oona cried.

Samuligan shook his head, eyebrows drawn closely together, his expression uncharacteristically bewildered.

"Is he . . . ?" Oona began, but trailed off, unwilling to finish the thought. It felt as if someone had reached inside of her chest and was crushing her heart in a tight fist. It was hard to breathe. She glanced up into the faces of the applicants, but their expressions were too difficult to read through her blurred vision. Tears welled in her eyes. This could not be happening. It was simply a bad dream. She would wake up and laugh it away. It was just not possible that the Wizard was . . . was . . .

She tried to force the word from her lips. "Is he . . . ?"

"Dead?" said Samuligan. He shook his head. "I cannot say."

He wrenched the dagger from the floor. There was a sizzling sound, like bacon in a hot frying pan. With a cry of pain Samuligan flung the dagger away. It bounced across the carpet before skittering to a stop near the table. Oona pushed herself quickly to her feet, confusion blurring her thoughts. She wiped at her eyes, her gaze rolling from the smoking dagger on the floor to Samuligan, who cradled his singed hand against his chest—thin wisps of smoke floating upward from his palm.

"That is no ordinary dagger," Samuligan said, his voice like a whip. His haunting eyes scanned the room as he rose to his full height. "And this is no accident. Someone has deliberately stabbed the Wizard."

"What?" Oona said, shaking her head. She could see the Wizard's empty robes at her feet, and the slit that the dagger had made in the purple fabric. "Someone did this to him? How is that possible?"

Deacon launched himself from Oona's shoulder and landed beside the dagger, where he hastily inspected the emblem of a half-lidded eye etched into the hilt. The dagger was small and thin, with almost no cross guard to speak of, and shiny as polished silver.

"This blade is not used for stabbing," he said at last, and Oona saw his thick, black feathers shudder. "No, not for stabbing, but for throwing! It is the kind of dagger thrown not with the hand, but one that is thrown with the mind. There are only two daggers such as this that have ever been known to exist. They are known as *Fay Mors Expugno* and *Fay Mors Mortis*."

Isadora Iree gasped. "The Faerie Catcher and the Faerie Death!"

Samuligan fixed her with his hard gaze. "You have heard of them, Miss Iree?"

Isadora glanced around nervously. "We . . . ah . . . learn all about faerie lore at the Academy of Fine Young Ladies."

Deacon hopped uneasily away from the dagger before

returning to Oona's shoulder. "Then, Miss Iree, you would know that both daggers were created during the Great Faerie War, by the Magicians of Old. They were weapons created with the specific purpose of either kidnapping or assassinating the most powerful highborn faeries and military captains. Nearly a hundred years after the war ended, the daggers became the very first acquisitions of the Museum of Magical History, and they have resided there—out of public view—for hundreds of years."

Oona's gaze darted toward Hector Grimsbee, whom she herself had seen standing in front of the museum that very morning. Grimsbee's face appeared inscrutable. Her heart was thrumming, and it took all of Oona's concentration to focus on what Deacon was saying. It was all very important information, she knew, but it was so hard to think straight with her uncle's empty robes lying at her feet.

Perhaps he is still alive, somehow, she thought. *What was it Deacon said about kidnapping?*

"The two daggers were twins," Deacon continued. "But they had very different powers. *Expugno* was the name of the dagger enchanted to capture and imprison. Thus, its name: the Faerie Catcher. It was intended to be used to capture highborn faeries, but was instead used only once to capture a certain high-level general in the Faerie Army. That general was Samuligan the Fay. Is that not true?"

Samuligan nodded grimly. "To be sure, it was the *Expugno* dagger that captured me over five hundred years ago."

"But Samuligan is now a servant of Pendulum House," Oona said, and she seized upon the faint hope that perhaps the Wizard had only been transported to another part of the house. "Do you mean that Uncle Alexander might be in Pendulum House somewhere?" she asked.

Deacon and Samuligan shared a look.

"I'm afraid not," Samuligan said. "When I was captured by the Magicians of Old, the dagger transported me to a prison: a dark place with no light at all. I later learned that that heinously dark place was, in fact, a tiny cell at the top of a great, windowless tower. But at the time it did not matter where I was, since I was no longer in my own body. For you see, not only was I locked away in the tower of eternal night, but also imprisoned within the body of a lizard. In that reptile state I was unable to use my magical powers to try and escape."

Samuligan pointed a gangly finger at the portrait of Oswald the Great and his lizard, Lulu, before continuing: "It was Oswald himself who captured me. He had a fondness for lizards, as I'm sure you all know . . . and so it was a lizard that he chose as the form of my ultimate prison. How long I remained in that state, I cannot say, but one day Oswald himself came to the tower and released me from my enchantment, returning me to my original faerie form, but only after he and his fellow magicians worked such heavy magic upon me that I was forever locked into a life of service to the occupants of Pendulum House."

The story—which Oona had never heard before in its entirety—caused a shiver to snake down her spine. A thought occurred to her. "The Black Tower in the cemetery," she said. "You were locked in the Goblin Tower!"

Samuligan nodded. "It was the Goblin Tower, indeed."

Oona looked down at the shiny blade on the floor and said: "If that is the same dagger that was used on you, Samuligan, then that must mean that Uncle Alexander is locked up inside that tower right now!" A wave of frantic urgency washed over her at the realization. "We have to get him out! This instant! What are we waiting for?"

Once again, Deacon and Samuligan shared a look.

"What? What is it now?" Oona asked. Her frustration was threatening to boil over. "Why are you looking at each other?"

Reluctantly, Deacon said: "But you are forgetting that the *Expugno* dagger had a twin: *Fay Mors Mortis*. The Faerie Death. The Magicians enchanted *Mortis* to not only kill whomsoever it struck but to wipe the victim out of existence completely." He paused, looking gloomily down at the dagger on the floor. "The two daggers were formed from the same mold. I cannot say which of the two daggers this one is."

Oona's heart plummeted. Her knees turned to water, and suddenly Adler Iree was at her side, supporting her. His touch was cold but comforting. For a moment she thought to turn to him and bury her face in his shoulder, and there let the tears consume her, until it suddenly occurred to her that someone in this room must have done this to her uncle. It could have been anyone of them . . . including Adler.

Deacon fluttered to the back of a chair, raking his black eyes across the room and echoing Oona's thought. "How someone in this room came to possess the dagger, I cannot say. But surely one of you is the attacker."

Oona stepped away from Adler, whose cloak hung from his shoulders, raggedy and frayed. The boy did not appear to notice her move away. He seemed deep in consideration. At last, he said: "If that dagger, whichever one it is, *Expugno* or *Mortis*, is thrown with the mind, then the attacker could have thrown it from anywhere. Or they could throw it again at any moment."

Lamont John-Michael Arlington Fitch III took in a startled gasp.

Deacon glanced suspiciously in the boy's direction. "No. The magics used to enchant the daggers were very complicated, even for the likes of the Magicians of Old.

There were strong stipulations set on the objects in order to make them work properly. It could be thrown only once within a twenty-four-hour period, which would give it time to . . . well, to recharge, you could say. The spells also stated very clearly that the daggers would work only under the following conditions, and I quote from the *Encyclopedia Arcanna*: 'For purposes of accuracy, the throwing of either dagger must take place within a confined space, such as a room. The dagger must be carried into the room by the attacker, who in turn must visually see the victim from a distance of no more than ten paces away.' Also, for fear of their own creations being used against them, the Magicians of Old enchanted the weapons so that no faerie could touch them without burning their flesh."

All eyes turned to Samuligan, who raised his hand, displaying his char-black palm. The smell of burned flesh still permeated the air.

"You mean that only someone in this room could have done this?" Oona asked.

"That is correct," Deacon said. "Someone must have brought the dagger into the room and seen the Wizard with their own eyes in order to have thrown it with their mind."

"I want to go home," said Sanora Crone, the young witch. Oona realized it was the first time she had heard the girl speak, and she sounded terribly frightened.

"No one is to go anywhere until the police have been fetched," Deacon said in his most authoritative voice.

"But Deacon, we must get to the cemetery at once," Oona said. "The only way to find out if Uncle Alexander is dead or alive is to discover if he is inside that tower."

"That will have to wait, Miss Crate," said Samuligan.

The words angered her. Oona whirled around to glare up at him, the hem of her skirt swirling about her ankles in a storm of fabric. "What are you talking about, Samuligan? Wait for what? We don't know if my uncle is dead or alive, and you tell me to wait?"

Samuligan met her gaze with a soft, pitying look. It was not unkind, and no doubt was meant as comforting, and yet it was a look that Oona had never before seen upon the face of the faerie servant. It was not mocking or amused. It was a look of utter compassion and under-standing, as if he knew all too well the horrible sense of panic that was rising up in her, threatening to overwhelm her completely.

Deacon flew to her shoulder, and when he spoke, it was in a gentler voice than he had been using before. "Samuligan is correct. The Black Tower resides in the center of the cemetery, and it is now past seven o'clock. The sun has set."

Oona shook her head. "What does that have to do with . . . ?" But she trailed off. Her mouth opened and closed several times as she realized what Deacon was talking about. Finally, she said: "Oh. Of course. No one may enter the cemetery by night."

"They would be ridiculously stupid to try," said Isadora. "And doomed to fail."

Oona glared at her, but she knew Isadora was right.

Adler dropped into a chair. "The army would certainly see to it that no one enters the City of the Dead after dark."

At the mention of the name, City of the Dead, the room seemed to grow somewhat colder and the lights slightly dimmer. But of course that might just have been Oona's imagination. It was at that moment that Lamont John-Michael Arlington Fitch III stepped meekly forward before asking: "I beg your pardon, but what is the City of the Dead, and why is it guarded by an army?"

Oona peered at the boy suspiciously. She knew absolutely nothing about the New Yorker, and for all she knew it had been he who had attacked her uncle, no matter how wide-eyed and confused he may appear. Indeed, Oona felt like accusing him on the spot. Or accusing them all. But she contained herself with the realization that that was precisely the kind of behavior employed by Inspector White. No doubt Oona's father, a far superior police inspector, would have kept his suspicions to himself until he had more proof.

Surprisingly, it was Hector Grimsbee who answered Lamont's question. In a cold, hushed stage whisper—like a man preparing to tell some horrible ghost story—he said: "The City of the Dead is what the residents of Dark Street call the cemetery after dark. It is where the ghosts of a thousand souls rise from their graves each night to dance and play amongst the headstones and mausoleums. A place where the living are not permitted to enter, and where the ghosts of a regiment of soldiers—poltergeists with shimmering shields and glowing swords, dead for five hundred years—stand vigilant guard at the gates of the cemetery. From dusk until dawn they stand their watch, allowing no spirit out, nor any living person in. And pity the fool who attempts to cross their path, for they will soon join the dead at their play."

Lamont gazed at the blind man, disbelieving. But when he turned to the others, and they all nodded their agreement that this was, in fact, the way of it, the New York boy shuddered, and like Adler Iree, he, too, took a seat.

"And besides," Deacon added. "Even if the Wizard is locked inside the tower, you will need to discover how to get inside, and then of course there are the goblins to consider."

Oona gazed up at the goblins in the tapestries on the walls. They seemed to be mocking her with their pointy ears and penetrating gazes. She sighed heavily, feeling very tired and very angry at the same time. "Well, it seems we must wait until tomorrow to check the tower. But for tonight, there is still a way to find out if the Wizard is dead or alive."

"And how is that?" Deacon asked inquisitively.

Oona took in the applicants one by one. "We make the attacker confess."

CHAPTER NINE

Waiting for the Authorities

U pon Deacon's insistence, and in spite of Oona's own reluctance, a note was sent via flame to police head-quarters, informing the inspector of the crime that had been committed. Oona was certain that if Inspector White got involved, he would only make matters worse. But of course, Deacon was right. The police must be informed, and so she wrote the note herself, using all capital letters, which, because of her shaking hand, was the only way she could make her writing legible.

URGENT. WIZARD HAS BEEN ATTACKED. POSSIBLY MURDERED. BODY MISSING. COME AT ONCE. SUSPECTS STILL IN PENDULUM HOUSE. [signed] O.C.

Oona had then handed the note to Samuligan, who had in turn struck a match, set it ablaze, and placed it in the fireplace. Several minutes later a response appeared in the same spot. It explained that the inspector was out on a case and would be dispatched to Pendulum House as soon as possible. In the meantime, a police constable would be sent to secure the crime scene. No one was to be permitted to leave the premises.

"You mean we all have to wait here?" Isadora asked in alarm. "But there is a possible murderer among us. And what if they have that other dagger on them?"

Hector Grimsbee, who for some reason had declined to take a seat in a proper chair and was hunkered down on the carpet with his elbows on his knees, said: "The young lady with the melodious voice does have a point. It's quite possible that we are all in grave danger. Perhaps we should return to the safety of our own homes."

But Samuligan, who had taken on a bit of the authority figure, would not hear of it and suggested that they all retire to separate rooms until the inspector arrived. Oona thought this was an excellent plan, as it would allow her the benefit of interviewing each suspect individually.

Together, they all exited the parlor, crossing through the central antechamber, where the smells of dust, and wood, and iron, and stone collided like a soup in the belly of the manor. They ascended the grand staircase, the wood steps creaking beneath their feet as they paraded to the second floor, where the faerie servant showed the visitors to their separate rooms; he then joined Deacon and Oona in the hallway.

The various shapes in the long red carpet shifted constantly beneath their feet, forming new and ever-changing patterns. This in turn gave the impression that the three of them were still moving down the hall, despite the fact that they all stood in one spot. Black iron sconces threw harsh lines of light against their faces.

"Who should we begin with?" Oona asked.

"What?" Deacon said. And then, realizing what she was planning to do, he added: "You don't plan on interrogating the suspects yourself, do you?"

Oona raised an eyebrow. "What did you expect, Deacon?"

"But . . . but . . . do you think it a very wise thing to do?" he asked. "I mean, one of them attacked your uncle with an enchanted dagger. A dagger that has a twin, mind you. They could have the other one on them at this moment. I understand how you must feel, Miss Crate, but you promised your uncle that you would not go snooping around deadly criminals."

Oona sighed. She looked down at the moving lines on the floor, watching them twist and mutate from one unique pattern to another. Of course Deacon was right. She had indeed told her uncle that she would stay away from just such a situation, but what choice did she have? The situation had come to her, not the other way around. And she was fairly certain that Deacon was wrong about understanding how she felt. That was quite impossible, otherwise he would not be questioning her actions. She simply *had* to take charge of the case. It was the only way; otherwise, if she didn't occupy herself with some immediate action, then she was quite certain she would burst into tears at any minute.

Uncle Alexander is not dead, she told herself. *He's only been imprisoned in the tower. We'll figure out a way to get him out tomorrow, once the sun has risen and the ghosts have returned to their graves.*

But a second thought floated through her head like a cruel serpent . . . its words like venom: *Don't fool yourself. He's dead. Dead like your father. Dead like your mother, and your baby sister, too. Whose fault is that? Whose fault is it that the Wizard was looking for a new apprentice in the first place? This would never have happened if you hadn't broken his heart and abandoned your duties. Abandoned him. And now he's dead, too. Gone forever, and it is all your fault.*

Oona could feel the tears beginning to well, but she blinked them back. Now was not the time. "I will begin with the young witch, Miss Sanora Crone," she announced.

A knocking sound came from downstairs. It was, no doubt, the police constable at the front door come to secure the crime scene. Samuligan turned toward the stairs to attend to the front door. That was good. Sanora Crone seemed quite terrified of the faerie servant—indeed, seemed terrified of just about everything—and it would be better if he were not in the room. Between Samuligan and the constable, at least the dagger downstairs would be protected.

Oona turned to the first door on the right, where a sign over the door read: CAPTAIN'S CABIN.

"Well, here we go," said Deacon. "But do be careful. Almost nothing is known of the witches of Witch Hill."

"I will be as cautious as a cat," Oona said.

Deacon bristled, squawking at her. "The phrase is either 'curious as a cat' or 'cautious as a fox.' Which did you mean?"

Oona smiled wryly at him—a genuine smile that somehow slipped through her cage of grief—and then removed a hairpin from her pocket. In one well-rehearsed motion, she twisted her hair into a respectable-looking bun at the back of her head. She then squared her shoulders, feeling as ready as she would ever be, before raising her fist to knock on the door.

Knock, knock.

"Who's there?"

"Oona."

"Oona who?"

Oona and Deacon shared a look. Another smile stitched its way across Oona's face. Deacon's smile showed in his eyes. Oona searched inwardly for a clever response, but when nothing came, she decided to stick with her original idea.

"It is I, Miss Oona Crate. I wanted to make sure you were all right."

The door creaked open less than an inch, and an eyeball peered out at her through the space beside the doorjamb. It made a study of Oona, rolling in its socket, taking her in from head to foot.

"Hello?" Oona said.

The eye blinked at her.

Oona was on the verge of pushing the door open herself when the gap widened several more inches, and the oddest little creature she had ever seen poked its head through the opening. It gazed up at her, looking wide-eyed and utterly frightful. Oona's surprise at seeing the creature nearly sent her stumbling backward off her feet.

"Oh my!" she said. But then, realizing what she was looking at, she said: "Is that you, Miss Crone?"

It was the young witch, indeed, who stood in the

doorway gazing up at Oona, her face covered in what appeared to be some sort of thick, greenish goo: a glistening, pasty substance that covered nearly every inch of her girlish face.

For an instant Oona thought: *Oh dear. She's somehow turned into a goblin.*

"Sorry," Sanora said earnestly. "Did I scare you? Didn't mean to, I didn't."

Her voice was high pitched and girly, and she spoke in a strange sort of cockney accent, such as one might hear among the working class on Dark Street, though it was certainly an original variation of the accent and one that Oona had never heard before. The goop on her face emitted a strong cinnamony, herbal smell.

"What on earth have you got all over your face?" Oona asked.

Sanora touched her cheek. "Oh, this?" she said. "It's just me Witchwhistle Beauty Cream."

Deacon shuddered, before saying: "You mean *my* Witchwhistle Beauty Cream."

The girl looked at him, puzzled. "No. I'm pretty sure it's mine."

Deacon shook his feathers. "No, no. You misunderstand. I was simply correcting your English. You said '*me*' instead of '*my*.'"

The girl shook her head. "Anyways. All us witches

use it. It's very soothing, so it is . . . and I thought it would help, right?"

"Help with what?" Oona asked.

"With me jitters," said Sanora. "It's sort of strange, you know? Being aboveground for so long, and all."

"I see," Oona said politely, and did not mention the fact that the so-called beauty cream looked more like congealing swamp slime. Not wishing to put the girl on her guard, however, Oona left the subject alone. "May I come in?" she asked.

The girl hesitated, her gaze falling on Deacon as if not sure what to make of the ominous bird. Then with a short nod she opened the door and backed away. Oona stepped inside and closed the door behind them. The floor swayed beneath their feet, and the young witch pressed her hand to her stomach, as if she might be ill.

"Oh," Oona said. "I see you got the Captain's Cabin. I haven't been in this room for a very long time."

In truth, it had been years since she had entered the room. The Captain's Cabin had been one of her mother's favorite rooms to visit whenever she would pay a call to Pendulum House. Her mother had had a great love of boats, Oona remembered. But of course Dark Street had no sailing port to speak of, nor any lake to sail upon. The duck pond in Oswald Park, which supported only small canoes and rowboats, had been a favorite destination of her mother's. But if someone wanted the sensation of sailing on a grand ship across the high seas, then the only place on Dark Street to go would have been the Captain's Cabin on the second floor of Pendulum House, which stuck out of the side of the great manor house like a giant shipwreck.

The windows were all shaped into round ship's portholes, and on the walls hung various charting tools and spyglasses and a spoked steering wheel nearly twice Oona's size. But it was not the room's decor that made it so peculiar. The smell of salt water clung to the dampened air, while the floor rocked beneath their feet like a ship adrift on calm waters. After Oona's baby sister, Flora, had been born, her mother would often visit the Captain's Cabin, and the rocking motion would lull the baby to sleep.

The herbal, cinnamony fragrance of Sanora's facial cream mingled with the salty sea air, and Oona felt both delighted and saddened by the memory of her mother. But then the room gave a sudden lurch to one side, as if a rogue wave had slapped full force against the side of the ship. Sanora placed both hands over her midsection, and Oona felt a moment of pity for the girl.

"I'm sorry for the accommodations," she said. "Pendulum House is a most unique place. I suppose any house with so much magic in it is bound to be an oddity.

But believe me, you haven't gotten the worst room. Two doors down is a room that is a complete jungle—quite literally—and you can hear all sorts of creepy things crawling all around you. Impossible to sleep in, if you ask me. Though, during a stormy night, it's somewhat difficult to hold on to your dinner in the Captain's Cabin."

The witch swayed on her feet, putting out a hand to steady herself.

"Perhaps we should sit down on the bed," Oona suggested.

They crossed the room on wobbly land legs and sat. Oona felt a cold wetness seep through her skirts as she realized too late that the bedding was damp from the moist sea air. Sanora's fingers fidgeted anxiously with her own dress.

"You can relax, if you like," Oona suggested. "Perhaps take your hat off."

"Oh, no, never!" Sanora said, grabbing the brim of her hat. "We witches never remove our hats. It's . . . unthinkable."

Oona threw a glance at Deacon, as if to say: *Why hadn't he ever told her about such a fact?* Deacon only shrugged; apparently this was news to him as well.

"Please forgive me, Sanora," Oona said. "It's just that, well, there is very little known about witches. Perhaps if you could tell me a bit about your customs, I could be sure not to upset you in the future. What is it that you witches all do, by the way?"

Sanora tugged nervously at her ear. "It's kind of boring."

"Boring?" Oona asked. "You should try listening to Deacon lecture on the improper usage of adverbs and dangling participles."

"What's a dangling participle?" asked Sanora.

"My point exactly," said Oona.

"Well!" said Deacon. "Someone has to protect the English language from sinking into utter chaos. Sometimes I believe it degrades by the minute."

"See what I mean?" Oona said to Sanora. "If I can put up with that, then I can surely stand to hear about life under Witch Hill."

Sanora cracked a smile. "Ain't much to tell, really. We spend most our time underground, right? But sometimes we're allowed up topside, you know, to gather supplies and the like . . . but then we're to be coming straight back to the hill. No dillydallying."

Oona squinched up her nose. "That doesn't sound like a very good deal to me. Do you like it?"

Sanora only shrugged. "Like I said, it's kind of boring. That's why I wanted to apply for the apprentice position. But things ain't turning out the way I'd hoped."

"Hmm," Oona intoned before asking: "You said you

are sometimes *allowed* out of the hill. Who allows you? The older witches?"

Sanora said nothing, eyes downcast.

Oona let the question go, and asked: "What is the inside of the hill like? Is it nice and neat, or just a big hole in the ground?"

Sanora drew her legs up beneath her, but Oona got the impression that she was considering something. Reading the girl's expression through the thick slather of goop on her face was all but impossible . . . but Sanora's eyes, those great big, sad-looking eyes, appeared surprisingly wise.

"Well, ain't really a hole," Sanora said finally. "It's more like a patchwork of twisting tunnels and the like. They run all over. You could get yourself good and lost in there, if you didn't know where you was goin'. Get lost forever."

"And the other witches?" Oona asked, feeling a bit daring now that she'd gleaned some actual information. "The older ones. Why is it that they never come above-ground?"

But Oona knew the moment she asked it that she had made a mistake. Sanora's mouth clamped shut, her lips completely disappearing beneath the slimy facial cream. Oona decided to change tactics.

She stood, ruffling the back of her dress, attempting to

air out the uncomfortable ocean dampness. "You know, there is one thing you *could* tell me, Sanora, that would be of enormous help. Nothing to do with the hill, I promise."

Sanora nodded. Oona knelt, and the light from the outside streetlamps spilled through the portholes and lit up her face. It was a serious look she wore, and the younger girl pulled her feet out from beneath her and placed them flat on the floor.

"Is there anything that you might have seen," Oona asked, "when my uncle was attacked?"

Sanora's hands began to fidget.

"You did, didn't you," Oona said, more a statement than a question. "It's all right, Sanora. You can tell me. Nothing bad will happen."

"It weren't what I saw when he was attacked," Sanora said, her voice almost a whisper. "It was what I saw yesterday. That creepy ol' blind man, Mr. Grimsbee."

"Go on," Oona encouraged. She could feel the excitement bubbling inside her.

Sanora's gaze shifted to the door, then back to Oona. "The entrance to the hill is a secret, right? It was enchanted long ago so that only a witch can find it. Well, anyway, as you probably well know, Witch Hill sits on the opposite side of the street from that big museum. And it was as I made me way out of the hill that I see ol' Grimsbee in front of the museum . . . on the top steps, right? I'd most like never have even noticed him, if it weren't for him yelling at someone who weren't there."

Oona shook her head. "Are you sure you didn't see him today? And not yesterday?"

Sanora did not hesitate. "No, it was yesterday, as I went out for supplies."

Peculiar, Oona thought. *And I saw him doing the same thing today, before he disappeared.*

Sanora looked highly uncomfortable. "Reason I bring it up is . . . well, is . . ."

She trailed off, as if unsure of her next words, but Oona spoke clearly, her words locking together like pieces in a jigsaw puzzle: "Is because my uncle was attacked with a dagger that could have come only from one place: the Museum of Magical History."

CHAPTER TEN

Pink

Oona closed the door to the Captain's Cabin, her mind racing. She strode several steps to the center of the hallway and stopped to peer at the long line of doors. Behind one of them was her uncle's attacker.

"How could Grimsbee be the attacker?" Deacon asked from her shoulder. "The laws governing the dagger state very clearly that the assassin must *see* the victim in order to throw the dagger with their mind."

"Do you believe that Mr. Grimsbee is truly blind, Deacon? Have you ever seen a blind man act in such a way?"

Deacon considered this for a moment. "But why would Grimsbee want to attack your uncle?"

Oona racked her brain for any kind of motive, but she could not think of a single one. But then again, she still did not see a motive for *any* of the applicants to have attacked him. The frustration began to build in her like pressure in a steam engine. She kicked her foot against the wall, startling Deacon from her shoulder, and the shock from the kick sent phantom fingers tingling up her leg.

"Ouch!" she said.

"Do be careful," Deacon replied, returning to her shoulder.

"Hello?" said a voice.

Oona turned in surprise, only to discover the New York boy, Lamont John-Michael Arlington Fitch III, poking his bulldoglike face outside his door. His cheeks flushed as pink as a summer rose beneath his thick, round eyeglasses. "Is everything all right?" he asked rather skittishly. "I heard someone bang on the wall. But oh, I must have been mistaken. So sorry. I didn't mean to disturb you. Good day."

He moved to close the door again, but Oona stopped him, seizing the opportunity to talk to the boy.

"No, wait," she said. "It's my fault. I was the one banging. Or rather, kicking. This whole matter is so upsetting. I would love to have some company . . . Mr. Fitch, is it? May I come in?"

The boy's face remained pink. "Ah . . . I don't believe

that's . . . um . . . proper. A young lady in a gentleman's room? What would people say?"

Oona smiled at him. "Well, if the gentleman truly is a gentleman, then there is nothing to worry about, is there?"

Lamont's mouth fell open, as if he could find no logical response, and Oona pressed her hand to the doorknob. The movement startled the boy, and he abruptly stepped away. Oona entered the room and pushed the door closed behind her.

Lamont John-Michael Arlington Fitch III had been given the Pink Room, in which all the colors of the room varied only in slight shades of pink, as if a pink paint bomb had exploded in the center, covering the walls, the curtains, the bed, the plants . . . even Lamont John-Michael Arlington Fitch III's well-fitted clothes. . . . And now Oona's dress, too, was pink.

Though it was, by all means, the least dangerous room in the house, the Pink Room was by far Oona's least favorite.

Lamont backed away from both Oona and the absurd-looking pink raven on her shoulder.

"I don't believe we have been properly introduced," Oona said, and she put her hand out. "I am Miss Oona Crate. The Wizard's niece."

Lamont's pink eyes met with hers. He took her hand

tentatively and shook it. Oona's gaze flicked toward the pink table near the wall, where two equally pink chairs sat empty.

"Oh . . . um . . . forgive me, Miss Crate," Lamont stammered. "Would you care to sit?"

Oona smiled. "Thank you. That would be most . . . appropriate."

She crossed to the table and waited patiently as Lamont pulled the chair out for her. Here was a case where the boy was working so fiercely at being a gentleman that Oona felt her best course of action would be to aid him in his goal.

"You are very kind," she said. "Won't you sit as well?"

Lamont glanced nervously toward the door, as if someone might burst in at any moment and find the two of them together in his room . . . alone. Oona would have to put him at ease.

"The Pink Room," she said conversationally, "was created by one of the original Magicians of Old, isn't that right, Deacon?"

Of all the occupants in the room, it was Deacon who appeared the most uncomfortable. His normally foreboding coat of midnight black now radiated a most unbecoming shade of fuchsia.

"Alice Annabel Thicket was the magician's name," Deacon answered, though he sounded nothing but displeased with the situation. "Apparently she loved all things pink."

"I see." Lamont said thoughtfully. "And these Magicians of Old. They are different from the Wizard?"

Oona nodded. "Technically, a magician is what we call anyone who can work magic, while the Wizard is the title we use for the head of all magic, and the protector of the World of Man: the world that you come from, Mr. Fitch. The Magicians of Old is the name given to powerful men and women who lived in the times before and during the Great Faerie War."

Lamont sat down heavily in the chair opposite Oona, the legs creaking beneath his bulk. Finally, he said: "Everything is so peculiar here. I admit, I was surprised to have been invited at all. You see, I read the advertisement in the *New York Times* about the Wizard seeking an apprentice, and immediately created a résumé. I hadn't much experience in any kind of work, but the advertisement stated that none was necessary."

Oona and Deacon shared a look. It was typical of her uncle to add such a stipulation to the advertisement. If he couldn't have Oona, then Uncle Alexander apparently preferred someone with no preconceived notions of magic whatsoever.

Lamont continued: "I showed the résumé to my father, who was oh so proud that I had shown interest in something, but my mother refused to let me send the résumé at all. She threw it into the fire before I had a chance to send it off. So how the Wizard knew that I wished to apply, I don't know. But six months later I received a letter stating that a carriage would be arriving at precisely eleven p.m. to pick me up with my luggage."

Oona smiled at him. "Had you already addressed your résumé to Pendulum House when your mother tossed it into the flames?"

"I had indeed," Lamont said.

"That explains it then," she said. "Dark Street has no post office to speak of. We send our letters by fire."

Lamont scratched his chubby cheek for a moment, and then replied: "I had a feeling it was something of that sort. Wizards and all. Well, against my mother's wishes, my father agreed to let me make the trip on my own. Said it would be good for my character. And yet, you can only imagine my surprise when later that same evening I found myself waiting in a carriage in front of two buildings in a part of New York that I was unfamiliar with. At the stroke of midnight, the buildings no longer sat side by side, but instead an enormous iron gateway stood in between them, as if it had been there the entire time. Beyond the gateway, a broad avenue stretched out for miles and miles. The driver drove us through, and a minute later the gates swung shut behind us."

Oona raised her eyebrows in polite amusement. She could only imagine his surprise at discovering an invisible street in New York City. For her, however, the extraordinary mystery of the Iron Gates proved to be something short of special.

Lamont continued: "The driver took me to a place called the Nightshade Hotel and Casino. Wonderful accommodations, I can assure you. It puts some of the finest hotels in New York to shame."

Oona shot Deacon a furtive glance. The Nightshade Hotel was owned and operated by none other than Red Martin himself . . . and, Oona believed, was the headquarters for the Dark Street criminal underground. But of course, since it was the only hotel on Dark Street, it was no real surprise that Lamont had stayed there. Just then, it occurred to Oona that the Nightshade Hotel was situated at the north end of the street. When she had seen Lamont in his carriage earlier that day, however, he had been miles away, on the south end, directly in front of the Museum of Magical History.

She cleared her throat, preparing to ask him why he had been in that area of town, when the door to the room fell open. It was Samuligan, his cowboy hat and knee-length jacket silhouetted in the light from the hall.

"The inspector has arrived," he said. "He has asked us all to convene in the parlor. It seems there has already been some further development in the case."

CHAPTER ELEVEN

A Roomful of Suspects

The inspector stood in the parlor of Pendulum House, his hands clasped behind his back. His ghastly white face gave the impression that not only did he never go outside in the daytime, but that he had also been locked inside a coffin for six months. Against the thick blackness of his hair, he appeared more like an artist's sketch than a real man. Tonight the inspector wore no jacket, and when he dropped his hands to his sides, it was nearly impossible to tell where his stark white shirt-sleeves stopped and his wrists and hands began. Without his customary black jacket, which Oona assumed he must have left in the entryway, the man looked eerily like a ghost.

The dagger no longer lay on the floor, but Oona could see its shiny metal surface glinting on top of the fireplace mantel. Everything else remained the same. The table, the contracts, and Adler Iree's book were all just where Oona remembered they had been. The Wizard's robes remained where he had fallen, and Oona's stomach tightened at the sight of them.

The parlor's customary sense of warmth and comfort had been replaced with something far less pleasant. The shadows seemed somehow deeper, the portraits more cold and judgmental. The painting of Oswald the Great appeared particularly ominous to Oona as he stared down upon the crime scene, looking like he was about to pass a death sentence upon them all. The creatures in the tapestries stared out at the room wearing expressions of bitter suspicion.

A police constable leaned casually against a wall near the parlor's entrance, his attention buried so deeply in a cheap, yellow-backed novel that, despite his uniform, he might have been mistaken for a man on vacation. Unlike the novel-reading constable, Inspector White's attention appeared fully present in the room. He regarded the occupants suspiciously as Oona took her seat on one of the ornate sofas against the wall. Deacon shifted restlessly on her shoulder.

The smell of ash from the fireplace permeated the air,

along with the lingering stench of Samuligan's singed hand.

"Is this everyone, Samuligan?" the inspector asked.

Samuligan scanned the room. Hector Grimsbee sat slumped in a chair near the door, the bloody bandage around his head looking like the ragged attire of an Egyptian mummy. Sanora Crone, her own face once again squeaky clean, occupied a seat on the other side of the fireplace. Isadora Iree played nervously with her hair beside Adler, the two of them squished together on one half of the split sofa. The pendulum swung so close to Adler that he appeared to be in danger of getting struck by the bob each time it moved past. Lamont John-Michael Arlington Fitch III took a seat near the door, his hands folded neatly in his lap.

"Yes," Samuligan informed the inspector. "This is everyone."

The enchanted lights from the ceiling threw uneven shadows across the inspector's face. He clapped his hands together loudly before beginning. "I am Inspector White. I believe you all know why I am here."

He picked up the enchanted dagger from the mantel and threw it to the floor, where it stuck in the rug, quivering like a tuning fork.

Sanora gasped.

Lamont let out a startled: "Whoa!"

And Deacon exclaimed: "That was a perfectly good carpet!"

The inspector ignored him. "This dagger," he said, swaggering around the room with his stark white shirt gleaming in the magic lights, "was reported stolen earlier this evening from the curator's locked office at the Museum of Magical History."

At the mention of the museum, Oona glanced toward Hector Grimsbee, looking for a reaction. He appeared stone-faced, indifferent, and for all she could tell, blind or not, he was staring right back at her through those pupilless eyes.

The inspector slid a notebook from his back pocket and continued. "The curator's office is located downstairs, in the basement of the museum. The basement is off limits to visitors, and a guard is posted at the head of the stairs. The curator locked his office and left the museum for several hours to examine a possible acquisition. When he returned at four o'clock, he discovered that the door to his office was wide open, the glass case containing the two enchanted daggers had been smashed, and the daggers were gone." The inspector snapped his notepad shut and thrust it out before him, as if the notepad itself were a piece of undisputable evidence. "The curator was the only one with a key, and the security guard at the head of the basement stairs swears that he allowed no one to pass."

Oona sat stock-still, listening to every word, her mind grabbing at each of the inspector's points, searching for clues.

The inspector cleared his throat, then said: "Clearly it was someone in this room who stole the daggers." He pointed at the dagger in the floor as proof. "And then that same individual used one of them to murder the Wizard!"

Oona shook her head, realizing what the inspector had just said. "Did you say *murder*?"

"I did, indeed," the inspector replied, sounding peeved for even having to answer the question.

Oona turned to the faerie servant. "Didn't you tell him, Samuligan?"

Samuligan clucked his tongue ruefully. "I did try, but—"

"Tell me what?" the inspector demanded.

"My uncle may not have been murdered," Oona informed him. "It is quite possible that he is still alive."

The inspector crossed to the center of the room and picked up the Wizard's empty robes. He shook them at Oona. "Then where is he?" he asked.

"Well, if he is alive, then he would be in the Goblin Tower," Oona said.

"In the Goblin Tower?" the inspector said. "Don't be ridiculous. A roomful of people saw him get stabbed. Is that not the case?"

He turned his attention to Lamont. Startled to be so singled out, the boy was forced to confess, "Yes, it is true," and then he pulled a handkerchief from his pocket and began nervously cleaning his eyeglasses.

"But Inspector," said Deacon. "While it is true that *one* of the daggers would have killed him, the other would have sent him to the Goblin Tower, as Miss Crate has just told you."

The inspector dropped the Wizard's robe back to the floor. "So, Mr. Bird, you admit to having knowledge of these weapons."

"Deacon has knowledge of the entire *Encyclopedia Arcanna*," Oona explained.

"How very convenient," the inspector replied.

Oona gaped at him. "Are you actually accusing Deacon?"

The inspector slowly shook his head and began to rub his thin, white hands together. "The museum has a registry at the front entrance. All persons entering the museum must sign their name. There is a museum security guard stationed at the entrance to make sure no one gets in without placing their name in the registry." The inspector abruptly turned his back to everyone and watched the pendulum swing from one end of the room to the other. "It would seem that very few people are interested in magical history these days . . . or at least on Mondays anyway . . .

because there were only two names written on today's page in the registry. And do you know whose names they were?" The inspector suddenly spun around so that his gaze fell on the Iree twins. "It just so happens that they are both sitting in this very room. Isadora and Adler Iree!"

Isadora slapped a hand to her chest. "Yes, I did go to the museum this morning . . . but only because Head Mistress Duvet at the Academy of Fine Young Ladies is very eager to have the next Wizard's apprentice be someone from her school. It's because of her that I ever even applied for the position in the first place, and it was at Head Mistress Duvet's explicit instructions that I went to the museum this morning so that I might refresh my knowledge of magical history before my interview with the Wizard. And I must say, I was completely bored out of my mind. Magical history is quite dull. There never is anyone in that huge building, and it's sort of . . . well, it's creepy being in there all alone."

"But Miss Iree," the inspector said, flipping open his notepad, "you did not go to the museum alone, did you? You went with your brother."

Isadora shook her head. "No, I went by myself. I only knew that Adler had been there because I saw his name written in the registry. But I didn't see him. The place is so big I could have been in there with a hundred people and never seen a single soul."

The inspector studied her for a moment before asking: "And what did you do after you left the museum, Miss Iree?"

"I went next door to my mother's dress shop for tea. Remember, you saw me there. All of my mother's dresses were stolen." Isadora drew in her breath. "Do you think that the daggers and the dresses were stolen by the same person?"

"I think it very likely that *you* stole them both, and then came to Pendulum House to murder the Wizard!" the inspector said.

"Me? Why on earth would I want to hurt the Wizard?"

The inspector strode across the room toward Isadora, hands outstretched as if preparing to grab hold of her shoulders and shake a confession out of her. But as he moved, the inspector failed to remember the dagger sticking out of the carpet. His foot struck the narrow hilt, and he tumbled to the floor.

"Who did that?" he howled, pushing himself quickly back to his feet and shoving his stringy, black hair back from his face.

"I believe it was the dagger you tripped on, Inspector," Oona said.

The inspector turned on her. "I thought I told you to stay out of official police affairs, Miss Crate."

Oona raised her eyebrows in surprise, before reminding herself just whom she was dealing with. Truth be told, up until this point she had been quite impressed with all the information the inspector had compiled. Indeed, it was something of a shock to discover that the Iree twins had been at the museum that day. It was certainly possible that Isadora had it in her spiteful nature to attack the Wizard, but the thought of Adler being involved, or even being the attacker himself, was upsetting, to say the least.

She took a calming breath to steady her nerves before realizing that the inspector was still waiting for her to explain herself. She spoke calmly and clearly. "My uncle was attacked, and quite possibly murdered tonight, Inspector, to which I am a witness. Not only do I have every right to be here, I am required to be here. And also, if you need it to be pointed out to you, no one tripped you. You tripped yourself on the dagger." She pointed to the floor.

The inspector turned to the dagger, a look of surprise on his face. "Oh, of course."

Adler adjusted his top hat so that it rested upon the back of his head. "I was at the museum, 'tis true," he said. "I'm at the museum most days, when I'm not at the

Magicians Legal Alliance, that is. The museum's library is quite amazing. I was doing research."

What sort of research? Oona wondered, but what she asked was: "Inspector, are you sure there is no way someone could have gotten past the security guard at the front of the museum without signing the registry?" She glanced sideways at Grimsbee, gauging his reaction. His face remained inscrutable beneath the bloodstained rag on his head.

The inspector frowned. "It is possible, but highly unlikely, I would think. The security guard would have to answer that question."

And Oona thought: *Yes, I'll have to ask him that when I visit the museum tomorrow.*

And then a second, crueler voice in her head asked: *When are you going to do that? After you break into the Black Tower, defeat the goblins, and discover that your uncle is not in the tower cell after all, and that Inspector White is right . . . that the Wizard is dead?*

The thought angered her so much that she blurted out: "Mr. Grimsbee, how did you injure yourself? I saw you earlier today on the museum steps, and you did not have that bandage around your head."

The room fell markedly quiet. Someone cleared their throat. A mouse could be heard skittering through the walls. Grimsbee slid forward in his chair, and for the first time since they had been gathered together, his expression changed. He appeared to look right at Oona with his horrible white eyes, his lips pinched together in a mask of fury. His faced turned bright red, and his nostrils swelled to the size of walnuts. And then suddenly, horribly, his mouth drew out into an oily grin that was the very replica of his pointy, bullhorn mustache.

Through gritted teeth, he said: "I cut myself shaving."

Oona blinked several times, shaking her head. "Shaving your forehead?" she replied, her voice brimming with disbelief. She turned to the inspector. "Surely you do not believe him? Who shaves their forehead?"

The inspector appeared thoughtful, scratching at his white, white chin with the tip of one white, white finger.

"I do not know what to believe," he said. And then to Oona's further astonishment, he said: "You are all free to go."

"Go?" Oona cried. She was suddenly on her feet. "What do you mean, go? You're going to let my uncle's attacker just walk out of here?"

"We do not have sufficient evidence to hold any of them in custody," the inspector declared. He paused to consider something for a moment. "But I *will* see to it that police Constable Trout over there is posted at the Iron Gates, to make sure no one flees Dark Street until the killer is discovered."

Police Constable Trout stood near the doorway, his dreamy gaze lost in the pages of his novel, as if completely unaware of the murder investigation going on in the same room. Somehow the inspector's assurance that the constable would be watching the Iron Gates gave Oona little comfort.

"That is all," the inspector said, and began marching toward the door.

"But Inspector," Oona tried one last time. "Don't you think you should place everyone under house arrest? Keep them here in Pendulum House? At least until we discover who—"

The inspector cut her short. "Miss Crate. When will you learn to leave grown-up work to . . . uh . . . well, to grown-ups? Now run along and play with your pet birdie, and leave this case to the professionals. We have everything under control, don't we, Constable Trout?"

The novel-reading constable turned the page of his book, giggling at something he'd read.

"You are all free to go," said the inspector again.

Oona looked at Hector Grimsbee, who grinned in her direction.

"I will inform the Dark Street Council of the Wizard's death," said the inspector, "and the council will decide what is to be done about the position."

"But he's not necessarily dead!" Oona shouted.

The inspector nodded sadly at her. "Denial is the first stage of grief," he said, and then turned to go.

Oona stared after him as he made his way toward the door, his highly polished shoes squeaking their way across the long, ornate carpet, and his white shirt glaring against the light. Frustration gripped at her insides. The man was a great big inkblot on the name of law and order. Oona chanced to look down at the floor, and thought: *Look, he's even left the evidence there in the carpet.*

She bent to retrieve the dagger.

"Don't forget the weapon, Inspector." Oona pulled it from the floor and held it out. At first she felt only a tingle: a slight warmth that slowly intensified in her hand so that soon it felt as if she had pulled the dagger not out of the floor but out of a pile of hot coals. By the time the inspector had made his way back across the room and put out his hand, the handle of the dagger had grown too hot for her to hold. Oona took in a sharp breath, letting the dagger fall from her fingers. The instant the weapon hit the floor, bouncing against the carpet with a soft thud, the pain disappeared. She looked at her hand in surprise. Her fingers did not begin to smoke, nor did her hand turn char-black as Samuligan's hand had done when he had touched the dagger. But the flesh about her fingers *did* appear slightly red. It had not been her imagination. The heat *had* been there.

"Well, that was very rude," said the inspector, bending to retrieve the dagger.

Oona hardly heard him. She turned to Samuligan, wide-eyed and wondering. "It burned me, Samuligan," she said in a tone of complete bewilderment. "I felt it. It . . . It burned me."

CHAPTER TWELVE

The Inner Garden

T hough tangled and overgrown, the garden in the inner courtyard of Pendulum House was Oona's favorite place to be alone and to think. Surrounded on all four sides by the lofty walls of the great manor house, it was as solitary a place as Oona could hope to find. After all of the distressful events of the evening, she'd needed to breathe its comforting air, and stroll through patches of sighing-lady grass, which sighed softly in the starlight like broken-hearted ladies, and stands of sallow flowers, whose bright petals changed colors and could be used to predict the weather. It was a secret place, known only to the occupants of the house, and Oona found it to be the best place in all the world to let her thoughts simply wander through the hills and valleys of the endless mysteries that occupied her mind.

Presently, she gazed at her hand, opening and closing her fingers, as if they were strange to her. She thought back to earlier that evening and remembered how completely uninterested the inspector had behaved toward her complaint that the dagger had burned her. Indeed, everyone in the room had been so eager to get away from the house that—with the exception of Adler Iree, who seemed to be watching Oona quite intensely, as if anticipating some new marvel of magic to spring from her hands at any moment—no one had shown the slightest interest in what had just happened.

Once they'd all gone, however, and Oona had been left alone in the house with Deacon and Samuligan, she had at last asked the impending question: "Why did the dagger grow so hot in my hand? I thought it was enchanted to burn only faeries."

Samuligan didn't have an explanation for what had occurred. The dagger had not affected the inspector, nor had it burned Constable Trout when the inspector had handed him the evidence to take to the station. Only Oona and Samuligan had suffered the effects of the dagger's strange magic, though Oona's own hand had not been nearly as badly burned as Samuligan's had, despite the fact that Oona had held on to the dagger for far longer than the faerie servant.

"There is only one rational explanation that *I* can think of for why the dagger would burn you," Deacon had offered. "There is a theory, which I daresay you have heard before, that the reason that Natural Magicians, such as yourself, are able to invoke such strong magic is because they possess some small amount of active faerie blood in their veins. The idea is that, long ago, before the closing of the Glass Gates, a faerie man and a human woman had a child together, and that human-faerie child grew up and had a child with another human, and so on, and so on, until there was almost no trace of faerie left. The immortality that all pure-born faeries possess is washed away by the limited nature of the human body. But faerie blood is, above all else, the very essence of magic. It would not disappear completely, even after a hundred generations. Or perhaps even a thousand. No one knows for sure. It is, of course, only a theory."

Oona shook her head. "But if that is the case, and I do possess some trace of faerie blood, then why did my parents not have the powers that I have? Or my grandparents?"

Deacon shrugged. "Why do some children have an uncanny ability to play the piano, while their parents possess no musical skill whatsoever? What causes a brilliant ballet dancer to be born from simple country farmers, or a mighty warrior to be born amongst a horde of meek brothers and sisters? Again, no one knows. It is, perhaps, an unsolvable mystery."

Oona disliked the idea of an unsolvable mystery. Currently, as she stood alone in the starlit confines of the inner garden, she turned her mind to a more solvable mystery: the attack on her uncle. But somehow it was the two incidents with Isadora, just before she and her brother had taken their leave of Pendulum House, that popped into Oona's mind. Isadora was such an infuriatingly selfish girl, and troublesome to say the least. But Oona had not realized just how troublesome she truly was until the so-called fine young lady had smeared dirt across Oona's face and then, shortly after that, nearly knocked her out with the coatrack.

The inspector had departed the house some minutes before, along with Constable Trout, Lamont John-Michael Arlington Fitch III, Sanora Crone, and that horrible Hector Grimsbee. Isadora had needed to use the bathroom before leaving, and so Oona, Samuligan, and Deacon had patiently waited for her, along with Adler, in the house entryway. Several times Adler's and Oona's own eyes had met, and each time the awkwardness of the silence was palpable. She had wanted to grab hold of his shabby cloak and shake him, make him swear that he'd had nothing to do with what had happened to her uncle. But she could not do that. Adler had been at the museum that day, and it could very well have been he who stole the dagger and used it to kill the Wizard.

Uncle Alexander is not dead, she tried to convince her-self. *He is in that tower, and first thing tomorrow, we will find a way to get him out!*

"Perhaps I should go and see what is taking Isadora so long," Oona had said, though truthfully she simply wanted to get away from the uncomfortable silence of the entryway. Thinking that she might use the bathroom herself after Isadora, Oona asked Deacon to wait in the entryway with Samuligan and Adler while she checked on Isadora. She crossed the circular antechamber and turned down the side hallway. When Oona got to the bathroom, however, she discovered that the door was open and the room was unoccupied.

"Isadora?" she called. Glancing up and down the hall, Oona noticed the doors to the inner courtyard standing wide open. She approached the doors slowly. "Isadora?" she called again. Again there was no answer. Her fists clinched.

She'd better not be out there in the garden, Oona thought, feeling quite angry at the idea. The inner garden was full of secret plants that only the Wizard and his apprentice were allowed to know existed. And Isadora most certainly was not yet the Wizard's apprentice.

Oona stepped through the doorway and into the open air of the courtyard. The stars were bright, the night crisp. Oona saw movement near the far end of the garden. Her feet moved silently beneath her as she stepped from the brick patio to the dirt path that led through the various plants and hedges. The shadowy leaves of a dancing fern slid silently out of her way with a graceful, dancerlike fluidity, and when her foot crunched upon a fallen leaf, the sighing-lady grass masked the sound with its beautiful sighing lament.

No surprise to Oona, the movement she'd seen turned out to be that of a dress. A red-and-gold-striped dress, to be precise, that glinted prettily in the starlight. Isadora was bending down over an empty patch of soil.

Oona cleared her throat. "Ahem."

Isadora jumped, nearly toppling forward and knocking over the low wooden sign sticking out of the dirt in front of her. She wheeled around, and Oona glanced down at the sign, which read: TURLOCK ROOT.

"Can I help you, Isadora?" Oona asked in what she hoped was her best patronizing voice.

Isadora looked around, blinking innocently, as if she were unsure of where she was or how she had gotten there. "Oh, I seem to have gotten lost on my way back to the entryway."

Oona folded her arms and began tapping her foot. "Lost your way, have you? Well, I think it's safe to assume that if you did not walk through the garden to get to the bathroom, then you would not need to walk through it to get back out."

Isadora straightened up. "Well, there's no need to get snippy. I simply took a wrong turn. Then I saw this sign here, and well, I thought I might . . ."

Oona looked down at Isadora's hands and saw the dirt on them. "You thought you might dig up some turlock root?"

A memory floated to the surface of Oona's mind: Isadora's mother, Madame Iree, saying how much she would like to get her hands on a bit of turlock root so that she could make herself young enough to wear the glinting-cloth dress.

"Well, what if I was?" Isadora said defensively. "It was for Mother. She told me that this stuff grew only in Faerie, but look, here it is, right here." She pointed to the sign.

Oona opened her mouth to tell Isadora that the reason it grew there in the secret garden was because Pendulum House was built on Faerie soil—that Pendulum House was the only place this side of the Glass Gates built on such enchanted ground—but she stopped herself. Isadora didn't need to know such things, and probably wasn't interested.

"Well, you can't take any," Oona said.

"Who is going to stop me?" Isadora asked, raising her chin defiantly, and then her eyes suddenly went wide.

"I would enjoy that pleasure," said a voice from behind Oona. Oona turned to discover Samuligan standing behind her. He must have come to see what was taking so long. His toothy grin was a horror to behold in the starlight, and Oona found herself thankful that the grin was not directed at her.

Isadora pinched up her lips and said: "Fine. Mother wouldn't want this stinky stuff anyway. It smells horrible, like you. Here, have a whiff."

In three swift motions, Isadora reached out, wiped her filthy hand across Oona's face, and then sidestepped Samuligan as she stormed off toward the courtyard doors. Oona was simply too stunned to say a word. She stood for a moment, blinking in surprise, unsure as to whether she should run and tackle the other girl, or simply let her go. It was infuriating, not to mention highly embarrassing. The dark soil ran from her cheek to her mouth like a hideous scar. Catching a whiff of the pungent soil, she spat on the ground, and wiped the sharp taste of dirt from her lips.

Samuligan had evidently decided to stay with Oona, rather than pursue Isadora, and for the moment she was glad for it, as the faerie servant handed her a handkerchief to wipe her face. Together, the two of them walked back across the courtyard, Oona hoping that by the time they made it to the front of the house the Iree twins would be gone. No such luck.

They found Deacon perched atop the entryway coat-rack, with Isadora shouting at him. Adler was telling her to calm down, but she would have none of it. She whirled around, the red-and-gold stripes of her dress spiraling about her feet, and arrowed her finger at Oona.

"You stole my shawl!" Isadora announced.

Oona's eyebrows nearly came together. "I *what*?"

Isadora pointed at the coatrack beside the broom closet. "Don't play stupid with me. I hung my shawl on that rack when I came in this evening. It matches my dress perfectly. Now it's gone."

Oona looked at the coatrack. She remembered seeing the shawl earlier that evening, remembered placing it back on the rack herself after the rack had fallen on top of her when she'd tumbled from the closet. The only thing hanging on the rack now was a lone, black jacket. Where the shawl had gone, Oona had no idea.

Isadora fell into a fit. *"Where's my shawl!"* She lashed out, kicking over a nearby umbrella stand, and then shoved the heel of her shoe hard against a footstool near the closet. Oona jumped out of the way to avoid being hit by the stool, and the umbrella stand toppled over, spilling two lacy white parasols to the floor, along with one pointy red umbrella that nearly poked Adler in the leg.

"Now see here, young lady!" Deacon said from the top of the coatrack. "Calm down!"

But Isadora was not ready to calm down. "I left it right here!" she shouted, and then grabbed hold of the jacket on the coatrack and yanked. Suddenly, the entire rack toppled over. Deacon leaped into the air, shrieking and batting his wings as the rack slammed to the ground.

"Where's my shawl?" Isadora howled, kicking violently at the fallen rack.

"Isadora!" Adler shouted.

"Stay out of this, Adler," she scolded.

"But Isadora, look," Adler said. "There's your shawl. Right there."

Deacon landed on Oona's shoulder as Adler pointed to where the rack had struck the floor. The shawl was lying on top of the jacket.

"Look," Adler said, kneeling down to pick up the red-and-gold fabric. "See there, Isadora. Someone placed their jacket on top of your shawl. That's why you didn't see it. That's all." He handed the shawl to his sister before returning the coatrack to its upright position and hanging the jacket back upon its hook. "The inspector must've forgot to take his jacket with him when he left, that's all." He glanced at Oona, giving her a half smile. "He'd probably forget his own head if it weren't connected to his neck, so he would."

Oona did not return the smile, however. She was too shocked by Isadora's behavior—indeed by all the events of the evening—to do anything but blink at him confoundedly. Looking at the inspector's jacket on the hook, she could only think: *Just what I need is for Inspector White to have some reason to return to the house tonight.*

As the twins took their leave, stepping over the scattered parasols and umbrella on the floor, Isadora turned in the doorway, her shawl draped over her shoulders like a striped flag. For an instant it appeared she might be on the verge of apologizing for her behavior, but what she said was: "Don't forget. You're still supposed to find out who stole my mother's dresses. They must be found before tomorrow night's masquerade ball."

Oona closed the door in the girl's face.

Several hours later, Oona could still not believe that Isadora would be so ridiculous as to believe she, Oona, would put her energy into finding some silly missing dresses when the only thing that mattered was learning if her uncle was still alive . . . and discovering his attacker. But churning the slim evidence over in her mind, she knew that, so far, there was very little to go on. The thing that irritated her most was that she saw no reason for any of the applicants to want to harm her uncle. She had to find out more about them.

The fact that she'd seen Grimsbee disappear in front of the Museum of Magical History—the very place where the daggers had been stolen—haunted Oona's thoughts like an insistent ghost. It didn't prove that Grimsbee had done the job, but it was a start. Deacon insisted that the power to become invisible was magic long lost. But Oona had seen Grimsbee arguing with someone who was not there.

And then there was the fact that both Isadora Iree and Adler had been inside the museum earlier that day.

When her feet tired, Oona sat with her back against the tall glass tree in the center of the garden. The tree sprouted not limbs of wood, but branches of swirling glass. Crystal leaves sparkled like diamonds in the starlight. Her dislike of magic aside, Oona had always thought the tree was the most beautiful thing she had ever seen. She could spend hours just staring up at its crystalline beauty, watching the light prism through its limbs like a fantastic ice sculpture.

Tonight, however, the tree could not hold her attention. She stared, instead, vacantly across the garden at the barren splotch of dirt where she had caught Isadora digging for turlock root. Oona had once asked her uncle why he did not use the root to keep himself looking younger, and he had explained that the root not only made people look young, but made their minds young as well.

"I prefer wisdom to beauty," he had told her. "And

besides, I believe I grow rather more handsome the older I get."

Poor Uncle Alexander. Why would someone wish to harm him? The thought that he might be dead was overwhelming, and as she sat there, beneath the limbs of the great tree made of glass, she began to feel quite numb. Uncle Alexander's eyes seemed to hover before her, looking so disappointed in her for abandoning him. Why had she deserted him? She knew why, of course, but the guilt was like a knife in her side. She felt hollow, as if all of the blood had drained out from inside of her. Staring numbly at a naked patch of dirt, she thought of what lay beneath. It was like a mystery: always appearing one way, when beneath the surface lay something extraordinary.

And then her thoughts turned, as they so often did when she sat alone in the inner garden, to the accident— the terrible accident beneath the fig tree in Oswald Park. Both of them, her mother and her baby sister, Flora, had been gone in an instant. Oona knew that it was her own fault that it had happened, despite her uncle's insistence that she was not to blame. If she had not conjured the spell, they would still be alive. She had meant only to show them what she could do, to delight them.

"Lux lucis admiratio!"

With the use of a fallen twig, she had shot sparks of light from its tip, as if from a magic wand. The sparks flew high, circling the great fig tree like shooting stars, changing colors as they spiraled around and around, faster and faster.

Her mother had smiled at the trick. Oona had only been ten years old at the time, but even then she had known that it was the first genuine smile she had seen upon her mother's lips since the death of Oona's father some five months before. Flora, who was not yet even one year old, began to giggle and clap in their mother's arms—mother and baby resting on the lawn beneath the broad canopy of the tree—as the sparks shooting from Oona's twig grew bigger, and brighter, and more plentiful . . . though what Oona had not realized then was that the dazzling lights were growing more and more powerful. The sparks grew so bright that they challenged even the sun, causing the shadow of the fig tree to shift and dance in the bright light of day. People stopped to watch the lights in wonder.

"See what I can do?" Oona had said.

"I see, Oona," her mother had said. "It is—"

But her mother never finished her words. Whatever she was about to say Oona would never learn, for at that very moment the lights spun violently out of control, slamming into the tree with a burst of energy so strong that the tree simultaneously burst into flames and crashed over onto its side. It happened so quickly that her mother had no chance of getting out of the way. And just like that, her mother and sister were gone from her life. Gone, and never coming back.

It had been Uncle Alexander who had consoled her. It had been he who had assured her that they had not suffered. The tree had been enormous, as fig trees were likely to become. And when Inspector White had asked to question Oona, it had been the Wizard who had refused him, claiming that the act had been a magical one, which fell under his own authority. No one else had been injured—there was that much to be thankful for, at least—and the force from the blast against the tree had sent Oona flying several yards away, where she'd landed hard but unharmed on the open lawn.

Presently, as she leaned against the trunk of the tree of glass in the inner garden, the tears began to roll down Oona's cheeks. The sadness she usually managed to keep at bay began to fill her chest, and as she stared upward into the night sky, she realized that the crystal leaves of the glass tree did not sparkle so much like diamonds as they did like tears. When the feeling finally passed, and she was done crying, Oona at last felt the tug of sleep, and forced herself to slump up the stairs to her room, where she fell fast asleep.

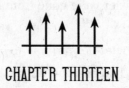

CHAPTER THIRTEEN

The Tale of the Really, Really Long Sleep

Oona sat up in bed, blinking against the early-morning light.

There was a knock at her door.

"Who's there?" she asked in a groggy voice.

"It is I," Samuligan replied from the other side of the door.

It was Samuligan's voice rather than the knocking that startled Deacon into wakefulness. He spread his wings, rustling his feathers in a sumptuous morning stretch.

Oona groaned, wrestling her way back to consciousness. Untangling herself from her blankets, she quickly glanced down to make sure her nightgown was buttoned properly.

"You may come in," she said, rubbing at her eyes.

The faerie servant entered the room, looking as tall and imposing as ever. His cowboy hat sat forward on his brow so that it was nearly impossible to see his eyes, and his boots clicked against the floor, an eerie, hollow sound, like someone knocking from inside a coffin. He held a red envelope in his long faerie fingers.

"I found this tied to the front gate," he said.

Oona pushed herself up to receive it. The letter was simply addressed to: Occupants of Pendulum House, Number 19.

She slid the letter from the envelope. It felt crisp and expensive. Printed in bold, black letters at the top of the red paper were the words EVICTION NOTICE.

Deacon dropped down from the bedpost to Oona's shoulder and began to read aloud. "You have been served. All occupants of Pendulum House shall vacate the premises, along with their possessions. They have until 11:59 tonight, May 15, 1877, after which time, at precisely midnight, the pendulum will be stopped and the demolition of the house will begin. This in accordance with the new owner, the Nightshade Corporation." Deacon paused before adding: "It is signed: Red Martin. President and Owner of the Nightshade Corporation."

"An eviction notice?" Oona asked. "Is this some sort of awful joke?"

"I'm afraid not," Samuligan said. He pointed to the top of the paper. "That is the official stamp and seal of the Dark Street Council. It appears to be a fully legal document."

"How is this possible?" Oona asked. "Red Martin owns Pendulum House? I don't understand."

"Not only that," Samuligan continued, "but he apparently intends to tear it down to make way for his new hotel and casino. Just have a look."

He pointed out the window. Oona slid off the bed and peered through the glass, which overlooked the front yard. A man wearing a shabby bowler hat was pounding a large wooden sign into the overgrown rose beds.

The man's broad shoulders blocked Oona's view of what the sign said, but a moment later, when he stood back to survey his work, she was able to see it very clearly. Two palm trees had been painted on either side of the sign, and stretching between the trees hung a comfortable-looking hammock filled with gold coins; in the background stood an enormous hula hut silhouetted against the orange glow of the setting sun.

In bright red letters, it read:

FUTURE SITE OF
INDULGENCE ISLAND
HOTEL AND CASINO

In smaller letters below, it said:

Oona was aghast. She returned her attention to the letter. "How can this be? I thought only the Wizard could own Pendulum House. What will happen if the pendulum is stopped?"

Samuligan only shrugged.

Deacon answered: "I do not believe it has ever been done."

Oona shook her head, trying to comprehend the implications. "Well, this must be stopped." She looked absently around the room, gathering her thoughts. Finally, she said: "First thing we must do is find out if Uncle Alexander is in that tower."

"And how do you plan on doing that?" Deacon asked. "According to the *Encyclopedia Arcanna*, the only person with any knowledge of the Black Tower's secrets is the presiding Wizard. Only he or she knows how to get inside. But if your uncle is truly inside the tower, then there is no way to ask him."

"Ah, but you forget," Oona said to Deacon. "Only the Wizard and his apprentice have the knowledge. And I *was* my uncle's apprentice for nearly five years."

Deacon squawked in surprise. "You mean that you know how to get inside the tower?"

Oona twisted her mouth to one side. "Well . . . no. Not exactly. I mean, that was one subject we hadn't gotten around to yet."

"Oh, I see," Deacon said, sounding much disappointed.

Oona pinched at her bottom lip, considering something. "But he did show me the book in which such secrets are kept."

"Book?" asked Deacon, clearly surprised.

"Indeed," said Oona. "It is a book with no name. A secret book handed down from one Wizard to the next. I'm sure you must have seen it before, Samuligan, in all of your years of service."

The faerie servant nodded slowly, almost reverently. "I have never been allowed to read it. There is a magical binding on the book, much like the curse on the mind daggers, which prevents any faerie from opening its cover."

Oona nodded. Her uncle had told her as much when he had first shown her the book.

A sudden thought occurred to Oona. *What if it is true, and the reason I am a Natural Magician is because I have faerie blood in me? Would I be able to open the book?*

Her uncle had shown her the book only a handful of

times in her five years as apprentice . . . but he had never allowed her to handle it. When he was not using it, the book remained safely hidden away.

"But yes, to answer your question," Samuligan added in a dreamy sort of voice, "I have seen the book, to be certain. And what interesting secrets it must hold." His eyes seemed almost to shimmer beneath the shadow of his hat, as if perhaps the counterspell to the enchantment that kept him bound to a life of service were somewhere in its pages.

Oona could not know for certain that this was what Samuligan was thinking, but she did know that the counterspell to release the faerie servant was not in the book. She had once asked her uncle about that very subject, and he had told her that, so far as he knew, there was no counterspell, and that if there ever had been one, then it was lost long ago. But the Wizard had asked Oona not to give this information to Samuligan.

"But why?" she had asked as the two of them sat together in his study.

The Wizard had replied: "Because it will destroy any hope that Samuligan might have of ever being free. And neither man nor faerie can live for long without hope. To take that away would be cruel. After all, just because I do not know how to break the curse does not mean a way does not exist."

"Would you release him if you could?" Oona had asked.

"In a heartbeat," the Wizard had replied. "If there was a way to send him back to Faerie as well. But those are two things I cannot do."

Afterward, Oona had sought Samuligan out and found him polishing a set of silver teapots by magic in the parlor. As her uncle had requested, she did not mention the knowledge that there was no known counterspell to his predicament. But she had asked Samuligan if he liked his job.

"I have been a warrior and a champion," he had replied. "A general in the Queen of Faerie's Royal Army. I have been present at great victories, and even greater loss. I fought against the most powerful of the Magicians of Old." He paused to gaze admiringly up at the portrait of Oswald the Great. "I have dueled spells against the greatest of them all, and lived to fight another day." Samuligan lowered his gaze to the silver teapot and looked into his own distorted reflection. "And yet in the end, it seems that I have found nothing more satisfying than being a simple servant, in spite of the fact that so many of these Wizards have been such buffoons." He had grinned at her—that perfectly mischievous grin that seemed to be such a part of his faerie nature. "I hope you are not a buffoon, Miss Crate, when you become Wizard."

That had been the most personal conversation Oona had ever had with Samuligan, and she thought now that it had been the most vulnerable he had ever appeared.

At present, Oona looked up from her bed at the faerie servant. The brim of his hat cast the top of his face into complete shadow.

"Could you use your faerie powers to open the tower, Samuligan?" Oona asked.

"The tower is immune to Faerie Magic. It is coated in glass, and the spells guarding it are too strong by far. It was made to hold faeries inside, remember. I cannot help you here."

Oona nodded. "All right then, we have no choice but to use the Wizard's book."

"You know where it is?" Deacon asked.

A memory drifted through Oona's head like a dream: of peering through the crack of a door . . . and her uncle making some motion with his hand, and a bookshelf swinging open.

Oona rose from the bed. "I need to dress," she said. "Both of you, meet me in the study in ten minutes."

Ten minutes later the three of them stood in the quiet of the Wizard's study. The slumbering dragon-bone desk could be heard breathing beneath the silence. The room smelled of books and ash from the fireplace, and the loan tea saucer continued to hover above the fireside table, endlessly in search of its missing cup. Oona stood in front of the bookcase where she had seen her uncle open the compartment.

"He stood right here," she said aloud. "And then he made a motion with his hand."

"A magical motion?" Deacon asked from atop the desk.

Oona scratched at her head. It was possible, yes. And if that were the case, then they would surely be out of luck. She turned to Samuligan.

"If there is a magical hiding spot, then can you open it, Samuligan?"

He shook his head. "Not if it is well constructed. Though I can try. First, I will need to determine exactly where the hiding spot is."

"It is right here," Oona said, pointing at the row of books in front of her.

Samuligan placed his hand on the shelf and closed his eyes, concentrating. He stood frozen for nearly a minute before at last stepping away from the shelf and shaking his head. "There is no magical hiding spot there. At least, none that I can detect."

"But I saw him open it," Oona said.

"Perhaps the magic is too well constructed for Samuligan to detect," Deacon suggested.

The faerie nodded that this was possible.

"Or perhaps," Oona said, running a finger along the spines of the books, "just perhaps . . . the compartment is not magical at all. Perhaps it is . . . mechanical."

Her finger stopped on the spine of a large book enti- tled: *The Tale of the Really, Really Long Sleep and Ten Other Miserably Dull Tales for Bedtime. Edited by Milford T. Tedium.*

"Well, now," she said, amused. "Here is a book that no one is likely to attempt taking off the shelf."

She took hold of the book along the spine and pulled.

Something clinked, followed by several clonks, and a single satisfying creak as the entire shelf swung outward to reveal the hidden compartment behind.

"Ingenious," said Deacon.

"Bravo," said Samuligan.

A quick little smile stole across Oona's face, and she peered inside the compartment. The drinking glass and bottle of scotch were just inside, beside which sat a large black ball. Intrigued, Oona picked the ball up and exam- ined it. It had been painted to resemble an oversize bil- liard ball. A large figure 8 was printed on it, and beneath the 8 were the words: ASK ANY QUESTION, AND TURN OVER TO DISCOVER THE ANSWER.

"What is it?" Deacon asked.

Oona showed them the large 8 ball, and what was written on it. "It appears to be some new novelty product my uncle was working on."

"Ask it a question," Deacon urged.

Samuligan appeared eager to see the device work as well.

Oona's heart began to pound. Perhaps this magic billiard ball of her uncle's could actually solve the mystery for them. Oona held the ball in both hands and asked: "Is my uncle alive or dead?"

She hesitated, looking first at Deacon and then at Samuligan. They both nodded their encouragement. She turned the ball over.

A small window had been placed into the bottom of the ball, through which could be seen a cloud of liquidy mist. The words ASK AGAIN LATER appeared in the window.

"What?" Oona said, her voice ripe with irritation. She rolled the ball back over in her hands, reread the instructions, and then asked: "Is my uncle dead?"

Again she turned the ball over, and again the words ASK AGAIN LATER appeared in the misty window.

Oona shook the ball violently, nearly shouting: "Who attacked my uncle?" She peered into the window, and yet a third time the words appeared: ASK AGAIN LATER.

Oona raised a suspicious eyebrow at the ball before placing it back in the hidden compartment. "Apparently, Uncle Alexander hasn't worked the kinks out of it yet."

"Apparently so," Deacon agreed.

Oona peered toward the back of the compartment

and saw what they had been looking for. The book was pushed all the way to the back, and Oona was nearly forced to stick her head inside the compartment in order to reach it. The heavy leather binding felt old and coarse, and as she slid it forward, a slim stack of papers fell to the floor at her feet. Samuligan bent to retrieve them as Oona hefted the book from the shelf to the dragon-bone desk. The book seemed much heavier than it ought to have been, and she let it fall to the desktop with a heavy thud. The steady breathing of the desk faltered for a moment, as if there were a hitch in its breath, and then once again settled into its habitual pattern.

"Okay, let's see what's inside." She placed a finger on the corner of the front cover but found it much too heavy simply to flip open. It took both hands and nearly all of her strength to heave its cover back, and by the time she had finished this seemingly simple task, her brow was damp with sweat.

"It must be the magical binding that Samuligan had mentioned before," Oona said, catching her breath.

Deacon seemed quite excited by this news. "Yet even more proof that Natural Magicians have some active strain of faerie blood in them. But because you are human, the magical protection is weakened."

"Tell that to my hands," Oona said, flexing the soreness from her fingers. Yet it seemed that Deacon was right. She only hoped that the magical binding on the book was limited just to opening it, and did not extend to turning its pages; otherwise, this was going to take forever.

She flipped a page, and it turned as easily as any page in a normal book. Breathing a sigh of relief, Oona flipped to the back, where she hoped to find an index. Her luck held out. Listed in alphabetical order were row after row of all the topics to be found in the book. She ran her finger down the line of Bs. Binding Magic . . . Birch Trees . . . Birds . . . Black Magic . . . and there it was: Black Tower (*see* Goblin Tower), 413.

Deacon hopped to her shoulder as Oona found the page in a flurry of turns, and discovered . . . not what she was expecting. On the entire page there was only one reference to the tower's entrance. One single line near the bottom of the page. It read: "To enter the tower, you must first find it."

This was followed by what appeared to be a poem.

Upon my head I have no face
For your ease I come in a case
And though I'm well and upon my way
Upon my flight I'm here to stay
I slow you down, and tire you out
Yet getting you there is what I'm about.

Oona turned the page over to make sure she was not missing something. When she found nothing else, she turned back to page 413 and slammed her fist against the corner of the book.

"But this is just as helpful as that magic billiard ball," she said. "It tells us nothing!"

"It appears to be some sort of riddle," Deacon said.

"What it says, Deacon, is that in order to enter the tower you must first find it. But we know where the tower is. It's in the cemetery."

Deacon hopped from her shoulder to the desk so that he might get a better look at the book. "But perhaps the 'it' that the text is referring to is the entrance. And the riddle—"

Oona snapped her fingers. "Yes, of course, Deacon. Answer the riddle and we will know where to look for the secret entrance!"

Oona grabbed a pen and paper, and quickly copied the riddle. "Samuligan!" she said excitedly. "Bring round the carriage, please. I want to get to the cemetery as quickly as possible."

But at first the faerie servant did not seem to have heard. He was reading one of the pieces of paper that had fallen on the floor.

"Samuligan, did you hear me?" Oona asked. "Please bring the carriage around front. And you really shouldn't be snooping about in Uncle Alexander's private letters."

Samuligan tipped his hat back on his head and gave her a calculated look, as if to say that she was hardly the person to be giving lectures on snooping around.

"You will want to read this," he said. "I believe you will find its contents quite enlightening."

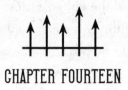

CHAPTER FOURTEEN

The Barrier, the Riddle, and the Circle of Stones

The journey to the cemetery, which was located at the very south end of the street, took nearly forty-five minutes by carriage. Oona did not notice the time pass. It was early yet, the sun just having topped many of the buildings, and most of the street's varied inhabitants still slept. A few early risers and shady-looking characters wandered the mist-covered sidewalks, along with several sleepy-eyed police constables.

But Oona observed none of this, nor did she so much as glance out the carriage window as they rolled the six-mile stretch of empty street, with the exception of once, when the carriage bumped over some missing cobblestones and she looked up to see the stone steps of the museum and the enormous carved stone top hat. She caught a glimpse of the girl-size dress in the window of Madame Iree's Boutique for Fine Ladies. The enchanted glinting cloth caught Oona's attention for the length of time it took the carriage to roll past, and then she was once again lost in thought.

It was solely the two sheets of paper in her hands that divided her attention. In her right hand she held the riddle that she had copied out of the Wizard's book. But it was the paper in her left hand that currently held her gaze: a document printed on crisp red paper and written in quite specific and legal terms. At the top of the document were the words CERTIFICATE OF DEBT, beneath which was a scramble of musical notes. Luckily for Oona, learning to read the musical language of magical law had been part of her training as an apprentice.

She sighed. "From what I can make out—and I am not a lawyer, so I am not certain—but it appears that Uncle Alexander borrowed some money. According to this document, he has been borrowing money for quite some time . . . a period of two years. But not from a bank. It would seem he has been borrowing from a company called Dupington Moneylenders."

"Dupington?" said Deacon. "Never heard of them."

"Neither have I, Deacon. But this certificate of debt and the eviction notice we received this morning are both printed on the same thick red paper. It's my guess that if we look into it, Dupington and the Nightshade Corporation will be one and the same. That is why Red Martin has evicted us."

"But what does that mean?" Deacon asked from the seat opposite Oona. His voice shook against the rattle of the carriage.

"If my suspicions are correct, then it means that, more than likely, Red Martin had a dirty red hand in the attack on Uncle Alexander," Oona said. "That's what I think."

"But he was not in the room at the time of the attack," Deacon pointed out.

Oona nodded. "No doubt he put someone else up to it. It is too much of a coincidence that Red Martin should benefit so much from all of this. Clearly, he and one of the applicants are in cahoots. But which one?"

"Are you sure the document is authentic?" Deacon asked. "Do we know for sure that the two companies are the same, and that Red Martin has the right to take own-ership of the house?"

Oona frowned at the certificate, glancing over the musical notations. "It appears so. But I do not know all that much about legal documents. We will need to consult a lawyer."

"Ravensmith does not open until after nine o'clock," Deacon informed her.

Oona nodded. "Until then, we have a riddle to solve."

The carriage creaked to a halt, and a moment later Samuligan opened the door for her. Dressed in an auburn-colored dress, and with her long black hair worn down about her shoulders, Oona stepped to the sidewalk, leaving the Certificate of Debt behind in the carriage. She placed the paper with the riddle on it in her dress pocket. The arched stone gateway stood ominously before her, above which soared the mammoth Goblin Tower. The solid black structure rose up from the center of the cemetery to meet the sky—ending at a daunting, if not to say unnatural, height. She craned her neck all the way back to see the very top of the tower as it scraped against the bottom of a drifting cloud.

"It is over seven hundred feet tall," Deacon announced as he alighted upon her shoulder. Oona gulped audibly. Suddenly, the thought of going into that bleak, window-less structure—not to mention somehow getting to the top, where the prison was supposedly located—did not seem like such a good idea. Oona turned to Samuligan.

"You are certain that your magic cannot penetrate it?" she asked.

Samuligan looked at the tower with an expression that Oona could not at first read, and then she realized that the reason she could not read it was because it was an expression she had never before seen on the faerie servant's face. Samuligan looked afraid. The realization sent a shiver running from the bottom of Oona's feet to the top of her head.

"I assure you," Samuligan said. "Not my magic, nor any that I know of, can penetrate that tower. That riddle you have is likely the only key to getting in . . . and should you manage to find the entrance, then I cannot say what you will find inside. It is called the Goblin Tower, after all. I was blindfolded when Oswald took me out of the tower so that I would not be able to see its secrets. I never saw the goblins, but I believe that they are no laughing matter."

Oona remembered the horrible little eyes and pointy ears of the beasts in the parlor tapestries. She nodded. But if there was even a chance that her uncle was in there, locked away and helpless, then she was determined to get him out. And if he wasn't in there . . . well, then she would know which dagger had struck him, and she would hunt down whoever had murdered him and make him pay for it.

She took a deep breath and said: "Let's do it."

But the faerie servant did not move from his spot beside the carriage.

"Aren't you coming, Samuligan?" Oona asked.

"No faerie may approach the tower's walls," he said. "That is known. There is an invisible barrier around the perimeter. It was only in Oswald's presence that I was able to pass out of it. And besides, I have been inside of the black cell at the top of that tower before. I do not wish to see it again. No, I will await your return here." He climbed back atop the carriage and thumbed back his hat, looking down at her with his intelligent faerie eyes. "But don't forget that if you do manage to get to the top, your uncle may not be the same as you remember him. Oswald turned me into a lizard when he captured me with the dagger. There is no telling what form your uncle may have been transformed into. It will have been a form of his attacker's choosing."

Oona had forgotten all about that little detail. "How do we change him back if he has been transformed?" she asked. "Clearly, it can be done. You are no longer a lizard."

It was Deacon who answered. "According to the *Encyclopedia Arcanna*, there is a single phrase that may transform the victim back into their original form."

"And what is the phrase?" Oona asked.

"Unfortunately," Deacon replied, "the dagger communicates the phrase to the attacker the moment the dagger is thrown with the mind."

"You mean that only the attacker would know how to transform him back?" Oona rolled her eyes. "Oh, I do detest magic."

She walked through the arched stone gate into the

cemetery. Crumbling gray headstones emerged from a sea of mist-covered hills like ragged, broken teeth. The cemetery was immense, seeming to go on forever, and Oona felt a sting of sadness as she set foot inside. It had been a long time since she had visited the so-called City of the Dead. Her parents' and her sister's graves were located on the far side of the tower, and she had not visited them since the day each of them had been placed in the ground. Certainly there was no time to do so today, and so she shoved the sadness aside the best she could and began to pick her way toward the base of the tower. The cemetery was vast, but getting lost on her way would have been nothing short of impossible. All she had to do was walk toward the seven-hundred-foot tombstone.

She circumvented several small mausoleums on her way, some of which had crumbled completely in on themselves. This was an old place, the kind of place only a ghost could call home. And of course, Oona knew that they *did* call it home, every night after sunset. It was a disquieting thought, and she quickened her steps.

At last she crested a low hill and got her first glimpse of the tower's huge foundation, which stood about forty feet in front of her. She'd never been so close. The ground seemed to bowl around it, as if the weight of the massive structure were causing the very earth to sink in. It was there, on the crest of the hill, that Oona felt a strange kind of resistance. It felt like the air around the tower had suddenly grown thick. Her stride slowed, and for a moment she didn't think she was going to be able to walk any farther.

"Is there a problem?" Deacon asked from her shoulder.

"Don't you feel it?" Oona asked, her legs all at once beginning to ache from the force it took just to move one foot in front of the other. "There's something strange with the air."

Deacon fluttered into the air and flew in a wide circle around her head before returning to her shoulder. "I don't notice anything."

Oona considered this new puzzle before realizing that what she was coming up against was likely the magical barrier Samuligan had mentioned. The barrier was detecting her active faerie blood and attempting to keep her from passing through, but because she was a human it could not block her out completely. At least that was what she thought, until she actually did come up against something that stopped her altogether.

It felt like there was an invisible brick wall in front of her. Oona put her shoulder into it and pushed, but to no avail. She gritted her teeth and once again shoved as hard as she could. This time something shifted. She slid forward . . . and then she was actually *inside* the invisible wall. It was a strange and uncomfortable sensation, to say the least. A trapped feeling. It felt as if the barrier were closing in around her on all sides, and she was suddenly reminded of being locked inside the broom closet the day before—remembering how the door had stuck, and how she'd needed to turn around in the cramped space and squeeze down on the knob as hard as she could—but at least then the closet hadn't been getting smaller.

Here it felt very much like the barrier was trying to crush her. But the feeling only made Oona push harder, the tips of her shoes digging into the soft, grassy hill. She grunted, a low guttural sound from the back of her throat. The muscles in her legs began to burn, and her shoes started to slip beneath her where the grass had been gouged away. For one horrible moment it seemed as if she might be stuck there, unable to move forward or backward. Unable to move at all. The thought terrified her so much that she let out a sharp cry, heaving her body forward with one last wild burst of energy . . . and then it was over. She was through. The air gave way, and she tumbled helter-skelter down the hill to the base of the tower.

"Umph." She collided with the smooth, glassy wall— its surface so deep and black that it seemed more like an emptiness where a tower should have been. But it was not emptiness at all. The walls were as solid as stone. Oona rubbed at her shoulder and pushed herself to her feet. About ten feet from the tower, a circle of stones sat in the low grass. It was slightly smaller than the size of a wagon wheel, and Deacon fluttered down beside it.

"Are you all right?" he asked.

She glanced down at herself. "I have a grass stain on my elbow, but I'm fine." She did a quick circle of the tower, looking for any sign of a door. It was a perfect square, each wall running approximately seventy feet across, and when she came back to where she had started, she was no wiser as to where the entrance might be. The only irregularity she could find at all was the circle of stones in the grass, which, so far as she could tell, appeared on only one side of the tower.

Finally, she removed the riddle from her pocket and read aloud:

"Upon my head I have no face
For your ease I come in a case
And though I'm well and upon my way
Upon my flight I'm here to stay
I slow you down, and tire you out
Yet getting you there is what I'm about."

She glanced around for any sign of what this might mean.

"'Upon my head I have no face,'" she said aloud.

"Well, there certainly are a lot of headstones around here. And *they* don't have faces."

"But have you ever seen a headstone in a case?" Deacon asked.

She ignored him, running the riddle over in her mind. *Upon my flight I'm here to stay,* she considered. *What can fly but stays in the same place? It doesn't make any sense.*

Deacon, who seemed to be stuck on the second part of the riddle, said: "If it comes in a case, then it must be something small."

Oona didn't know if that was right, but she did not argue aloud. There were many sorts of cases. There were instrument cases and traveling cases, and both could certainly be well upon their way, but neither of those had a head. There were bookcases, but Oona didn't see any books lying around anywhere. There were legal cases that took place in courtrooms, and yet none of those things had anything to do with getting you to some place. And certainly none of them could fly.

"Many riddles contain a play on words," Deacon suggested. "For instance, the line 'I slow you down, and tire you out' could be referring to going down to the bottom of the hill, where we'll find the way out of the tower. And of course, the way out would also be the way in."

Oona shook her head. There was an element of truth to what Deacon was saying—there could indeed be a play on words happening—but she thought Deacon's attempt had been too complicated. He was adding an element to the riddle that wasn't there. Good riddles were usually quite simple. All of the clues were there already, and you didn't need to add anything. She was simply missing it, and it was right in front of them, she could sense it.

"'I slow you down, and tire you out,'" she said, walking around the circle of stones. "'Yet getting you there is what I'm about.'"

Again it did not make any sense. Why would something that is meant to get you someplace slow you down and tire you out? It was simply counterproductive. Unless . . . unless . . .

Oona felt a kind of buzzing in her head, though it was not the same sort of buzzy feeling she got whenever she performed magic. No, this was quite different. It was the buzz of her thoughts slowing down, of turning a puzzle around in her mind, looking at it from different angles, poking at it with an imaginary finger, feeling its texture, pulling it apart and clicking it back together in new and different ways. To Oona, this was the best feeling in all of the world, and yet the feeling did not get in the way of the process. It simply buzzed in the background, a growing energy, urging her forward, assuring her that the answer was there. Inside.

A breeze rolled up the hill to play with the folds of Oona's dress. She didn't notice. Nor did she feel the warmth of the rising sun, or the smell of the blooming dandelions in the grass. The buzz was all consuming, everywhere inside of her. The words danced around the riddle, and the riddle danced around the meaning. Her mind moved from one possibility to the next, stepping gingerly upon the cryptic clues, pressing down upon each one the way that someone might test their weight upon a set of rickety stairs.

And then suddenly there it was. The buzzing dropped away as swiftly as it had come . . . and in its place was the answer. She had it! And of course it was so obvious. Deacon had been right about the play on words, except he'd been looking at the wrong part of the riddle. And like most riddles, once she had the answer, it became painfully clear. She laughed.

"What?" Deacon asked.

Oona beamed triumphantly at him. "Stairs, Deacon! Don't you see? A set of stairs has a head but has no face. They also come in a stair*case*. The phrase 'And though I'm well and upon my way' is indeed a play on words. What it is actually saying is: 'I am a *well* and also a *way*.' A stair*well* and a stair*way*. They also can come in a *flight* of stairs, which of course do not move. And lastly, perhaps the most obvious part of the riddle, they slow you down when you are walking up them, yet they get you to where you are going."

"Yes, yes! I see!" Deacon said, and the two of them looked excitedly around. Just as quickly as the excitement had come it seemed to disappear. "Ah, yes. A stairway," Deacon said wearily. "Do you see one?"

"Ah . . . well . . . not exactly," Oona said, the skin above her nose crinkling up as the confusion set in.

"Not exactly?" Deacon questioned.

"Well, all right, not at all," she said. "What else could it be?"

The two of them stood in silence for what seemed like a very long time. The sun had grown higher since they'd arrived at the tower, and its shadow, which cut across the face of the cemetery like a dark scar, had begun to shrink. Oona chewed on her lip. An idea came to her, and she had no idea if it would work or not. At this point anything was worth trying. She stepped into the circle of stones in the grass and faced the tower. It seemed as if the tower itself were staring down on her, like some huge black pupil in an enormous eye. She became very nervous, not because she thought her idea might not work but because she thought that it would. She locked her gaze upon the blackness before her, and said: "The password is: stairs."

In the blink of an eye, a set of smooth black steps appeared in front of her. They rose up nearly a full story high, to where a heavy iron door appeared in the side of the tower. And something else. A black iron key had appeared at her feet in the stone circle.

Deacon took in a startled breath. "You did it! You found the entrance."

"Yes. The riddle was a password, Deacon!" She snatched up the key. "Come along. Let's hurry up the steps before they disappear."

And before I lose my nerve, she thought.

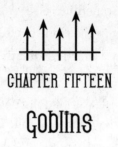

CHAPTER FIFTEEN

Goblins

Oona had only just unlocked the heavy iron door in the side of the tower, pushing it inward on creaking hinges, when the goblin nearly startled her off her feet.

"Beg your pardon, miss," it said as it stepped out of the darkness and into the light that streamed through the door. Dressed in a yellow medieval tunic and a pair of woolen breeches, the goblin peered at Oona and Deacon through tiny, malicious-looking eyes. Its pointy ears twitched on either side of its greenish bald head. "Oh my, did you ever give me a fright!" the goblin said, its voice low and gruff. The malevolent-looking creature placed its hand to its heart, as if it had indeed been frightened by her sudden appearance. Considering the fact that the goblin was nearly a foot taller than Oona, she came very close to saying: "*I* gave *you* a fright?"

But what she did say, the moment her wits had returned to her, was: "I'm sorry. I didn't mean to frighten you."

The goblin considered her, the green skin around its squashed-looking nose wrinkling up into a distorted snarl. Oona stiffened, ready to bolt back through the door. Deacon did the same on her shoulder.

At last the goblin let out a loud sneeze, and its face relaxed. "Oh, dear me, I do apologize. It must be all that fresh air coming through the door. It's making my allergies act up. Anyway, enough about my problems. I suppose you've come to see the prisoner."

Oona's eyes widened. "You mean there *is* a prisoner?" She couldn't believe it. It was almost too good to be true. Her uncle was alive after all.

But the goblin only shrugged. "I don't know. I mean, why else would you be here if there wasn't a prisoner?" He pointed to the key in her hand.

Oona felt her excitement drain away, and once again her nerves began to steal back over her. The goblin's eyes had a perpetual edge of malevolence about them, yet he seemed polite enough, and after a moment she decided the frightening face was only frightening because that was simply how goblins looked. In a way she almost felt sorry for him.

"Very well," the goblin said, and then turned its frightening gaze upon Deacon. "That your bird, miss?"

Oona nodded, clearing her throat. "Yes."

The goblin gave Deacon a glimpse of its yellow-fanged teeth before smacking its flat, wormy lips together. "Well, you might want to have him wait outside. Not unless you fancy him becoming supper for one of my brothers. I can control myself, so I can, but Glok and Clagwell . . . well, let's just say that neither of 'em has had black raven pie in neigh on five hundred years. Me? I prefer cat, myself. Though my favorite is worms, of course. Big, fat, slimy glowworms." His small, beady eyes seemed to glaze over at the mention of the worms. "You didn't happen to bring any extra, did you? One for an old doorkeeper like myself?" He looked at her expectantly.

Oona swallowed a lump in her throat. "I'm afraid not. I'm fresh out of . . . um, worms. Though I do have to make sure that you . . . you don't eat . . . um . . ." She couldn't get herself to say it.

"What? Humans?" the goblin said, and then stuck out his tongue. "No, miss. And begging your pardon, but I can't think of anything more disgusting. I'd sooner eat my brothers. But luckily, we goblins do not need to eat at all; otherwise, we would have all gobbled each other up long ago."

Oona gave Deacon a sideways look. "Perhaps it is best that you—"

"Wait outside," he finished for her. He took immediately to the air, and added, "Good luck," before disappearing out the door.

Oona smiled nervously at the goblin.

"Very wise, miss," the goblin said. "My name is Marrgak, by the way. Follow me."

Marrgak led her down a short hallway. The walls were as black as night, and all that could be heard was the patter of their footsteps. It was a short walk, however, and a moment later they emerged into a wide-open room. Glowing torches hung against the walls in row after row of flickering lights that rose endlessly into the darkness above. In the center of the room was a rowboat—the very same kind that her mother had been so fond of floating around in at Oswald Park—except that this rowboat hung like a basket beneath a lime-colored hot-air balloon. Oona had only ever seen illustrations of hot-air balloons before, and it was a very exciting sight. This balloon, however, was much smaller in scale than the ones she'd seen in books. It appeared to be about one-quarter of the size of the ones she remembered.

Oh, Mother would have loved to have seen this, she thought.

But the thought was erased in an instant when she realized that the boat was presently occupied by four thick-armed goblins, each one identical to Marrgak. In fact, the only way Oona could tell them apart was by their different-colored tunics. The boat's four oars had been pushed out of the way, and as Oona and the doorkeeper approached, she was surprised to see that the creatures were presently engaged in a game of cards. Indeed, though she had known of the existence of goblins from her history lessons with Deacon, she had never actually seen one outside of the enchanted tapestries in the parlor. Seeing so many of them now made her feel quite nervous, to say the least.

As Oona and Marrgak stopped at the edge of the boat, the four other goblins scarcely bothered to look up from their card game.

"This girl's going up to see the prisoner," Marrgak announced.

One of the goblins in the boat—this one was wearing a red tunic—looked up from his cards and then lowered his head again. "We're in the middle of a game," was his only reply.

Marrgak gave Oona a little shrug. "Good luck getting them to row you up when they have a game going." He pointed to the seat at the front of the boat. "There's where you sit. See you on your way out." He turned to go. "Be careful, though," he called over his shoulder. "If someone is a prisoner up in that cell, they must be pretty bad."

And then he was gone, swallowed up by the darkness. The four goblins in the boat continued their game, mumbling in low voices to one another, as Oona climbed into her seat at the bow. Once in place, she looked down at her feet to discover several objects: a hand drum, a whip, and an iron lockbox.

"Um, can you please take me up now?" she asked politely.

The goblins ignored her.

"Um . . . hello?" she said.

No response.

"Row!" she snapped at them. It did no good. They were too engrossed in their game.

She glanced at her feet and picked up the whip. Looking from the whip to the goblins, she hoped that she wasn't expected to whip them. They all looked very strong, and very bad-tempered, and would certainly have had no trouble taking the whip right away from her. And besides, the idea just seemed quite mean, no matter how lazy they were acting. The only thing she could think to do was to crack the whip along the side of the boat, and so that's exactly what she did. She snapped the end with an awkward flick of her wrist, readying herself to jump from the boat should the goblins make any sudden move toward her.

Krack!

The four goblins groaned in unison, clearly irritated, but they placed their cards on the seat beside them and pulled once on their oars. A flame mechanism in the center of the boat fired once, and the boat rose about a foot from the floor. The goblins then picked their cards back up and returned to playing their game.

"This is going to take forever," Oona said, looking up. The bottom of the lime-green balloon blocked her view of much of the ceiling, but still, she knew that seven hundred feet was a long way up. Once again, she glanced over the objects at her feet. Trusting in her instinct that these random items were the keys to getting the goblins to work, she briefly considered the hand drum and what it might be for, but when she bent to retrieve it, she changed her mind and picked up the iron lockbox instead. There was only one thing she could think to do. Quite determinedly, she set the box in her lap and slid the black iron key that she had taken from the circle of stones into the lock. The box clicked open to reveal four plump, wriggling worms. The worms had a faint mystical glow about them, and Oona knew immediately what they were—glowworms, the kind that could be found deep in the gardens at Pendulum House, beneath the patches of turlock root and sighing-lady grass.

Remembering what Marrgak had said about how much he liked worms, Oona plucked one of the slimy glowworms from the box and closed the lid again so that it locked shut. She held up the worm.

"If you row me all the way to the top, I'll give you these," she said.

The goblins ceased their murmuring and turned to her, cards raised. Their eyes flashed, betraying their excitement. They turned to confer, mumbling low to one another before turning back.

"You must give us the worms first," said the goblin in the red tunic.

"First?" Oona said dubiously. She did not trust the sly tone in the goblin's gravelly voice. If she gave them the worms now, they might still refuse to row her to the top.

"It is how it is done," said the goblin. "It is how it is always done. You give us the worms, then we row."

"Oh, yes," another of the goblins agreed. "It is how it is done."

Maybe the goblins were telling the truth, and that *was* how it was done. The way that their horrible little eyes peered at the worm in her hand made her feel very uneasy, and she had just begun to fear that they would go right ahead and take the worm and the key by force when a thought occurred to her.

They can't just take it. It's part of the tower's enchantment. And this is all some test, like the riddle. If I don't pass, then I can't go up to see the prisoner.

She considered the words that the goblin had said: *It is how it is always done.* If anyone would know how it had been done hundreds of years ago, when the tower was still being used, it would be these goblins. She made her decision.

"All right," she said, unlocking the box and reaching in. The glowing worms squirmed in her hand. "I'll give you the worms and you'll take me to the top?"

The goblins' black eyes sparkled against the glow of the worms. Their mouths gaped, revealing fleshy gums and jagged teeth.

"Oh yes, indeed, miss," the goblin in red assured her. "It is how it is done."

The goblin extended his covetous, large-knuckled hands, and Oona handed over the four worms. The goblin passed the worms around, one for each of his companions. They popped the worms into their large, flat mouths like popcorn, and then grimaced as they swallowed. Oona realized that they wore the same sour expression the Wizard got on his face when gulping down a shot of whiskey.

The goblins began to sway slightly from side to side, grinning at one another.

"All right," Oona said, "a deal is a deal. I gave you the worms, now take me up."

The goblins burst into laughter, slapping one another

on the back, as if in congratulation for a job well done. The one in the red tunic began to hum a little tune, while the one in purple stifled a hiccup and nearly slid out of his seat. A great, burly belch issued from the mouth of the goblin in blue, and Oona was blasted with the smell of it. She wrinkled up her nose as the stench engulfed her, and she understood what was happening. The smell was very similar to the stink that drifted out through the doors of some of the pubs on the north end of the street. It was the smell of beer, and wine, and hard alcohol.

"You're all drunk!" Oona said aloud.

The goblins' grins grew wider still, revealing even more of their hideous pink gums. They threw their arms around each other's shoulders and began to sway back and forth.

"Hay-ho, the dairy-oh," they began to sing together. "A worm in my belly, and no more woes. Hay-ho, the dairy-he. The workin' life is not for me."

She listened to them sing their song, the words beginning to slur together as they bellowed out the ridiculous lyrics. Looking down, she saw that the lockbox was once again occupied by four worms.

"Just great," she said. "A never-ending box of worms." She slammed the lid closed. "What help is that? All they do is get them drunk, and now they're worse than before."

"Hey, miss!" said the goblin in blue, his words coming

out slurry and overly loud. "Who you talking to? You crazy or somethin'?"

Again they all howled with laughter, slapping him on the back in praise of his superior wit.

The frustration was too much. Oona picked up the whip and cracked it over her head.

"Row!" she shouted. At the sound of the whip, all four goblins sat bolt upright in their seats, hands on their oars. They went stone still. Oona looked at them in amazement. It was as if they were hypnotized. Somehow, she was quite certain, it was connected to the sound of the whip. Oona glanced at the lockbox, and it came to her. She suddenly understood. Once the goblins ate the glowworms, they became intoxicated. Once intoxicated, the crack of the whip caused them to snap into some kind of hypnotic trance. But now the question was, how to get them rowing.

Oona picked up the third object from the bottom of the rowboat: the hand drum. She gave it a slap. The goblins heaved forward on their oars. The firing mechanism shot a flame toward the balloon, and the boat rose in the air. She slapped the drum again, and again they heaved, this time backward, and again the boat rose several feet.

Oona looked from her hands, to the drum, to the goblins. "This is most excellent," she said.

The excitement filled her, and she began beating

rapidly on the drum, but her erratic slapping only caused the goblins to move out of synchronization, in which case the firing mechanism would do no more than sputter. She paused before taking a deep breath and beginning again, this time beating slowly and in rhythm to the movements of the goblins, increasing her speed bit by bit as they began to build momentum.

It was working. The boat rose higher and higher, and soon the floor disappeared completely into the darkness below. It took nearly five minutes to reach the top of the tower, where the balloon bounced softly against the ceiling, and Oona's hands were sore from slapping the drum. Fiery torches hung from the ceiling and walls, illuminating a wooden walkway that stuck out of the side of the building like a floating boat dock. At the end of the walkway stood a heavy iron door.

"That must be the prison cell," she said, but the goblins were all still locked in their trance state, neither denying nor confirming her suspicions. "Well, there's only one way to find out."

She hopped from the boat to the dock and made her way to the iron door. The black iron key was in her hand, but she hesitated before sliding it into the lock. This was it: the moment of discovery. Was the Wizard inside this cell, alive after all, or would she find the cell empty and be forced to admit the worst . . . that he was dead, just like everyone else she had ever loved? Her fingers trembled as she inserted the key into the lock. Just as she had been certain that the key would open the tower door and the iron lockbox, she was certain that the key would work here as well. The fit was perfect. Again she hesitated, unsure if she really wanted to know the truth. What would she do if he was dead? Her uncle was all she had left.

He must be in there, she thought. *He simply has to be.*

A memory surfaced, projecting itself on the door in front of her. A beautiful remembrance of the days before she had become the Wizard's apprentice. She had been small . . . so small that he could pick her up in his hands. Both her mother and her father had been there. They had all been outside somewhere. Perhaps even at the park. They had all taken turns tossing her into the air. Up she would go, and she would scream with delight as she hovered briefly in the air before falling safely back into their hands. Her mother's hands had been soft and comforting, her father's hands strong and sure. It was becoming harder and harder to remember their faces, a fact that made Oona feel quite sad, but she remembered the feel of their hands, and their smells, and their eyes. Her uncle's beard had not been so gray on that day. He'd been younger, of course, but not *that* much younger. The dark color in his beard had mostly begun to fade in the past few years; since after the accident. The two of them had been through so much together, and the thought of losing him, too, was nearly too much to endure.

She imagined opening the door and seeing his wizened, gray-bearded face look up in surprise, and feeling the surge of relief as she rushed into his arms. The anticipation was too much. She turned the key and shouldered open the heavy metal door, its iron hinges screeching from centuries of neglect. The door fell inward to reveal . . .

A small empty room. Oona's heart plummeted, and her knees came unhinged. She fell to her knees, her legs hitting the floor so hard that the sound echoed around the tiny cell, but Oona did not feel the shock of pain. It was the disappointment of not finding her uncle that consumed her. The darkness of the room pressed in on her, and she found it difficult to breathe. She could feel the emotion bubbling up inside of her, an overwhelming twisting of grief, but she found that she could not release it. She could not cry, nor make any sound. She wanted to scream, desperately, but it would not come, and she was unable to free what she was feeling: that horrible, horrible mixture of loss, and anger, and confusion. But for some reason her eyes remained as dry as desert stones as she fell forward onto her hands, lost, unsure of what to do next. Fighting for breath.

And perhaps it was because of her trapped grief—because she did not cry out, and remained so silent—that she heard the croak. It came from the corner of the cell. Oona looked in the direction of the sound, her dry eyes peering into the shadows, but could see nothing. And then she thought she saw something move. She blinked, still feeling that horrible sensation of locked-up grief, but also a hint of curiosity. Something moved again, and Oona sat up onto her knees, the skirt of her dress fanning around her in the doorway. A moment later, a small, slick-skinned toad hopped into the light that flickered in through the open door. Its enormous eyes blinked up at her in a way that Oona had never seen a toad look before. It was a look of . . . recognition.

And suddenly, Oona remembered what Samuligan had said about how, if she found him, the Wizard might not be in a recognizable form. She leaned forward and peered into the toad's wizened face. It stared back, and though it was strange to think, Oona was almost certain that the toad was relieved to see her. It opened its mouth and let out a low croak.

"Uncle Alexander?" she asked.

Again the toad croaked, the sound bouncing softly off the walls of the cell.

Oona extended her hand, and the toad hopped onto her open palm. She raised it to her face and—with equal parts concern and relief, not to mention a goodly portion of bemusement—she said: "Well . . . isn't this interesting?"

CHAPTER SIXTEEN

Quick and Bop

Oona watched the storefronts and apartment buildings roll by as the carriage traveled up the broad cobbled avenue, vibrating the lacy frills of her dress and the toad in her lap. From his place on the seat beside her, Deacon leaned in to get a closer look at the toad, which presently gave a croak of displeasure.

"Don't get so close, Deacon," Oona said, turning from the window. "You're making him nervous."

Deacon pulled away, swaying to the motion of the carriage. "Are you certain that is your uncle?"

Oona's brow furrowed. "Of course it's Uncle Alexander. Just look at that face." The toad gazed up at her, wide-eyed and looking highly uncomfortable. "Try imagining the Wizard without his beard," Oona said.

A moment later Deacon replied: "By Oswald, you're right! I can see it. The toad does look like your uncle."

"Or my uncle looked very much like a toad," Oona said. The toad croaked its disapproval.

The journey from the top of the tower back to the bottom had taken only half the time of the assent. Getting back through the invisible barrier, though, had proven just as difficult as getting in, and at present, Oona felt exhausted and hungry.

"Sometimes a case does not allow time for such mundaneries as eating," she said.

"*Mundaneries* is not a proper word," Deacon chided.

"Ah, here we are," she said, glancing out the window. "The lawyer's office."

The carriage creaked to a halt, and a moment later Samuligan opened the door. Setting her uncle on the seat beside her, Oona quickly searched the riding compartment for something to keep him in. She discovered a round hatbox beneath the seat. She opened it only to discover that it was one of her mother's old hats. Broad-brimmed, with a large auburn-colored silk flower on the side, Oona knew it was quite out of style, but she also thought it would go perfectly with her auburn-colored dress, and so she placed it on her head, adjusting it to the desired angle, and then placed the toad inside the box.

"You'll be safer in here. Until we figure out how to change you back," she told her uncle. He croaked softly as she placed the lid on top. Setting the certificate of debt on top of the box, she stepped to the curbside. Several moments later she stood in front of a narrow, redbrick building that slanted so far over the sidewalk, it looked as though it might topple at any moment. A sign above the door read: RAVENSMITH LAW.

With the box beneath one arm, she knocked. No one answered.

Oona glanced around and saw that the street clock down the sidewalk read 9:30.

"I thought you said Ravensmith opened at nine o'clock," Oona said.

Deacon flew to the sill of the small window beside the door and pointed his beak at the sign posted there.

WORKING HOURS: 9:00 A.M. TO 5:00 P.M.

"Hmm." Oona knocked again several times, then tried the knob. It was locked. Just as she was ready to give up, the door was answered by a man in a wheelchair. The lower half of the poor fellow's body was sealed up in a hard plaster cast, and his legs stuck straight out in front of him. In one hand he held a feather duster. Oona recognized it as one of the enchanted "giggling" dusters from her uncle's shop. A dirty rag hung from the man's jacket pocket, and a crooked pine-branch broom lay across his lap.

"Can't you read the sign?" the man asked irritably. "We don't open until nine o'clock!" He was a plain-looking man, except for his eyebrows, which were the bushiest Oona had ever seen, and great gobs of white hair spilled from his ears.

"But, it is nine thirty just now," Oona said.

The man in the wheelchair shook his head at her as if she were very stupid. "You can't fool me," he said. "Mr. Ravensmith is not yet in. And Mr. Ravensmith is always in by nine o'clock. So you see, I'm afraid it cannot be past nine, as he has not yet arrived."

Oona shook her head at the man's logic. "But that doesn't make any sense, Mr. . . . ."

"I am Mr. Quick," the man in the wheelchair replied. "And I have worked as Mr. Ravensmith's secretary for over ten years. Believe me when I say he is always in by nine o'clock, so whatever you say, I know that it cannot *possibly* be after nine. Now, if you will excuse me, I need to get back to dusting the office. If there's one thing Mr. Ravensmith detests more than anything, it is dust and dirt, and today is Miss Colbert's day off."

"Miss Colbert, the cleaning maid?" Oona asked, remembering how Mr. Ravensmith had hired the old

Pendulum House maid. And now that she thought about it, the pine-branch broom in the secretary's lap looked suspiciously like the one that had gone missing from the Pendulum House broom closet just after Miss Colbert was dismissed.

"Is that the maid's personal broom?" Oona asked curiously.

Mr. Quick rolled his eyes at her. "Of course it's the maid's personal broom. There is nothing more personal to a maid than a broom, except for perhaps a duster."

He turned his attention to the window and began dusting. The enchanted feathers started to giggle, a highly annoying sound, and Oona needn't wonder why her uncle sold so few of them. She watched the man dust the window for several seconds, when finally he turned back to her.

"Are you still here?" he asked. "I told you that we do not open until nine o'clock."

"Oh, of course," Oona said, attempting to keep her frustration at bay. "Well, perhaps we could wait for Mr. Ravensmith inside?"

"I told you—" Mr. Quick began.

"Yes, yes. You don't open until nine." Oona sighed heavily, looking down at the certificate of debt on top of the box.

"He may be next door," Mr. Quick offered. "Mr.

Ravensmith often visits the Magicians Legal Alliance before coming to the office."

Oona felt almost shocked to receive a bit of useful information. "Oh. Thank you, Mr. Quick. We shall try next door." She turned to go but stopped, unable to help her curiosity. "By the way, what happened to your legs?"

"It's not the legs!" said Mr. Quick in a craggy, irritated tone. "How many times do I have to tell people? It's the hip."

"Oh, I apologize," Oona said. "What happened to your *hip*?"

"I broke it, tripping on a pothole," he replied. He appeared slightly embarrassed. "And let me say, there is no worse pain than a broken hip, I can assure you."

Deacon tutted from Oona's shoulder. "Ridiculous. I can think of many unfortunate accidents that would result in far worse pain than a broken hip. For instance, being slowly crushed beneath a hundred-ton boulder, or perhaps having one's arm chewed off by a hungry bear, or maybe even—"

"I think we get the point, Deacon," Oona said, suddenly feeling queasy.

Mr. Quick sneered at Deacon before flaring his nostrils at Oona. "I have work to do, young lady. Now, good day!" The secretary attempted to slam the door, but the door bounced off his plaster cast, then ricocheted off the wheel of the chair, sending Mr. Quick shooting backward. The door slammed shut, and they heard the faint sound of a crash and a curse from the other side.

"Okay then. Next door, it is," Oona said.

The Magicians Legal Alliance resided in a plain, six-story building, whose entrance consisted of nothing more than a simple white door.

Oona turned to the faerie servant. "I would feel much safer if the Wizard were to remain out here with you, Samuligan."

The faerie servant took the box in his long fingers, and Oona removed the certificate of debt from the top. She watched Samuligan return to the carriage, the box beneath one arm, his long faerie face shadowed beneath his cowboy hat. No one in their right mind would dare harass Samuligan the Fay. The Wizard would be safe. Satisfied, she removed the eviction notice from her pocket and turned to the door. It was time to get some legal answers.

The door fell open, but there was no one behind it. Oona stared through the empty doorway into the Magicians Legal Alliance building, perplexed. She glanced back toward the carriage, but Samuligan only shrugged.

"Well," Oona said. "This is going to be interesting."

She stepped through the doorway, Deacon riding on her shoulder like a strange appendage. Once inside, the door swung shut, leaving the two of them in a small foyer, in the middle of which stood the fattest man Oona had ever seen. Though his head was bald as a crystal ball, a set of thick side-whiskers hung down below his jiggling jowls. Dressed in a shabby-looking suit—of which the trousers were at least a foot too short—he smiled at her, exposing a set of straight white teeth. Most striking of all were the tattoos on his face. One cheek appeared nearly solid silver, while the other glittered as brightly as a new gold coin. Even his ears were covered in the alliance's strange pattern of squiggles and lines, making them look purplish blue.

"Welcome to the Magicians Legal Alliance," said the man in a booming voice. "I am Mr. Bop, senior under-secretary to the secretary of the Board of Secretaries, and acting vice secretary in charge of all matters of secretarial law." He sounded very proud of his title, and Oona nodded appreciatively. Mr. Bop extended his hand. "And you are?"

"Miss Oona Crate," she said, shaking the man's hand. *Mr. Bop,* she thought. That name was familiar. Where had she heard it before?

"And how may I help you today?" the man asked.

"I am hoping to find Mr. Ravensmith."

"Ah, Ravensmith?" Mr. Bop looked apologetic. "I'm afraid he is not here. But it is possible that he may come in later."

"Oh," Oona said, feeling quite disappointed. She let go with a heavy sigh, considering her next course of action, when she suddenly asked: "Is Adler Iree in?"

Mr. Bop's face brightened. "He is, indeed. He is, indeed. Adler Iree is one of our finest and brightest young members. Just follow me, and I will take you to him."

The enormous senior undersecretary turned quite nimbly on his heels and made his way across the foyer, the entire floor shaking noticeably beneath his feet. Oona and Deacon followed him through a set of double doors, only to find themselves in a wide-open room with various-shaped desks and comfortable seats. Many of the desks were occupied by solitary figures, each of them hunched over their tables with their noses buried in one book or another. The walls were covered floor to ceiling with books—the most remarkable part being that the ceiling soared some six stories above their heads. Books, books, and more books; and rickety, crooked ladders—some of them hammered together piecemeal, one on top of the other—that ran on tracks all the way to the top shelves. It made Oona's head spin just to look.

Something Hector Grimsbee had said the night before

suddenly popped into Oona's head, and she turned excitedly to Mr. Bop. "Are you the same Mr. Bop who lives in the apartment above Madame Iree's dress shop?"

Mr. Bop's eyebrows rose in surprise. "I am, indeed. But how did you know that? Do you know my wife?"

Oona shook her head. "I am acquainted with Hector Grimsbee, who lives in the apartment above yours. Do you know anything about him?"

"The man upstairs?" asked Mr. Bop. He frowned slightly. "Never seen the fellow, to tell the truth. We must have different schedules. What did you say his name was?"

"Grimsbee," Oona said. "He's a blind man. Use to be an actor at the Dark Street Theater."

Mr. Bop shook his head. "Can't say I've heard of him. I don't go to the theater much, but if he's an actor, my wife may know him. She's an actress. It keeps her busy while I'm working. She plays the role of the Faerie Queen every year in *Oswald Descends*. I've never seen it myself, but according to her, not only does she have the best speeches, but it is she who gets to battle Oswald, the most famous of the Magicians of Old, during the play's spectacular finale upon the fabled steps of Faerie."

To Oona's surprise, Deacon threw both wings out in a dramatic gesture, nearly slapping her in the face, before quoting the final lines of the Faerie Queen: "'Sleep not, ye thieves of magic! I shall avenge ye! I shall avenge ye all!'"

Oona's eyebrows rose, and Deacon looked suddenly abashed as he folded in his wings and attempted to recompose himself. Oddly enough, despite Deacon's outburst, not one of the figures at the tables looked their way.

"Ah, there he is," said Mr. Bop. He pointed toward a speck of a person at the top of one of the more unsafe-looking ladders. For half a heartbeat Oona thought Mr. Bop was speaking of Grimsbee, but even from this distance, Oona recognized Adler's raggedy cloak and threadbare hat. He slid a book from a shelf near the top of the stacks and then began descending the rickety ladder at a breakneck speed. Before Oona could blink several times, the boy had made his way to the ground floor, the ratty old top hat resting securely on his head. He made his way hurriedly toward a desk.

"Mr. Iree!" called Mr. Bop.

Adler froze in mid-sit, looking around.

"You have a visitor," Mr. Bop said, and then to Oona: "If you'll excuse me, I'm off for a bite to eat. Very nice to meet you, Miss Crate."

The floor shook like a small earthquake as Mr. Bop swiveled around and quickly marched away, disappearing through the double doors. Oona hardly noticed. She was too busy observing the tattoos on Adler's handsome face, how they crinkled up ever so slightly as he tried to suppress a smile. He swiftly stood, pulled a second chair to his desk and held out his hand. Oona wasn't sure, because the room was so dimly lit, but she thought the boy might have winked at her as she made her way across the room. Suddenly, her mouth was very dry.

No one looked up as she padded across the ornate carpet and took the seat provided for her. Nor did anyone speak. Everyone seemed completely absorbed in their reading material—everyone except for Adler Iree, who took his own seat, placing his elbow on the table and resting his jaw in the palm of his hand.

"I was expecting you," he said.

CHAPTER SEVENTEEN

Adler Iree

"A h, riddle me, fiddle me," spoke Adler Iree, seemingly indifferent to anyone whom he might disturb in the quiet atmosphere of the Magicians Legal Alliance. "Come to check up on me, have you, Miss Crate? Thinking maybe my sister or I stole that dagger from the museum, and then later used it on the Wizard?"

Oona did not respond immediately, but instead she watched him. He was direct, and intelligent, and yet boyish all at the same time.

She adjusted her hat and said: "Your accent is Irish, Mr. Iree, yet your sister's and mother's accents, like most of the citizens on Dark Street, are distinctly British."

Adler rolled his eyes. "Isadora got the Irish twisted

out of her by our grandmother. Our father, may he rest in peace, was Irish blood, going all the way back to before his great-great-grandfather first stepped foot on Dark Street. Father died when we were but eight years old. That's when our grandmother—me mother's mother—moved into the house. Tried to make us speak what she called proper English, and told Isadora that she was going to go to that la-di-da Academy of Fine Young Ladies just as soon as she was old enough. You should have heard Isadora before Grandmother showed up. Her accent was thicker than mine, if you'd believe it."

Oona nodded, feeling her chest tighten at the mention of Adler's father's death. She of all people knew how hard it could be to lose a parent. But Adler simply shrugged. And the *way* that he shrugged . . . it was sort of . . .

Well, it's cute, she thought, but then quickly forced the thought aside, reminding herself that this charming boy could very well be her uncle's attacker.

"Well, now that that little mystery is solved," she said, perhaps a bit too hastily, "I'd first like to talk about yesterday."

Adler shifted in his seat. "I did not go to the museum to steal the daggers, if that's what you're after. I showed up at ten o'clock, just when the museum opened. I signed in at the front, and then headed straight for the library, where they keep the rarest law books in the back."

Oona glanced at the walls, looking at the stacks upon stacks of books, before saying: "Don't they have law books here, Mr. Iree?"

Adler's fingers rubbed at the edge of his book, where Oona could plainly read the title: *The Little Red Book of Large Legal Loopholes*.

"The books at the museum date back hundreds of years before any of the alliances' books do," he told her. "That's why the museum books are preferable."

"Bit of a scholar?" Oona asked.

Adler straightened in his seat but did not answer. Yet Oona could tell the comment had delighted the boy. He glanced inquisitively at the two red-colored documents in her hand. Oona had nearly forgotten that she was holding them. Adler said nothing, yet the scarlet moons at the corners of his eyes crinkled almost imperceptibly. It seemed as if he were holding back a smile. Oona could not have said why exactly, but she decided then and there to trust him. It was perhaps irrational, but what choice did she have? Ravensmith could not be found, and she needed answers. Adler was, after all, a studying lawyer.

"Tell me what you make of these." Oona slid the eviction notice and the certificate of debt across the desk. The boy took his time reading both documents line by line before handing them back.

"Hmm," he said. "I'll be right back."

He walked to a nearby bookshelf, ran his fingers along the book spines, and then slid a large, single volume from the shelf before returning to the table.

"What's that?" Oona asked.

Adler flipped through the pages. "It's a record of all of the businesses on Dark Street. Ah . . . here it is. Dupington Moneylenders. Looks like they are a legitimate business, registered with the Dark Street Council." He paused a moment before adding: "Says here that Dupington Moneylenders is owned by another company named Fool's Gold Enterprises." Adler flipped several pages back in the book, ran his finger down the page, and then stopped. "And Fool's Gold Enterprises is owned by yet another company."

"Let me guess," Oona said. "The Nightshade Corporation."

Adler snapped the book shut. "You got it. Dupington is a fitting name, Miss Crate, because it seems your uncle was duped into borrowing money from the Nightshade Corporation . . . in a clever, roundabout way. And now ol' Red Martin's finally found himself a way to build his dreadful Indulgence Island. Been bloody well tryin' to do it for years, from what I hear, but there was no vacant land on Dark Street large enough. Not till now, anyway. I hear he's wanting to import sand from some exotic beach and make the place look like a tropical island, if you can believe it."

Oona could believe it, remembering the image of palm trees and the enormous hula hut painted on the sign in front of Pendulum House.

"Can you imagine what an awful sight that would be?" Adler added. "Right smack in the middle of Dark Street?"

Deacon cleared his throat. "Surely the Dark Street Council would never approve of such a thing. It would ruin the street's characteristic charm."

"But they *have* approved it," Adler said, pointing to the top of the letter at the council's official seal. "Red Martin's got all them council members in his pocket. He's been putting it in their heads for years that Pendulum House is too unkempt and frightening looking, with its crooked tower and tangled gardens."

"I myself find palm trees much more frightening," said Deacon.

"You mean to tell me that these documents are legal?" Oona said so loudly that she turned to see if anyone was looking. No one was. Every head in the room appeared fixed in place, bent over their various books.

Adler leaned forward, his seat creaking beneath him like twigs underfoot. "Oh, aye," he said. "It's fairly simple. In the event of your uncle's death, ownership of Pendulum House would normally have gone to you, if you were still the apprentice, but since you gave it up, and no other apprentice was yet chosen, then Red Martin, as the ultimate owner of Dupington Moneylenders, legally has the right to repossess the Wizard's personal property—meaning he can take all the Wizard's stuff—as compensation for the money your uncle borrowed. Very cleverly done, if you ask me."

"So because I signed away my rights as apprentice, Red Martin owns the house?" Oona asked, feeling as if her heart had dropped into her stomach.

"Yes. Just so," Adler said. "And think on this. If the Dark Street pendulum stops swinging at midnight . . ." He raised his eyebrows at her, waiting for her to get it. Suddenly, she did.

"If the pendulum stops at midnight . . ." She trailed off, shaking her head and wondering why she hadn't figured it out sooner. "If the pendulum stops at midnight, then Dark Street will cease its rotation. It will be permanently open to New York City."

Adler snapped his fingers. "It's a theory, anyway. All those New Yorkers will come flooding through the gates to see the magical world, and Red Martin will make a bloody fortune off his new hotel/casino. That is, if it works."

"What do you mean, if it works?" Oona asked.

Catching on to Adler's train of thought, Deacon said: "Ah, well, since the pendulum has never been stopped, no one knows for sure what will happen. The Magicians of Old set the street to spinning as a measure against faerie attack. That way, if the faeries ever did manage to break through the Glass Gates, then their armies would have only one minute per day in which they could cross over. The magicians also bestowed an enormous amount of magic into Pendulum House, so that the Wizard could tap into that power and enable him—or her—to not only fend off the attacking army but also to protect the house itself, thereby ensuring the uninterrupted swing of the pendulum within. As Samuligan explained last night, part of the house's job is to hold the street on course as it spins through the Drift. It is for that reason that the house was constructed at the very center of Dark Street."

"Is this really the time for a history lesson, Deacon?" Oona asked.

Deacon ruffled his feathers. "I believe that it is. You see, because there is the distinct possibility that when the pendulum is stopped at midnight, the street will simply stay connected to New York indefinitely. Most likely, that is what Red Martin is banking on. But there is also the possibility that once the house is destroyed, the magic will no longer be contained, and Dark Street could simply go spinning off into the Drift, leaving us with no connection to the World of Man whatsoever. There would be no way to get food or supplies. Like a boat adrift at sea, eventually people would begin to starve."

For a long moment the three of them sat in silence. It seemed almost too horrible to conceive.

At last, Deacon said: "These are, of course, only two theories. Given time, I imagine we could come up with more. Let us not forget that even if Red Martin's plan works, and the street stays put, if Pendulum House is destroyed, then there will be no power source for the Wizard to tap into should the Glass Gates ever fall. And with both sets of gates open, the World of Man would be completely vulnerable to faerie attack."

"It seems to be a gamble that Red Martin is willing to make," said Adler.

Oona's empty stomach felt as if it had just twisted into a great big knot, and the magnitude of the mystery suddenly hit her. If Red Martin succeeded in his plan, then it was actually possible that everyone on Dark Street could end up dead. And the only way she could see to stop that possibility from occurring was to find her uncle's attacker and make them reveal the words that would reverse the enchantment before midnight.

A new thought occurred to her, and all at once she saw a glimmer of hope.

"But wait!" she said. "Red Martin can't have Pendulum House. My uncle is not dead. He's just been transformed into a toad. I rescued him from the Black Tower this morning."

Adler blinked at her in surprise.

"It's a long story," she assured him. "But it is him, I am sure of it."

Evidently taking her at her word, Adler shrugged. "That may be the case, Miss Crate, but according to this morning's paper, he's dead as all else. Here, have a look."

He slid a thin, folded newspaper out from beneath a stack of books: *The Dark Street Tribune*. Oona unfolded the paper and read the headline: "Police Declare Wizard Dead. No Successor Chosen."

Oona slammed the paper down. "But this is outrageous!" Her voice echoed back at her from the high ceiling, yet again, not a single head turned in her direction.

"Even so," Adler said, "if what you say is true, and your uncle is actually a . . . a toad? Then unfortunately he still forfeits his rights to the house. The reason I happen to know so much is because I went to the museum yesterday specifically to look up information on the Wizard and Pendulum House . . . seeing as I was applying for the apprenticeship and all. Anyway, one of the things I remember finding was an extremely old document, written by several of the Magicians of Old and signed by Oswald himself. That's some pretty heavy law, just in case you were wondering, and the document stated in no uncertain terms that only a human being could ever be named Wizard. It was a condition made into law to make sure that no faerie could ever hold the position. Unfortunately, that same condition applies to toads as well."

What about humans with faerie blood? Oona thought to ask. But it was a pointless question, she knew. She had already given up any possibility of ever becoming the next Wizard. Yet still . . . *Certainly there have been Natural Magicians who were named Wizard before. Uncle Alexander told me so. He said they were the best Wizards ever.*

Oona shook her head, unsure as to why she was suddenly so concerned with such thoughts. Surely her days of magic were over. It didn't matter what the laws said.

The three of them sat in silence for what might have been a full minute.

At last Oona rose from her chair and folded the two letters into her pocket. "Thank you, Mr. Iree," she said.

Adler caught hold of her hand. He did not rise from his seat, but her hand tingled, and all the tiny hairs along her arm stood endwise.

Oona quickly slid her hand from Adler's, doing her best to remain as calm as she could manage with her heart suddenly racing. Adler frowned, but it was not an aggressive look.

"That thing I saw you do yesterday," he said. "Fixing the broken glass. That was quite . . . um . . ."

Oona's face flushed red. "Stupid," she said.

"Stupid?" said Adler. "Oh, I'd not say that. Just the opposite, actually. I'd never seen anyone do something like that in all my years on Dark Street."

Oona felt a sudden need to fidget with her hat. "I should not have done it . . . and I won't do it again."

"But why?" he asked. "I'd heard it said that you was a Natural Magician. That's mighty rare, and nothing at all to be ashamed of."

For a moment she felt like telling him everything. About how the magic had gone wrong, how she could not control it, and how those nearest and dearest to her had paid for her mistake with their lives. But of course Adler would most likely already know this. The incident in the park was far from a secret, having happened so publicly. And yet still, she wanted to tell him how sometimes she would be walking down the street and think that she had smelled her mother's perfume, and she would turn around, heart thumping, only to discover some other woman, some stranger, and Oona would feel as if her heart might explode. Or how the sound of a crying baby would sometimes cause her to lose her breath, reminding her so much of the sister she'd had for such a short time.

But Oona mentioned none of this, and instead she simply said: "I believe that will be all."

"Oh, aye," Adler said, rising. "I'll walk you out. By the way, that hat looks very fine on you."

Oona couldn't help herself—the smile slipped through her defenses and landed quite plainly upon her face. "Thank you, Mr. Iree."

"Call me Adler," he said, smiling back at her.

Oona considered this. "All right. Thank you, Adler." She adjusted the hat on her head, feeling strangely giddy. "It was my mother's."

CHAPTER EIGHTEEN

The Museum of Magical History

Oona placed her mother's hat on the seat beside her and stared out the carriage window, her hand resting on the hatbox with her uncle safely inside. She felt lost. Everything she had learned from Adler served only to complicate matters in her head, and she hoped that a visit to the museum would prove helpful in clearing some of the confusion.

She watched the fortresslike structure roll into view. The carriage clattered heavily over several potholes as Samuligan pulled to the side of the road in front of the museum.

Oona threw the compartment door open before Samuligan had a chance to open it. She thrust the hatbox into his hands and said: "Keep an eye on that."

"Why are we here?" Deacon asked.

"I wish to ask the security guard some questions," she replied. "Perhaps we will discover something the *inspector* did not."

But the first thing Oona discovered was that the giant sculpture in the shape of a top hat was standing right in her way. The sculpture was nearly seven feet tall and perhaps five feet in diameter.

"What is this, anyway?" Oona asked.

"Petrified colossus clothing," Samuligan said. "Giant clothing so old that it has turned to stone."

Oona knew from her history lessons with Deacon that colossi—men and women who were reported to have been over seventy feet tall, and who had lived thousands of years before even the Great Faerie War—had at one time used the ancient Faerie road to travel back and forth between worlds.

"You mean to tell me that those ancient giants wore top hats?" Oona said, disbelieving.

Samuligan grinned. "They were quite ahead of their time . . . fashionably speaking."

"Well, it's not a very good place for an installation. It takes up half the sidewalk." Oona shook her head as she ventured around the giant hat and made her way up the stone steps to the front door. Regardless of being nearly five inches thick and at least eight feet wide, the wood door opened easily at her touch, swinging inward on its big iron hinges, and Oona stepped through the threshold into the museum.

The entryway consisted of a vast circular room, with high-beamed ceilings that vaulted upward in weblike patterns. A ring of massive monolithic stones stood in the center of the room, and Oona knew from her many visits to the museum with her uncle that this mysterious stone circle was one half of a set, the other half of which stood in the countryside somewhere in England. Though Oona had not seen the sister version of the enormous structure, she did know that it was called Stonehenge by those residing in the World of Man, and that it had not been kept nearly as nice as the one standing in the entryway to the Museum of Magical History. Both rings of stones had been gifts from faeries to magicians thousands of years ago when humans and fairies had traveled back and forth between the worlds in harmony. What their purposes were had long been forgotten.

But it was not the mysterious magical circle that Oona had entered the museum to find. A uniformed guard was posted just inside the front door, a thickset man with arms like mountains and no neck at all. Oona turned to him now and saw that he was staring at her, as if surprised to see someone walk through the museum doors.

"May I help you, miss?" he asked.

"I hope you can," Oona said. "I was wondering if you were on duty here at the front entrance yesterday."

The guard's caterpillar-like eyebrows rose ever so slightly. "I was."

Oona nodded. "Very good. I was also wondering if you remember seeing a certain man enter the museum. He would have been tall, about your height, with greasy black hair and a bullhorn mustache. Also, he would have been blind, his eyes white like snow."

"Oh, you mean the actor, Hector Grimsbee," said the guard.

Oona's heart gave a heavy thump. "Yes, yes. He was indeed an actor with the Dark Street Theater. That's him. You saw Mr. Grimsbee enter the museum yesterday?"

The museum guard frowned. "No."

"No?" said Oona.

"No. Otherwise he would have signed his name in this register book here." The guard pointed to the thick book sitting on a wooden pedestal beside him. "I'd have made sure of it. By the way, if you wouldn't mind, you'll need to sign in as well."

He handed her a pen, and she signed her name at the top of a blank page. Curious, she flipped the page back one day, and saw that the inspector had been correct: the only two names on the registry for the previous day were Adler and Isadora Iree.

Oona handed the pen back to the guard. "You know who Hector Grimsbee is? You would recognize him on sight?"

"Oh, to be sure," said the guard. "I would have remembered seeing him come in here. My wife and I are really big fans of the theater, you know. He was in a lot of plays up until about a year ago. Why do you ask? Do you know him?"

"We are acquainted," Oona said, unable to keep the disappointment from her voice.

"Oh," said the guard excitedly. His face went slightly red. "Do you think you could get me an autograph? Not for me, mind you, but for my wife. She would be so pleased."

"Sorry," Oona said, "but I don't think . . ." She trailed off as a short man no taller than Oona herself came striding through the circle of stones toward the front door. His beard was well trimmed, and his nose was quite pointy. His most recognizable feature, however, was an enormous overbite, which gave him a rather horsey appearance, and Oona recognized him from being at some of her uncle's social gatherings. He was Mr. Glump, the museum curator.

"Mr. Glump," Oona called. "May I ask you a few questions?"

Mr. Glump stopped abruptly, looking distastefully

from Oona to Deacon on her shoulder, then back to Oona again. "There are no pets allowed in the museum."

Deacon puffed up his feathers, as if getting ready to explain the difference between a pet bird and a living reference library, but Oona spoke first.

"I'm sorry, Mr. Glump," Oona said. "I will remember that the next time I visit. You might remember me, I'm—"

"Miss Crate. Yes, I know," said the curator. "I remember you from one of those Pendulum House parties. I read the paper this morning, and I'm very sorry to hear about what happened to your uncle, but if you have come here to blame me, I can assure you that the reason the daggers were stolen was not my fault."

"Yes, I know," Oona said. "Inspector White mentioned that you were out of the office."

Mr. Glump nodded. "I received a note via flame yesterday that an anonymous guest at the Nightshade Hotel had come across a mysterious black box with all sorts of magical symbols carved into it. They wanted to meet me at the hotel at one o'clock to discuss a possible donation of the artifact to the museum. Well, as everyone knows, Oswald's wand—the one that some say he stole from Faerie, and which then in turn was stolen from *him*—was supposedly kept in just such a box. I was immensely interested, so I sent a reply, agreeing to meet the anonymous person in the hotel lobby at one o'clock, as they had suggested. The Nightshade is on the north end of the street, so I left my office around twelve fifteen, locking the door behind me, as I always do. But the whole thing turned out to be some rude joke. The person with the box never showed, and when I returned, around four o'clock, I found my office door hanging wide open, and the daggers where gone."

Oona tilted her head thoughtfully to one side. "That's over three and a half hours, from the time you left. If the person never showed, then why did it take you so long to return to the museum? Surely, even the slowest of carriages wouldn't have taken several hours to make the trip."

Mr. Glump looked slightly uncomfortable. "I . . . um. Well, I waited in the hotel lobby for nearly a half hour after the agreed-upon time, and then two gentlemen from the hotel security approached me. I thought they were going to ask me to leave, but instead, after I explained why I was there, the two of them seemed to feel so sorry for me that they gave me several brandies on the house, and a handful of betting chips to pass the time while I waited. It seems that the time got away from me. Lost a bit of my own money when the free chips ran out. But anyway, that's neither here nor there. The fact remains that I was not here in the museum when the daggers were stolen."

Oona scratched at the back of her neck, considering

this new information. It sounded suspiciously to her as if someone had lured the curator out of his office on purpose.

"Are you the only one with a key to your office?" Oona asked.

Mr. Glump nodded. "Yes, but of course even the most sophisticated locks can be picked . . . and that is why we have security guards."

"And you're sure you locked the door to your office when you left?" Oona asked.

The curator's nostrils flared, and he looked all at once peeved at being questioned by a twelve-year-old girl. "I always lock the door! Now, if you'll excuse me, I have a headache, and I'm going home early." He raised one mocking eyebrow at her before adding in a rather sarcastic tone: "That is, if you are done with your questions, Miss Crate."

"Oh yes," Oona said. "Quite finished."

The curator pressed his hand to his head and headed out the front door. Oona was about to make her own exit when the guard called after her.

"You sure you couldn't get Grimsbee's autograph for me? I mean, for my wife, that is."

Oona paused for a moment, long enough to look back at the guard, but her head was too full of thoughts to answer his ridiculous request. She pulled the door open and walked through, letting it fall shut behind her.

"No need to be rude!" the guard called after her. *"All you had to do was say no!"*

Oona ignored the guard's shouts as they fell silent behind the thick wooden door and walked to the edge of the first step.

"Grimsbee didn't go in, Deacon," she said, sounding baffled. "I don't understand. First off, if Grimsbee truly was alone when we saw him, and not arguing with some invisible person, then how did he injure his head? Certainly not shaving his forehead. And why did he disappear?"

Oona began looking around for other possible places where Grimsbee could have disappeared to, but after several minutes she said: "There is nowhere else he could have gone."

Deacon shifted his weight on her shoulder. "He *must* have entered the museum."

"But why did the guard not see him?" Oona asked. "He clearly would have recognized him."

From her elevated position she could see the street stretching out in both directions. The giant top hat hid part of the carriage from view, but she could see Samuligan waiting patiently for her near the horse, the hatbox in his hands. The sun was high overhead by now, and a cool breeze ruffled at the skirt of her dress.

Across the street stood Witch Hill, looking both barren

and unremarkable, save for the single, dead tree at its peak. Next door to the hill, the Dark Street Theater rose several stories tall, with the joke-telling clock out in front on the sidewalk. A sign hung over the ticket booth:

THIS FRIDAY ONLY

OPEN-CALL AUDITIONS FOR *OSWALD DESCENDS*

Oona took one more look around and sighed. "I just can't understand how Grimsbee could have done it."

She felt immensely let down for having discovered nothing to prove Grimsbee's guilt, and, seeing nothing more she could do, Oona began to descend the steps one by one. Overly preoccupied in her disappointment, and paying very little attention to what she was doing, she failed to notice how the old stone steps had broken away in several places at her feet. She stepped down, felt herself about to fall, then briefly caught her balance, only to lose it again half a second later as the stone crumbled beneath her, and she landed hard on her side.

Deacon shot into the air, landing beside her on the cold stone step.

"Are you all right?" he asked.

A fierce pain seared through Oona's hip, and she could feel it instantly begin to bruise. She clenched her teeth together, biting back the pain.

"Just my hip," she said, sucking air through her teeth before giving Deacon a roguish smile. "At least it's not broken," she added. "I hear there's no worse pain."

Deacon scoffed.

It was then, as she stifled a laugh, that she saw something on one of the lower steps. The sight of it so surprised her that the pain quickly dulled.

"Look, Deacon. Do you see it?"

"See what?" he asked.

Oona pointed. "Blood."

She pushed herself up on wobbly knees, wincing slightly at the ache in her hip, but shoved the discomfort aside as she descended several steps to examine the splattered stain on the step. Oona pulled her father's magnifying glass from her dress pocket and used it to study the blotch.

It was dried blood all right. Taking a further look around, Oona spied another splatter of dried blood a few steps down, and another after that. By the time she reached the sidewalk, she saw that the trail of splatters came to a stop behind the giant top hat.

The hat loomed several feet over her head. She circled it twice, yet found nothing new. The trail of blood simply stopped there on the sidewalk.

Or started there, Oona considered.

She came to a stop beside the carriage.

"Is everything all right?" Deacon asked.

Oona did not answer him. She was afraid that if she did, then she might begin shouting that, no, everything was not all right. Her uncle was a toad, her home was going to be destroyed, and there was a possibility that the entire street might just spin off into the Drift, disconnecting them from New York and their only supply of foods and goods. The other possible scenario, where Dark Street became a giant tourist attraction for the benefit of Red Martin's new casino, was perhaps better, but the fact that this exposed the World of Man to faerie attack made it simply unacceptable. Oona's own father had been trying to bring down Red Martin's criminal empire for years, and Oona would love to finish the job. But first she would need to find out which of the applicants was in cahoots with the master criminal. Which one had a connection?

She stared thoughtfully across the street, toward the Dark Street Theater, and the sign out front:

THIS FRIDAY ONLY

OPEN-CALL AUDITIONS FOR *OSWALD DESCENDS*

Something clicked in her head. She walked partway around the hat once again, looked down at the blood, and then back up toward the sign over the theater. It came to her in a flash.

Oswald! she thought. *Of course. But it only makes sense.*

"Deacon!" she called as she moved hastily toward the carriage.

"Yes?" Deacon replied.

"Tell me. What building do you know of that has a large stairway leading up to its front entrance?" she asked.

"Well, there is the museum, of course," Deacon said, gesturing with a wing.

Oona nodded. "Yes. Yes. We know that. Any other such steps that you can think of? Something comparable in size to those leading up to the museum?"

Deacon considered this for a moment, then said: "The only steps I can think of would have to be the ones leading up to the Nightshade Hotel."

"Very good, Deacon," Oona said. She snapped her fingers. "And it is my guess that that is precisely where we will find him."

"Find whom?" Deacon asked.

Oona climbed back into the carriage. "Grimsbee!"

CHAPTER NINETEEN

Oswald Descends

They found Hector Grimsbee precisely where Oona had thought he would be. He stood halfway up the marble steps that led to the Nightshade Hotel. The hotel guests circled wide around Grimsbee as they made their way up and down the steps. Oona could understand why. Grimsbee looked quite angry, gesturing grandly with his arms and arguing with what appeared to be no one at all. The bandage around his head looked as if it had not been changed since the previous night, and it was drenched in sweat.

By far the most luxurious and opulent-looking building on the street, every window frame, handrail, and door handle of the hotel glistened with gold-flecked paint. At a mere four stories tall, the building was not the largest structure on Dark Street, but then again, Dark Street did not get many visitors. And besides, it was not so much the hotel that kept Red Martin in business, but the gambling and the other seedy activities that took place behind its golden doors.

With the box containing her uncle once again under Samuligan's watchful care at the curb, Oona cautiously ascended the steps, Deacon at the ready on her shoulder.

"Mr. Grimsbee!" she shouted in order to be heard over the blind man's babble.

Grimsbee stopped his gesticulating and turned to look at them . . . or *appeared* to look at them. His solid white eyes gleamed as he sniffed the air. "Ah. If it isn't Miss Crate, and her smelly birdie wordy. Or should I say, wordy birdie?"

"What are you doing up here on these steps?" Oona asked.

"I am rehearsing," Grimsbee replied. "There are open-call auditions this Friday at the Dark Street Theater, you know. I shall be in top form."

"I see," said Oona.

"I don't," Grimsbee replied, and then burst into laughter, as if this were the funniest joke he had ever heard.

"What will you be performing?" Oona asked.

Grimsbee gave his mustache a twist. "I shall be enacting

the final conflict of the play, where Oswald heroically battles the Queen of Faerie, throwing spells and repelling fire, all of which takes place upon the fabled steps to Faerie."

Grimsbee pressed his fist to his heart and bowed his head dramatically.

"Yes," Oona said, quite unimpressed. "I thought so."

Grimsbee continued: "Unfortunately, I could not remember where I put my umbrella. I was using it to represent Oswald's wand. I think I might have left it at Pendulum House last night, by mistake."

Oona remembered seeing Grimsbee the day before with the red umbrella on the museum steps. This memory in turn conjured up another image: this one of Isadora Iree kicking over the umbrella stand in the Pendulum House entryway, and a tall red umbrella shooting out and nearly poking Adler Iree in the leg. Oona was about to tell Grimsbee as much, but he cut her off.

"Once the director sees my performance," Grimsbee declared, "he will be forced to hire me in the lead role, and all my fans will flock to the theater for my triumphant return."

"Isn't it a bit dangerous for a blind man to rehearse on the stairs?" Oona asked.

"*Nonsense!*" Grimsbee shouted, making Oona jump. Clearly, the subject was a touchy one, and Oona felt certain that she was on to something. Grimsbee smoothed out the lapel of his jacket and recomposed himself. "I am able to fulfill the role as well as anyone. Even better. I am one of the greatest actors to have ever graced the stage. And why should I need a working set of eyes when my sense of smell is so clearly superior in every way. If that ridiculous director can't see that, then he is just as blind as I am, and deserves another sandbag dropped on his head."

Oona decided to ignore this last comment. "Isn't it true, Mr. Grimsbee, that you were rehearsing for your audition yesterday? Before your appointment at Pendulum House?"

"Why . . . uh . . . yes," said Grimsbee. "But how could you know that?"

Attempting to hide her excitement, Oona shrugged. "It was only an educated guess. You see, Deacon and I saw you on the steps of the museum. And I'm also guessing that while you were preparing, you had a rather unfortunate accident. Neither I nor Deacon saw it happen, because something distracted us while we were watching you, but I believe that you were practicing for the auditions when you fell down the steps of the museum and hit your head several times along the way."

Grimsbee's ears went red, and his eyes, despite their sightlessness, slitted as if leering at her. His eyebrows drew together, making one lone brow across his forehead.

"It . . . I . . . It was . . ." And then, the menace in his face suddenly dropped away. He fell to his knees, nearly falling down the steps as he did so, and folded his hands together as he began to plead: "You must keep your mouth shut about that. It wasn't my fault. The steps . . . they were old . . . they crumbled. That's why I came here, to the hotel, to rehearse today. I can do the part. Really, I can. But the director must not hear that I fell, or I will be ruined."

"So I guessed correctly—you did fall," Oona said. "You tumbled down the steps, hitting your head several times in the process and landing on the sidewalk."

Grimsbee ran his bony fingers across the bandage on his head. "Yes."

Oona turned to Deacon, triumphant. "That is why he disappeared so quickly. Grimsbee didn't go into the museum, Deacon. He fell down the stone steps in the exact instant that you and I heard the scream come from Madame Iree's dress shop. We looked away, Grimsbee fell, and when we looked back, we couldn't see him because he was lying on the sidewalk behind the enormous sculpture of the top hat."

"So that means . . ." Deacon trailed off.

"Grimsbee couldn't possibly have stolen the daggers," Oona finished.

Grimsbee stuck his jaw out indignantly. "That is

obvious. I was at the doctor's office getting my head wrapped until just before my appointment at Pendulum House. And do you know what the doctor said to me?"

Oona and Deacon shook their heads.

"He said that I was lucky I didn't break my hip," Grimsbee said. "No worse pain, the doctor told me."

Deacon shook his head. "I do wish people would stop saying that." He turned to Oona. "So if Grimsbee couldn't have done it, then who did?"

"Isn't it obvious?" said Grimsbee. "It's that little witch. You can smell it on her."

Oona threw her hands to her hips and shook her head. "You can't smell if someone is a criminal. And besides, that was probably just her pungent facial cream you smelled. It had a very strong . . . a very strong . . ." Oona trailed off, lost for a moment in thought. Finally, she said: "It had a very strong herbal smell."

"With a hint of cinnamon," said Grimsbee, pushing himself back up from his knees.

Oona was nodding. *With a hint of cinnamon.* That was exactly right. But the smell beneath the cinnamon had been herbal. And just now, it occurred to Oona that it had also been a familiar smell. The cinnamon had thrown her senses off, but she thought that she knew now where she had smelled it before.

"Yes, of course," Oona said, her bright green eyes

going wide with excitement. "Come, Deacon. We should return to Pendulum House at once."

"What for?" Deacon asked.

"We need to visit the garden." She scratched at her head, but before Deacon could question her any further, she added: "One other thing, Mr. Grimsbee. If you are so intent on being an actor, why did you apply for the position of Wizard's apprentice?"

Grimsbee shrugged. "Something to fall back on, I suppose. But then again, I don't see why I couldn't do both."

The words surprised Oona. *Do both?* she thought. It was an intriguing thought; one she'd never really considered seriously before. But the idea was interrupted by the sound of the hotel's large golden doors slamming open. Oona glanced up, only to find two enormous men in bright red suits hurrying down the steps. Clearly identical twins, the only difference between the two hulking figures was that one of them wore a bushy mustache in need of a good trimming, and the other was clean shaven.

They stopped on either side of Grimsbee. Matching badges on their red lapels read: NIGHTSHADE HOTEL SECURITY.

Grimsbee sniffed at the men uncertainly.

In a hushed, throaty voice, the twin with the mustache said: "We've received several complaints, sir, that you are frightening the guests. We're going to have to ask you to leave."

"But . . . ," Grimsbee began.

"Sorry, sir," said the man with no mustache, in a voice identical to his brother's. "No buts."

Faster than Oona would have believed such massive men could move, the twins picked Grimsbee up by his bony elbows and tossed him toward the street. Grimsbee howled as he collided with a carriage horse at the curb.

The horse neighed its disapproval, and Grimsbee pushed himself roughly back to his feet. Meanwhile, Oona was staring up at the hulking twins. They stood over her like two nightmarishly tall bulldogs, arms bulging beneath their jacket sleeves, looking as if she might be their next victim.

Deacon rose to his most menacing height, but the security guards appeared unfazed.

"Indeed," Oona said, backing gingerly away, feeling her presence at the hotel was suddenly less than welcome. It was as Oona backed down to the sidewalk that she got the curious feeling she was being watched, and not just by the monstrous twins. As if by instinct, she looked up and spotted a set of eyes leering down at her through the slit in a red-curtained window.

For the simple fact that she was standing in front of the Nightshade Hotel, she had a sneaking suspicion just whose eyes they likely were. She shivered at the thought of the notorious Red Martin himself watching her.

"Samuligan?" she said.

"Yes?" replied the faerie servant. He stood just behind her, holding the box with the toad.

"I think it is time to leave," she said.

Samuligan, who was also looking up at the ominous set of eyes, said: "Most wise."

Twenty minutes later, as she entered the inner courtyard at Pendulum House, Oona could still not shake the awful feeling those eyes had given her.

"What are we doing in the courtyard?" Deacon asked.

"I have a hunch," she replied.

She wound her way past the sprawl of the magnificent glass tree—which by day projected fantastic prisms of sunlight about the courtyard walls—and stopped at the edge of the soil patch where she had caught Isadora digging the night before. Heedless of her dress getting soiled, she dropped to her knees.

Deacon looked at the sign sticking out of the soil.

"Turlock root?" he said, sounding quite astonished. "But I thought it only grew in Faerie."

This was Deacon's first time in the inner garden, Oona realized. Deacon had been a present for her eleventh birthday, and they had been together for nearly two years, but she had never brought him out here. This had always been her place to be alone, and clearly Deacon had respected the house rules and had never ventured out here on his own.

"Don't forget that Pendulum House is built on Faerie soil," Oona reminded him.

Deacon nodded. "Oh . . . yes, of course. That makes sense. But still I had no idea. And why are we here?"

Oona lifted a handful of the dark soil to her nose. It was, of course, the same herbal smell she'd caught a whiff of the night before, when Isadora had smeared the soil across her face. But it was also familiar for another reason. She dug down into the dark soil, feeling around until her hand closed around something slick and smooth. She tugged. A moment later she was holding a bright green root above the ground. She squeezed it lightly in her hand, and a greenish substance oozed out around her fingers. The smell was quite powerful and conjured up an image of Sanora Crone, her face covered in this same slimy goop.

"You might want to wipe that off your fingers," said Samuligan. The faerie servant stood just behind her, holding the box containing the toad in one hand and offering a handkerchief with his other.

Oona dropped the root on the topsoil and received the handkerchief.

"Thank you, Samuligan." She wiped the goopy

substance from her hand and then examined it on the cloth. She sniffed it. "It is just as I thought. This is the same substance that Sanora Crone had on her face last night. Witchwhistle Beauty Cream, indeed!"

"Ah, yes," said Samuligan. "I thought I smelled something familiar on her. I could not place it last night. Now that I know what it is, however, it is obvious that she was attempting to mask the smell with cinnamon."

Deacon hopped to the ground beside the root. "Turlock root? But where would Sanora Crone get turlock root? And what does it have to do with the attack on your uncle?"

Oona had already considered both of these questions. Turlock root could only be grown in native Faerie soil. The only place to find Faerie soil other than Pendulum House was in the Land of Faerie itself. It was yet another mystery.

"I don't know where she's getting the root, Deacon," Oona said. "Certainly not from here. But as to your second question, what it means is that Sanora Crone is not what she seems. In fact, she is likely older than she appears to be."

"But why would she make herself so young?" Deacon asked. "To what purpose?"

Oona rose to her feet, letting the handkerchief fall to the ground. "For the answer to that, I think we will need to ask Sanora herself. Come, let us make for Witch Hill immediately."

"Ah, but the entrance is secret," said Samuligan. "Even I, who have lived on Dark Street for nearly five hundred years, do not know how to get inside. It is bewitched."

Oona took the hatbox from Samuligan and cracked open the lid. She peered inside. The toad sat in the center, looking up at her with its wide toady eyes. They were bright green eyes that, the more she looked at them, the more they reminded her of her uncle's. They seemed so unmistakable. Those were the eyes that had looked so disappointed when she'd decided to give up the apprenticeship for another life. A life as a detective. And here she was, living that life, yet it was not at all how she had thought it would be. In truth, she had never thought it would be so . . . personal.

And then a horrible notion invaded her thoughts. A stabbing sense of doubt. What if she was just seeing the similarity between her uncle's eyes and the toad's because she *wanted* to believe it? What if this was just some toad that had found its way to the top of that tower? Maybe the tower was infested with toads, and she did not know it. As unlikely as that might seem, the thought still managed to spoil her conviction that the toad and her uncle were one and the same. What if this was not the Wizard, but some long-forgotten faerie that had been imprisoned, like Samuligan, during the Great Faerie War? And that would of course mean that her uncle was, in truth, dead. Dead. Dead. Dead.

Oona shook her head, wishing she could stuff cotton balls in her ears to drown out the sound of her own thoughts.

"Stop it!" she whispered to herself. "This *is* Uncle Alexander. It only makes sense." She was afraid to open the lid of the box too far, in case the toad should jump out. She might never find him if they lost him out here in the garden. She spoke through the crack: "We'll figure out who did this to you, Uncle," she said. "Don't worry."

But the day was getting on, and if the Wizard did not show up in his human form before midnight . . . Red Martin would win.

She could only hope that this new information about Sanora was the break in the case she needed. For some reason Sanora Crone was using turlock root to make herself young. But how old was she really, and what was the purpose?

"Samuligan is correct," Deacon said. "The entrance to Witch Hill was enchanted long ago. No one can see the witches enter or exit the hill. No one knows how many witches are down there, or what they do, and the entrance would be nearly impossible to find."

Oona started back across the courtyard with the box clasped beneath her arm. "Certainly we won't let that stop us."

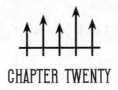

CHAPTER TWENTY

The Cobblestone Thief

The ride to the shopping district took a little over twenty-five minutes. Traffic was heavier than it had been earlier that morning, and Oona was feeling quite impatient. Her first course of action when she reached Witch Hill would be to climb to the top of the hill and knock on that old, crooked tree. Maybe the tree was a door of sorts. If that didn't work, she would simply resort to pounding on the ground and shouting Sanora's name until either the girl appeared, or Inspector White showed up to arrest Oona for disturbing the peace.

"Umph!"

Deacon was jostled from Oona's shoulder when the carriage came to a sudden halt. Oona just managed to save the hatbox from tumbling off the seat. She could see the museum just ahead.

"Why the abrupt stop, Samuligan?" Oona called out the window.

"See for yourself," Samuligan said.

Oona poked her head out the window. A carriage was stuck in the middle of the street, and traffic was coming the other way, making it difficult for Samuligan to veer around. The driver of the stuck carriage was attempting to lever the front wheel out of a pothole using a plank of wood.

"Sorry about this, miss," Oona could hear the driver saying to his passenger. "Got to complain to the street council about these potholes, I do."

"Stay here, and keep an eye on the box for me, Deacon," Oona said. "I'll be right back."

She stepped to the street and made her way toward the stuck carriage. The driver was doing his utmost to pry the wheel out, his face going red with the effort. Oona knelt down, peering into the hole.

"Hey you!" the driver said, clearly startled by her appearance. He stepped back, shaking the plank of wood, and Oona realized that it was the same cabdriver who had gotten stuck in the pothole the day before. The only difference was that today he was on the other side of the street, heading in the opposite direction. "You again?"

said the driver. "Who are you, and why do I keep seeing you every time I get stuck in these potholes?"

"Miss Crate!" said a voice, startling both Oona and the driver. Inspector White stepped from behind the giant top hat on the sidewalk. For some reason he was dressed in a ridiculous red-and-black-checkered hunting jacket. He sauntered to the side of the stalled carriage, where he stopped and stared down at Oona with an expression on his face that mimicked his next words: "I might have known."

"Might have known what?" Oona asked.

The inspector folded his lanky arms. "That the culprit would return to the scene of the crime."

"I beg pardon?" Oona said.

"Cobblestone theft," said the inspector.

Oona blinked at him in surprise. "What on earth are you talking about?"

The inspector shook his head as if she were very stupid. "The Cobblestone Thief, my dear. Surely you didn't think I wouldn't find you out. You've been stealing cobblestones from the street for weeks. I may not have any proof yet, but I am a very patient man. One of these days I'll catch those evil little hands of yours at their evil little deeds."

Oona's jaw jutted out in frustration. "First of all, I don't have evil little hands. I have very nice hands. And secondly, I don't know why someone would want to steal cobblestones, but you should probably know that my uncle was not murdered. He has been turned into a toad. I rescued him from the Goblin Tower this morning."

The inspector frowned. "That's ridiculous."

"What is ridiculous is that hideous jacket," said a familiar voice. Both Oona and the inspector looked up to discover Isadora Iree staring out the window of the stalled carriage.

The inspector looked suddenly embarrassed, glancing down at the red-and-black checkerboard jacket. "I did not have my own jacket today, so I borrowed this one from Constable Trout. On his off days, he likes to go hunting in the World of Man."

Isadora rolled her pretty blue eyes all the way up to the whites. "Well, perhaps if you weren't such an incompetent police inspector, then you would remember that you left your own jacket at Pendulum House last night, on top of *my* shawl! I had to iron the wrinkles out when I got home."

The inspector puffed up his chest indignantly. "I'm quite sure I did nothing of the sort. I took my own jacket to the tailor only yesterday, after tearing a hole in the sleeve." He turned to Oona, jabbing a chalk-white finger in her direction. "A hole that I received when I tripped because of the missing cobblestones that, no doubt, *you* stole."

Oona shook her head at him. "And, no doubt, *you* must

have forgotten that you picked your jacket back up from the tailor and wore it to Pendulum House last night, because Isadora is right; we all saw your jacket hanging on the coatrack. But that's all right. I suppose it will be just another bit of rubbish for Red Martin to cart away when he has Pendulum House demolished this evening. Now, if you will excuse me, Inspector, I would like to try to stop that from happening."

She turned, as if to head off in the direction of Witch Hill across the street.

"What's this about Red Martin?" the inspector called after her.

Oona lowered her gaze, wondering if it was even worth her time to explain all that she had learned, when something caught her eye. Her breath suddenly hitched in her throat, and she knelt down to get a better look at one of the places where the cobblestones had gone missing. The space where the stones *should* have been appeared as black as midnight, which was strange because normally beneath broken-out cobblestones one found hard-packed earth. From what Oona could tell, the space beneath these missing cobblestones was . . . nothing at all . . . a void . . . like whatever had happened to the missing cobbles had happened to the earth underneath as well.

If someone truly is stealing cobblestones from the street, she thought, and Oona couldn't understand why someone would want to do such a thing, *but if they are, then they are taking the ground beneath it, too.*

Intrigued, Oona returned her attention to the stuck carriage. The driver had gone back to levering the wheel out of the hole. "Yesterday you boasted to me that you knew every pothole on the street," Oona said to him. "Why is it you keep getting stuck here, in front of the museum?"

The cabdriver put his weight into the plank of wood. "I'd swear there's new holes right here almost every day. And these ones are twice as bad as anywhere else."

"What is the point of this pointless questioning?" the inspector asked.

"Because look," Oona said. "See where the cobblestones are missing?"

"The cobblestones that you stole?" the inspector said.

She sighed, realizing that what she was about to explain to this incompetent man was going to fly directly over his head. "No one is stealing cobblestones," she explained. "And they aren't simply disappearing. They are falling."

"Falling?" said the inspector. "Cobblestones don't fall from the ground. What do you take me for? An imbecile?"

Oona nodded. "For once, you are right, Inspector." The inspector guffawed, but Oona continued before he could protest. "Do you have a coin?"

"A coin?" he said. "If you are hinting that you would like to run off and buy yourself a treat, then you are sadly mistaken. I do, however, have a hard candy in my pocket, if that would satisfy."

Oona nodded enthusiastically that it would indeed satisfy, and from his pocket, along with a jumble of keys, a handful of pocket lint, and a used handkerchief, he produced a round candy in a wax wrapper. Oona took the candy, careful not to touch the pocket lint or the used handkerchief.

"Thank you very much," she said, and dropped the piece of candy into the hole where the cobblestone should have been. There was a moment of silence before a soft, echoing *pat* sound drifted up through the hole, as if the candy had hit something not too far below the street.

"You ungrateful little juvenile!" the inspector said. "That was a perfectly good piece of candy."

"But do you see?" Oona asked.

"What I see is that you are a menace," he said, "and that I have a good mind to arrest you for littering." His nostrils flared, and Oona thought for a moment that he might actually do more than threaten.

It was Isadora who saved her when she shouted at them from the carriage: "Why are you two lack-wits arguing about potholes when you should be finding my mother's dresses? Or have you forgotten that the Midnight Masquerade is tonight?"

Oona straightened, intent on telling Isadora—in as

rude of terms as possible—exactly just what she could do with her mother's dresses, when several thoughts suddenly clicked in her mind, like pieces of a puzzle locking together.

She looked from the pothole at her feet to the museum, and then from the museum to Madame Iree's Boutique for Fine Ladies next door. Most of the buildings on Dark Street were pressed together, wall to wall. As Oona had observed only the day before, the dress shop was no exception. On one side was a handbag shop, and on the other side was the museum, with the dress boutique looking rather squashed in between.

"Isadora," Oona said, her heart rate beginning to rise, "is your mother's shop open?"

Isadora shook her head. "Mother was too distraught to open the shop today. And besides, she's been too busy at home trying to stitch together new gowns to make up for the stolen ones."

Oona remembered something that Madame Iree had said the day before: how the dressmaker would love to get her hands on some turlock root, so she might age backward and wear the dress made of glinting cloth.

"Do you happen to have a key?" Oona asked hopefully.

"Just so happens that I do," Isadora replied. "But the dresses are all gone, except for the small, pretty one in the window. You'd never fit into it . . . and anyway, I told you yesterday, Mother makes dresses only for students of the academy, or—"

"Or alumna," Oona finished for her. "Yes, I know. But I think I might know who the thief is." *And more important, how they got in,* Oona thought. "I need to see inside the showroom to be certain."

"Very well," Isadora said. "If it will help get my dress back. But this better not be a waste of time."

Wearing a ruffled pink dress with lacy white trim, she stepped down from the carriage and handed the driver several coins. Meanwhile, Oona returned to her own carriage, leaving the inspector standing in the street, scratching at his wiry black hair and staring down at the pothole. Oona removed the hatbox from the carriage, peeked inside to make sure that the toad was all right, and then handed the box up to Samuligan in the driver's seat.

"Keep good care of that, Samuligan," Oona said. "And wait over there, at the curb. Deacon, with me."

Deacon leaped to her shoulder and the two of them met Isadora in front of the giant top hat.

"Should we bring the inspector?" Isadora asked.

Oona looked back to find the inspector with his arm stuck shoulder deep into the pothole, no doubt attempting to retrieve his candy.

"I believe we will do just fine on our own," Oona replied.

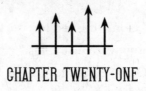

CHAPTER TWENTY-ONE

The Showroom

I t's gone!" Isadora shouted.

"What is g—" Oona stopped herself short, realizing all too quickly what Isadora had meant by "it."

The three of them, Isadora, Oona, and Deacon, stood in front of the dress shop. Isadora had just inserted her key into the lock when she looked into the storefront window, only to discover that it was empty. The glinting-cloth dress was gone. Isadora looked pale.

"Perhaps your mother took it home," Oona suggested.

Isadora shook her head. "No. That can't be. I was just on my way to fetch Adler from the Magicians Legal Alliance. Mother wanted us both home to help her sew the replacement dresses that she has been working on all night. On our way back home, I was supposed to stop by the shop and take the glinting-cloth dress home, for safekeeping."

"Your mother didn't take it with her when she left yesterday?" Oona asked.

Isadora gave her a look like she was very stupid. "No. Aren't you listening? Mother was so distraught when she left yesterday that she forgot all about it. That's why she gave me the key to pick it up today."

Oona had a vague memory of seeing the dress in the window on her way to the Goblin Tower that morning.

"Come, Isadora," Oona said. "If we're going to find any of these dresses, we need to go inside."

They closed the door behind them, and Oona found the first room of the shop much as she remembered it: the tables and the empty teacups, the red-and-gold-striped wallpaper, and the scent of lavender potpourri. The missing dress from the front window seemed to be the only difference.

Oona quickly moved to the showroom in the back, Deacon clinging tightly to her shoulder. The door stood wide open. This room, too, was as she remembered it: the naked mannequins and the crystal chandelier, the ever-burning lamps and the raised platform for dress alterations. Except, no . . . everything *wasn't* the same. The mirror that hung on the wall in front of the platform—

it was now cracked down the middle and hung slightly crooked. It reminded Oona of seeing Inspector White straighten the mirror on the wall only the day before. And there were several other differences. One of the mannequins beside the platform was lying on its side, and in the center of the room, where only one white candle had been lying on the floor, there now lay two.

"How do you suppose the thief got in and out?" Deacon asked.

Oona walked to the middle of the room and looked up at the chandelier. Two of the candleholders were empty. Isadora gazed down at the two candles on the floor.

"That happens all the time," she said. "The candles keep falling out of the chandelier's holders. It's a complete nuisance because we keep having to put them back up, and Mother won't allow us to actually light the candles since she's afraid they will just fall and light the dresses on fire. It's too bad, too, because candlelight is far more flattering than those magic lamps."

Oona smiled. "I suspect that the reason the candles keep falling is because Mr. Bop lives up there." She pointed to the ceiling.

Isadora's face scrunched up, as if she did not understand . . . but then her expression brightened. "Oh, you mean that great big fat man? I've seen him."

Oona nodded, remembering how the floor at the

Magicians Legal Alliance had shaken quite noticeably whenever Mr. Bop had moved. "Indeed. Mr. Bop is so enormous that when he walks around up there, he causes the ceiling to shake, which in turn rattles the candles out of their holders."

"So what does that have to do with the stolen dresses?" Deacon asked.

"So far as I can tell, absolutely nothing," Oona said. "But that mirror, on the other hand, I think has quite a bit to do with our mystery. It was not cracked yesterday, that much is for sure. I remember watching the inspector admire himself in its reflection as he straightened it on the wall. Also, look at that mannequin next to the platform. It was not lying over on its side like it is now. I'm quite certain."

"I believe you're right," Deacon said, gazing down at the toppled-over mannequin. "All the mannequins were upright yesterday."

Oona looked around the room, letting her eyes roll where they would. The floor was wood, polished to a brilliant sheen and flawless.

"The door appears to be the only way in," Deacon observed.

"*Appears*," Oona said.

"What is that awful smell?" asked Isadora. "Is that your bird?"

"I beg your pardon?" Deacon said, puffing up his feathers.

"No, wait," Oona said, and sniffed the air. "Isadora is right. This room has a distinctively different smell than the room out front, with its lavender potpourri."

Deacon began to sniff as well. "It has an earthy, herbal smell."

"With a hint of cinnamon," Oona added as she followed her nose across the room to one side of the raised platform, where she found what at first appeared to be a random piece of dirty black cloth on the floor. She held up the cloth to reveal a flimsy black dress. Upon closer examination, Oona found that, like her own dresses, this one was fitted with little hidden pockets. She reached inside one of them now and brought out a small metal canister.

"Perhaps the odor we smell," Oona said, "is that of the so-called Witchwhistle Beauty Cream?"

She twisted the top off the canister and the smell that came out was quite powerful. She needed only a glimpse of the green jellylike substance inside to know that it was the same stuff she'd seen caked on the young witch's face the night before. Oona quickly closed the canister and put it back in the black dress's pocket.

Deacon sniffed. "By Oswald, it is the same smell! And isn't that the dress belonging to the young witch, Sanora Crone?"

"Indeed," said Oona.

"But what is it doing here?" Deacon asked.

Oona nodded. "Good question, Deacon. She must have left it behind for some reason. But why?"

Isadora looked furious. "You mean to tell me that that dirty little witch is behind this?" She reached out for the black dress, as if she was going to take it from Oona's hands and tear it up. But Isadora's hand stopped short. She pulled her hand back, clearly not wanting to touch the smelly rag.

"I think Sanora is not just behind *this* thievery, Isadora," Oona said. She flung the malodorous dress over her shoulder before stepping onto the platform and running her fingers along the edge of the cracked mirror.

"What are you doing?" Deacon asked.

"If you look at this building from the outside," Oona began to explain, "you'll see that it is squashed between the handbag shop on one side and the museum on the other. This wall here presses right up against the museum."

Oona gave the mirror a push, hoping that her instincts were not wrong. The bottom portion slid sideways and up like a pendulum, revealing a large opening in the wall behind it.

Deacon took in a sharp breath. "A hole!"

"A hole, indeed, Deacon," Oona said. "It was curious

to me why the inspector had needed to straighten the mirror in the first place. Now we know why. Someone was coming and going through this hole."

Deacon glanced quickly around. "But why is the mirror now cracked?"

"I'm not sure," Oona said. "Could be that the thief knocked that mannequin over today when returning for the dress in the window. The mannequin then fell and struck the mirror."

Deacon nodded that it was certainly possible.

Lowering herself to her knees, Oona peered into the inky blackness of the hole in the wall and began to crawl through.

"I'm not going in there," Isadora said.

"You don't have to," Oona called back. "But if I'm not mistaken, then this hole leads . . ."

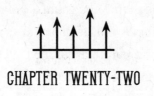

CHAPTER TWENTY-TWO

The Secret Entrance

N ext door, into the Museum of Magical History,"
Oona finished.

She pushed aside what felt like some kind of
heavy fabric and stood, smoothing out her dress. Deacon
hopped into the room before fluttering to the corner of a
large wooden desk.

"I do believe we are in the curator's office," Deacon
observed.

"Yes, we are," said Oona. "We are in the basement.
The steps in front of the museum rise up so high that the
basement is actually on the same level as the street . . .
and, more important, the same level as the showroom
next door."

An ever-burning lamp glowed dimly on the desk, its enchanted flame giving the room a greenish tint. A long tapestry depicting an entire galaxy of stars and constellations took up the greater part of the wall behind the desk. It was from behind this tapestry that she and Deacon had emerged. The floor was polished stone. To the right of the desk stood a broken glass case, above which hung a small brass-plated plaque. The inscription read:

FAY MORS EXPUGNO AND FAY MORS MORTIS

MAGICAL MIND DAGGERS

FIRST EVER ACQUISITIONS OF THE MUSEUM

OF MAGICAL HISTORY

AUGUST 12, 1418

Oona moved closer to the room's single door and examined the lock. "Look here. You see, the heavy-duty bolt has a latch on this side of the door, and can only be opened with a key on the other side. Once they took the daggers, the thief unlocked the door and then pushed it open to make sure that no one would go looking for how they actually got in. Everyone assumed that the thief came in through the open door."

"So the thief entered and exited through the hole in Madame Iree's wall," Deacon said. "But how did they get into the showroom?"

"I think the answer to that has to do with the missing cobblestones out front," Oona replied.

"How is that?" asked Deacon.

Oona didn't answer, but instead she pulled aside the tapestry and crawled back through the hole into the showroom, Deacon following closely behind. They found Isadora standing where they had left her, arms crossed over her frilly pink dress, fingers drumming.

"Did you find the dresses?" she asked.

"Shh, Isadora," Oona said, before removing her father's magnifying glass from her dress pocket and beginning an examination of the floor.

"Don't shush me!" Isadora scolded. Nevertheless, she remained sullenly silent as Oona conducted her investigation.

It has to be here somewhere, Oona thought. *There must be a second hole. It's the only way.*

But after several minutes of searching the floor, she found nothing. Not even a single crack. She sat down beside Deacon on the edge of the platform, feeling quite unsure of her theory. She had been so certain that Sanora Crone had come in through the floor of the showroom and then broken through the wall in order to enter the museum.

She stared at the magnifying glass, thinking of her father, and wondering if he would have been disappointed in her. She wished he was there, beside her. Surely her father would have known what to look for. But he wasn't, and he never would be. She bowed her head, running her fingers through her hair . . . and that was when she saw the faint scratch marks in the wood at her feet.

"There," Oona said.

She brought the magnifying glass to the scratches along the bottom edge of the platform, and Deacon peered through.

"Scratches in the polished wood," he said. "What does it mean?"

Oona hurriedly moved to the other side of the platform, planted her feet firmly against the floor, and pushed.

"Here is where Sanora got in!" she exclaimed.

The platform slid easily across the smooth wood, revealing the secret beneath. Deacon hopped excitedly from one foot to the other, staring down at the hole in the floor. The very top of a ladder could be seen descending into the darkness below.

Isadora looked from the hole in the floor to the hole in the wall. "I don't understand. Why are there two holes?"

Oona began rubbing her hands together. Here at last was something she could explain. "Remember last night, Isadora, when you asked the inspector if it were possible for the daggers and the dresses to have been stolen by the same person?"

"Everyone looked at me like I was crazy," Isadora replied, giving Oona a fiercely reproachful look.

Oona winced, realizing that, yes, the idea had seemed somewhat ludicrous at the time. "Well, it turns out, you were right." Oona pointed to the hole in the floor. "Sanora must have tunneled her way beneath the shop and come up here, beneath the platform. Though I doubt she was alone. This is a big job. One small girl could not have done it alone. It's my guess that she had some help from her fellow witches."

Oona scratched at her head. How the witches had known to come up in that exact spot, so that the platform would cover the hole, she didn't know. But she intended to find out.

Peering into the hole, she gulped. "Will you go down first, Deacon? Or shall I?"

"And why would I go in there?" Deacon squawked. "Now that we know how the thief got in, we simply need to tell the authorities."

Oona gave Deacon an incredulous look.

"Well, all right," he admitted, "perhaps Inspector White will muck everything up, but it's better than you or I going in there . . . alone."

Oona turned to Isadora, but the fine young lady put up her hands. "I'm not going down in there."

"And besides," Deacon said, "if Sanora did steal the

daggers, then that means she still has possession of the second one: *Fay Mors Mortis*. The Faerie Death. You promised your uncle that you would not go snooping around deadly criminals."

"I know what I promised, Deacon," Oona said. "But if Sanora was the one who threw the dagger at Uncle Alexander, then she is the only one who knows the words to transform him back. Red Martin intends to stop the Dark Street pendulum at midnight if the Wizard does not show up to reclaim Pendulum House." She pointed at the hole in the floor. "Sanora Crone could stay down there in Witch Hill for months, or even longer."

"Witch Hill?" said Deacon.

"Yes. Don't you see? There is a tunnel leading directly from this spot to the hill across the street."

"But how did you know it would be here?" Deacon asked.

"It all came from seeing those missing cobblestones. When I dropped the inspector's candy through the pothole, I did it to illustrate a point, which is that the witches have dug a tunnel beneath the street. That's why the cobblestones have gone missing, as well as the earth beneath them. The witches must have dug the tunnel terribly close to the surface, and the ground has begun to fall away in certain spots, like where the carriage wheels travel the most. That is why the carriages keep getting stuck."

"Hmm," Deacon intoned, glancing toward the filthy black dress that hung from Oona's shoulder. "I can see why she would want to steal the dresses, since her own is so very drab, but why would she wish to imprison your uncle?"

"Maybe she meant to kill him," Oona said. "Maybe she didn't know which dagger she was using. I don't know. As to *why* she would wish to harm him at all . . . that is precisely what I intend to find out."

Moving with a swift sort of confidence that she did not entirely feel, Oona snatched one of the fallen candles from the floor. She then dug a match from her pocket and struck it along the edge of the platform. Her face glowed as she lit the candle and took in a deep breath, as if preparing to plunge into deep waters. The lit match dropped from her fingers into the hole, winking out as it disappeared into the darkness.

"Miss Crate," said Isadora, almost tentatively.

Oona glanced over her shoulder. Strangely enough, she thought she saw an expression of concern on Isadora's face. It seemed quite out of place there.

"Do be careful," Isadora said. "No one knows what those witches do down there."

It was the concern in Isadora's voice that set Oona's nerves on edge more than anything else. She had a strange, albeit short-lived thought that perhaps Isadora wasn't quite as bad as she had judged her to be. Maybe there was a scrap of kindness in the girl after all. But the thought died quickly away when Isadora added: "And if you find the dresses, try not to get them dirty when you bring them back. That hole looks filthy."

Oona did not bother to respond, but instead she lowered herself into the hole in the floor, the burning candle held in one faintly trembling hand, and began her descent into the darkness below.

Deacon hopped to her shoulder, shaking his head from side to side. "Oh dear. Here we go."

CHAPTER TWENTY-THREE

Into the Dark

O ona touched bottom, the moist earth squishing beneath her shoes. She stepped around the ladder, holding the candle high above her head, where the flame licked at the earthen ceiling. The tunnel stretched out before her like a long, dark throat, and she began to have second thoughts about continuing forward. Down here in the dark, things seemed much different than they had up above. They were . . . well, they were darker, for one thing. And the air itself seemed denser and more threatening. She gulped audibly, considering whether or not to simply climb right back up, when something grabbed her attention.

"Look, Deacon. Do you see?" She moved closer to the

sidewall of the tunnel, exposing a pile of pickaxes, chisels, and handsaws.

"Tools of the trade," she said. "And look how many. It appears I was right, and there is actually more than one thief involved." She bent down, examining the ground. A set of wheel ruts cut into the floor and disappeared down the tunnel. "Some sort of cart has passed this way, many times."

"Careful," Deacon whispered. "Even I am having trouble seeing very far."

The two of them began to inch their way forward, the walls seeming to close in around them. It wasn't long before they came to a spot where the hooves of a horse could be heard clopping overhead.

"We must be under the street," Oona said, and looking up, they saw several square-shaped patches of sunlight leaking down through the holes in the street. At her feet lay the missing cobblestones, and beside one of them lay the candy Oona had dropped through the hole. She picked it up and put it in her pocket.

"I tried to tell Inspector White my suspicions," she said. "But he wouldn't listen."

Beyond the reach of the pulsing candlelight, she could see nothing. The hand holding the candle began to tremble as the wax dribbled down over her fingers. It was not the sting of the warm wax that caused the tremor inside of her, however, but the thought of the witches. Not only did she know nothing about them, but neither did Deacon, and he had the entire *Encyclopedia Arcanna* stored inside his head. They could have magic that no one knew about. Horrible spells.

Eventually, the two of them came to a spot where the tunnel split in two different directions. The wheel ruts turned left.

"What do we do now?" Deacon asked.

Oona thought for a moment. "Let's go left," she said, "and we will continue left on any other forked tunnels so that if we need to make a run for it, we can easily retrace our steps."

The tunnel curved and the ground sloped, so that it felt as if they were walking in a giant corkscrew, going down, down, down. They walked for what seemed a very long time, following two more forked tunnels, each time bearing left, until finally they came to a small, round room, where no fewer than six tunnels branched off in different directions. The floor here was smooth marble, and the walls were plastered smooth. An unlit chandelier hung down like a shadowy claw from the vaulted ceiling. It felt more like a palace entry hall than some underground cave, albeit a palace that had long gone to ruin.

A large sheet of paper hung on the wall between two of the tunnel entrances: a diagram of some sort.

"Do you know what this is, Deacon?" Oona tapped her finger on the paper. "This is a complete plan of all of the stores in the shopping district of Dark Street . . . including the dress shop and the museum basement. Look how detailed it is. You can even see right where the showroom platform is, and the mirror. This is how they knew exactly where to dig their hole."

"But how would they be able to acquire all of this information?" Deacon asked.

"My guess," Oona said, "Red Martin. This is very big, Deacon."

"You think he and the witches are working together?" he asked.

Oona shushed him. "Do you hear that?"

Deacon listened. "It's coming from there." He indicated a tunnel to their right with his wing.

"I guess we'll have to break our always-go-left rule," Oona said, and the two of them started down the first tunnel to their right. Oona's pulse rose. The deeper they went, the more distinct the sound became. It was the sound of voices arguing.

A dim light could be made out up ahead. Oona blew out the candle. Her nerves tingled, her muscles tensing with each step. The tunnel opened just ahead, the flickering light appearing to come from a room at the end.

She slowed, stepping as lightly as possible. Once she

came within a few feet of the tunnel's mouth, she could hear them clearly: two young voices, female. The first voice Oona recognized right away. It was Sanora. The second voice was one that Oona had never heard before. It sounded more mature than Sanora's girly soprano, though still young and feminine—perhaps someone Oona's own age or older. It was the second voice that spoke now, sounding exasperated.

"You are so clumsy, Sanora. You almost ruined everything."

"I'm sorry, Katona," Sanora replied.

"First, you pester me into returning to the dress shop so you can take the dress from the window, and regrettably, I agreed, so long as we were very careful. But then you insisted on trying it on in the showroom, and I warned you against it. But would you listen? No. You should have waited until we came back down here. Really! Whirling about in front of that mirror like that, and knocking over the mannequin . . . you cracked the mirror. It will need to be replaced now, and when they remove it from the wall to do so, they will find the hole leading into the museum. Must you act so childish, Sanora? I'll admit, the dress is magnificent. And you do look stunning in it. And yet . . ." The girl named Katona paused a moment before saying: "Sanora, where is your dress?"

"I'm wearing it," Sanora said.

"Not the one you stole. *Your* dress. Your work dress. The one you were wearing before you put that one on?"

"Oh," said Sanora. "I must have left it up in the . . ." She trailed off.

"In the showroom!" Katona said, sounding outraged. "Don't you realize that if they find it, they'll know it was us? Sanora, really, why must you act like such a child?"

"But I *am* a child," Sanora said.

"You are nothing of the sort!" Katona said. "You have simply been applying far too much of the cream. The turlock root has affected your judgment. Look at you."

"Look at *you*," Sanora said defensively. "I'd say you're looking quite a bit younger than—"

"I look and act like a young lady," Katona said. "You, on the other hand, have become a young girl, and at the rate you've been caking your face with that cream, you'll be an infant again in no time."

"I'm sorry," Sanora said, sounding quite meek.

"Hmm. I must discuss this with the rest of the coven, Sanora. We'll need to figure out what to do with your mess. Perhaps you'll have to go back for your old dress. That is, if it hasn't already been discovered."

"But—" Sanora began.

Katona cut her short. "I've heard enough! Stay here while I meet with the others. In the meantime, perhaps I should take that dress, so that you don't ruin—"

"*No!*" Sanora shouted, and now it did not sound like the voice of a ten-year-old girl, but instead like that of a much older woman. The sound of it sent goose bumps skittering up Oona's arms.

"All right," Katona said, and Oona thought she could hear unease in the older girl's voice. "I will bring it up with the others."

Deacon took in a sharp breath. "She is coming this way."

The two of them ducked back into the darker part of the tunnel. Oona pressed herself flat against the wall. For a second she could make out the silhouette of a figure wearing a dress and pointy hat outlined against the flickering light, and then the blackness swallowed her up. Oona held her breath. The sound of swishing skirts filled the tunnel, growing louder at first, and then fading away down the passage behind them.

Oona let out her breath, uncertain of what to do next. She turned the questions over in her mind: Should she move forward, or turn back? Was she doing the right thing? After several seconds of deliberation, however, she reminded herself that she had not come all the way down here simply to turn back at the last moment. This was her chance to learn the truth. Now was the time to be brave like a true detective, not meek like a frightened child. This is what her father would have done, she was sure of it. He would have met the challenge head on. And with that final thought, turning back was suddenly not an option. It was all or nothing. She took in several deep breaths to calm herself, and then said: "Come along, Deacon. It's time to confront Sanora."

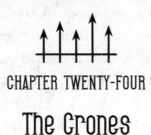

CHAPTER TWENTY-FOUR

The Crones

They found Sanora huddled on the floor of a candlelit room—though calling it simply a room would have been an understatement. Perhaps thirty feet across by fifty feet long, the room appeared to be an entire underground library. The stone walls had been carved into rising shelves, all of them stuffed with books, stacks of yellowing newspapers, and thousands of scrolls.

A long wood table occupied the center of the room, atop of which sat a pair of flaming candelabras. There were only two chairs that Oona could see, one at the end of the table and another sitting beside a bookshelf, as if someone had used it for a stepping stool. The floor was nothing more than hard-packed earth.

Sanora had curled herself into a ball on the floor in front of a shelf containing newspapers. She hugged her knees, rocking from side to side on the ground.

"Remarkable!" Oona said as she stepped from the opening of the tunnel into the light of the library. "Not only do you steal a gorgeous dress, but you choose to use it as a floor rag as well. Here. I believe this would be more suitable." Oona tugged the black dress she had found in the showroom from her shoulder and tossed it to the floor.

Sanora looked up, her large eyes round and red from crying. She sprang to her feet. The dress looked positively radiant on her, its shimmery cloth causing Sanora's normally pale complexion to look as if it glowed.

"Oh, Miss Crate," said Sanora in a small, shaky voice. "I'm sorry. I know I shouldn't have. But . . . But I can explain."

Oona raised an eyebrow. "You mean explain why there is a tunnel leading from the dress shop to Witch Hill? I've already figured it out, Sanora. It was quite devious of you to tell me that you saw Hector Grimsbee on the steps of the museum, especially when you knew quite well that it was you, and not he, who stole the daggers."

Sanora sank back to the floor, as if defeated, and she spoke in a trembling voice. "It's true, I told you about seeing Mr. Grimsbee so you would think he stole the daggers. But I also thought that it must have been Grimsbee who was the one who threw the dagger at the Wizard."

Oona shook her head, confused. "What are you talking about? If you stole the dagger, then why would Grimsbee or anyone else be the one who threw it?"

But before Sanora could answer, a voice interjected. "What is this?"

Oona whirled around, only to discover a girl, about fifteen or sixteen years old, standing at the mouth of the tunnel. Upon her head sat a tall, pointy hat. Her dress, a silky purple gown, was breathtaking in its finely detailed craftsmanship. The girl wore the dress well, and from the way she held herself, she knew it.

Oona braced herself. If these witches knew any sort of magic at all—or were in possession of the second dagger—then this was surely the moment she would find out. But nothing happened. On the contrary, it was Sanora who blurted out: "Katona, be careful! She's a Natural Magician. I saw her yesterday. She conjured a powerful spell right in front of everyone, so she did."

Oona glanced down at Sanora, feeling a shock of guilt shoot through her body like lightning, and for a moment the shame of doing the magic—letting it happen—came rushing back to her. It had been a dreadful betrayal of her promise to never do magic again. A betrayal to her mother and sister. It had been a mistake. A stupid mistake.

A trace of movement at the mouth of the tunnel

pulled Oona's attention back into the present moment. A second girl, roughly the same age as Katona, stepped out of the tunnel and into the library. She was followed by another girl, and then another, and another, each of them dressed in the finest of clothing—Madame Iree's missing dresses, no doubt—and each was wearing a pointy black hat. They stopped a few paces into the room and stared at the intruder and her bird.

Oona swallowed a lump in her throat, and Deacon whispered, "Oh dear," under his breath.

Again, Oona's muscles tensed in anticipation of being struck with some secret spell, but just as before, there appeared to be no threat of this at all. Indeed, they all seemed quite a bit more afraid of her than Oona was of them.

"Who is that?" asked one of the girls.

"It's that Crate girl," said another. "The Wizard's niece."

Katona's eyes widened beneath the brim of her pointy hat, like she'd suddenly remembered something. "You . . . You're the one who . . . who killed your own mother."

Oona took in a sharp breath, and it seemed as if the entire room gasped with her. No one had ever said it so directly to her before, so matter-of-factly. It sounded so brutal to her ears, so painfully cruel and true. It was like a blade slid right into her chest, sinking deep into her heart, and for a second she thought perhaps one of the witches had thrown the second dagger, piercing her straight through. But it was not steel that cut at her, nor any enchantment. This was cold, undeniable remorse. It was guilt and loss all tangled together in barbed wire. It was the drowned song of heartache. She wanted to shout out that it had been an accident, that she had not meant for it to happen. Part of her wanted to crumble to her knees and fall into a fit of tears, while another part wished to leap on Katona and pull at her hair, to tell her to take it back; to take back what she had said in order to make it untrue. But Oona did neither of these things. There was nothing she could do that would *make* it untrue, nothing at all . . . not even magic.

But she also knew that there was something that she *must* do, and that was save her uncle and Pendulum House. She might not be able to turn back the clock and save her mother and sister, but she could save the street from Red Martin's greedy scheme, and bring all those responsible to justice. That was what her father would have done.

Looking at the astonished expressions on the girls' faces, Oona realized for the first time that she just might be able to use their fear of her magic to her advantage. Even if she did not intend on using magic, that did not mean that she could not make the witches believe that she would. She only hoped that she could bluff them all.

And, she thought, *let's pray that none of them possesses* Fay Mors Mortis.

"What is it you want," Katona asked Oona wearily. "The dresses?"

Oona stepped forward, and the group of girls stepped back, all except for Katona, who seemed to be their leader. Oona could tell that the older girl was nervous, and yet there was an air of defiance about her as well.

Oona raised her chin. "The dagger that Sanora used to attack my uncle has turned him into a toad. What I want is for Sanora to tell me the magical phrase that will turn him back into his human form."

Katona laughed. It was a high-pitched chortle, filled with nervousness. "Sanora is not the person who attacked your uncle, Miss Crate."

Oona's eyes slitted. "Explain yourself."

Before Katona could answer, Oona noticed that several of the girls were attempting to edge their way back toward the tunnel. She arrowed a finger in their direction, like a Magician of Old preparing to cast some terrible enchantment. The girls stopped in their tracks.

"I want you all where I can see you," Oona commanded. "All of you, get on the table!"

The next moment, Deacon was soaring into the air, batting his wings at the girls, and cawing his high raven cry. The girls darted for the table; all except for Sanora, who remained where she was on the floor. There were nine witches in all, including Sanora.

"Where are the rest of you?" Oona asked.

The girls looked at one another. They did not seem to know what she was talking about, and then Oona suddenly understood.

"You mean to say that this is all there is? Nine witches?" She furrowed her brow, trying to adjust to this strange bit of news. Oona had always imagined scores of witches living below the hill. She'd imagined them beating on drums and dancing wildly around boiling kettles. The fact that none of them appeared older than sixteen was quite a surprise . . . or, that is to say, it was a surprise until she remembered the turlock root.

The odor of the beauty cream was faint against the smell of books and earth, but it was there.

"You, Sanora," Oona said. "Sit here. In this chair. Now explain to me how you did not attack my uncle, even though you were clearly involved in stealing the daggers."

Sanora rose to her feet and took her seat, her dress shimmering in the candlelight, mesmerizing to behold. She glanced nervously from Katona to Oona. "It was Red Martin," she said finally, her voice high and meek. "He forced us to do it . . . to steal the daggers. We did not know that one of them was to be used on the Wizard, I swear it. I was just as surprised to see it happen as you was. We was just told that if we didn't get the daggers, and take them to the Nightshade Hotel, then we would no longer receive our supply of . . . of . . ."

"Of turlock root," Deacon finished for her.

Sanora looked up in surprise.

Oona twirled the candle in her fingers like a baton. "Yes, we know that you have been using turlock root in your so-called Witchwhistle Beauty Cream to make yourself young. But we did not know where you were getting it from."

Now the question is, where is Red Martin getting it from? Oona thought, but did not ask. She waited for Sanora to respond.

Finally, Sanora nodded, smoothing the shimmery skirt of her dress. "Red Martin's the only one who knows how to get hold of the root. And I promise, Miss Crate, that he wouldn't say what them daggers was for. Just that he had to have 'em, and that *we* was to do the getting . . . or else. He gave us a drawing of the museum layout, and the buildings around it. It was very detailed. So, anyway, we started digging. We tried to dig directly into the curator's office, but the floor was solid stone. It would have taken too long to break through."

Oona nodded, circling around the back of Sanora's chair. "I'm guessing that's when you decided to tunnel beneath the dress shop next door."

Sanora nodded. "The showroom floor is made of wood. And that platform was hollow underneath."

"Of course," Oona said. "You could cut through the wood floor much easier than through solid stone. And from there you went into the museum through the common wall of the showroom."

Sanora began to fidget with the folds of her gleaming dress, and the light played eerily upon her face. "Once we got inside, we had to work by night, when the dress shop and the museum was both closed. It took longer than we thought it might to cut through into the museum, right? A whole week goes by, and we still wasn't in. And so, yesterday we get a message from Red Martin saying that we was taking too long, and that he needs the daggers that very day or we could kiss our beloved root good-bye. The message also says that he's gonna make sure that the curator is out of his office by one o'clock, and that he'll be gone for several hours. So, you see, we had no choice but to finish the job in the daytime. Thing is, Red Martin didn't know that we was going in through the dress shop next door. We just never told him."

"Lucky for you, Madame Iree was having a tea party at one o'clock, and the showroom was locked," Oona said.

"It's true," said Sanora. "And we was already almost through. We punched through the last bit of wall right behind that tapestry in about twenty minutes. We broke the glass case with a pick, took the daggers, cleaned up, and then . . . then . . ."

"And then you took the dresses," Oona finished for her.

Katona pointed her chin at Oona, her voice full of defiance. "We may spend most of our time down here in the hill, Miss Crate, but at least part of the reason for that is because people up there on the street treat us so rudely. They take one look at our pointy hats and scurry to the other side of the street. They point and whisper behind their hands. And that snobby dress shop owner was the worst of them. She never once let any of us witches so much as get three feet into her precious store before shouting at us to get out. Taking the dresses seemed only fair . . . and convenient."

Oona remembered her own experience of walking into the store for the first time only the day before, and the treatment she had received. The looks of distain on the ladies' faces had almost made Oona turn right around and head back out the door.

"Convenient, I will agree," Oona said. "Fair? That will be a matter for the courts to decide." She turned to Sanora. "Please, continue."

Sanora swallowed uneasily. "I dropped the daggers off in an envelope at the front desk of the Nightshade Hotel, and that was that."

"Surely you would have known that the daggers were

highly dangerous," Oona said. "Even their names speak of their treacherous possibilities. And yet you still stole them for a notorious criminal."

Sanora bit at her lip. "I swear, Miss Crate, none of us knew one of 'em was meant for the Wizard. If we had, then we would never have taken it."

"Really, Sanora?" Katona said, disbelieving. "You would have given up the beauty cream? I find that hard to believe. Look at you. Can't even act like an adult when you need to, in spite of being five hundred and seventy years old."

"Five hundred and seventy?" Oona said, hearing the astonishment in her own voice.

Katona shrugged. "Give or take a few years. When you're that old, it does not matter. Sanora, though she may appear to be the youngest among us, is by far the oldest . . . and by all rights should be head of the coven. But over the years, as her body grew younger, so did her mind. Lately, she got it in her head that she wanted to become the Wizard's apprentice. A ludicrous idea, really. The rest of us warned her against it, but she wouldn't listen. She's grown so insufferably obstinate, yet as timid as a . . . well, as a little girl."

Oona squinted at Sanora, trying to comprehend somehow that this was no girl, but a five-hundred-and-seventy-year-old woman. And then suddenly Oona thought that she understood what was really happening here. It came to her in a flash: the witches' real motivation. "If you are all truly so old, then that means that if you stop using the beauty cream . . . you will all die. Is that correct?"

Katona hesitated, her finger twisting nervously at a lock of hair. At last she said: "It is true. Without Red Martin's supply of the root, we will be unable to make the cream, and we'll return to our true age within a month's time. No doubt, we would die of old age much sooner than that."

Oona brushed a stray hair from her face, considering what Katona had just revealed. Stranger things had happened on Dark Street, and yet she couldn't help but feel sorry for them all. These . . . girls . . . women . . . old crones? What precisely were they?

"But I do wonder," said Deacon. "Where is Red Martin getting turlock root from?"

Sanora shared a look with the other girls. Katona began to shake her head, as if warning Sanora that this information was too precious to give away. After a long moment, however, Sanora said: "He gets it from Faerie."

CHAPTER TWENTY-FIVE

An Unexpected Visitor

K atona sprang to her feet. "Sanora, hold your tongue!"

"Faerie?" Oona said. "How can Red Martin be getting turlock root from Faerie? The Glass Gates bar the way."

"He smuggles it in, he does," Sanora said. "Only he knows how."

Katona moved forward as if to silence her, but Oona stepped between them. "Let her speak!"

Katona backed against the table, staring Oona down with eyes as cold as ice.

"Red Martin's found a flaw in the Glass Gates," Sanora continued. "He's been smuggling turlock root—and all sorts of other things, I'm sure—across the border for almost as long as the gates have been standing. The deal has always been that he provides us witches with the root, and we pay him with the various crystals and gold that we extract from deep within Witch Hill. We've been doing it for hundreds of years. Ever since Oswald closed the gates, and the magic began to fade. We used to be able to do magic, you know. All of us. But by the time we was a century old, the spells we once knew began to fade from our memories. Part of it was the closing of the gates, which softened all the magic. But mostly it was the turlock root. It somehow blocked our ability to remember the magic . . . and by that time we had no choice but to keep applying the cream." She touched the brim of her pointy black hat with a sort of loving fondness. "That's why we always wear our hats. To remind us of what we once were. Real witches who done real magic." She paused a moment, sitting up straight. She squared her shoulders and looked at the girls on the table: "That's why I wanted to become the Wizard's apprentice. To feel what it was like to do magic again."

For a moment, Oona could only stare at Sanora, blinking foolishly. It was all so extraordinary. Finally, she said: "But if you've been getting the root from Red Martin the whole time, then that means that Red Martin must use the beauty cream as well. He's at least as old as you are, and all of those ridiculous rumors that he is hundreds of years old are actually true."

"Just figuring that out, are you?" asked a new voice. "I thought for sure that little fact would have been in your father's files on me. But then again, I suppose he was just as dim-witted as you."

The voice emanated low and amused from the mouth of the tunnel, and Oona did not like the sound of it one bit.

She whirled around, only to discover a very plain-looking man dressed in an even plainer-looking tan suit and bowler hat. The man stepped casually into the room. His face was ordinary—the kind of face one might pass a hundred times on the street and never take notice of. Quite frankly, there seemed nothing extraordinary about the man at all. He smiled a perfectly uninteresting smile, and the only remarkable thing about his expression was that the smile did nothing for his eyes . . . eyes that, upon first and perhaps even second glance, seemed utterly unexceptional. And yet upon further examination, there was something altogether eerie about them. There was a kind of menacing glimmer in their gaze that caused a shiver to shoot up Oona's spine, and she realized all too quickly that these were the same eyes she'd seen peering down at her from the high window at the Nightshade Hotel.

Two enormous men dressed in red suits appeared behind the man. They stooped over in the tunnel, but once inside the room they straightened, rising to their full, ominous height. Oona recognized them as the twin hotel security guards, each carrying a thick wooden club.

"Red Martin!" said Katona.

"How do you do?" said the plain-looking man, keeping his eyes on Oona.

Oona's heart began to race. She had certainly not expected this. Red Martin himself. She did not know what to say. Here was the very man responsible for so many of the crimes on Dark Street, the man that Oona's father had been trying to bring down before he was killed . . . killed by known associates of Red Martin. Oona had often imagined this day, when she would finally come face-to-face with the man she believed to be responsible for her father's death. She had imagined just what she would say to him, sometimes going so far as to rehearse her speech in her head as she fell asleep at night, but now that the moment had finally come, she was speechless.

Red Martin turned to Katona and said: "I just stopped by to personally thank you for the wonderful job you did in obtaining the daggers, Katona . . . and to give you this." He snapped his fingers, and the twin with the mustache held up what looked like a bag of potatoes. "I thought you might be running low on the root. Yet what do I find when I arrive, but you telling this foolish girl all of our well-kept secrets? Too bad, really. I suppose I'll just have to keep this bag of turlock root for myself."

Katona looked horrified. "No. It was not me. It was Sanora. She's grown too young. She can't keep her big mouth shut."

Red Martin shrugged, as if it did not matter, and then turned to face Oona. "Let's deal with this little problem first, shall we? I'm sorry, Miss Crate, but I cannot allow you to leave the hill. Not now that you know our secret."

"Don't you touch her," said Deacon, puffing up his feathers to his full, menacing size.

Red Martin chuckled as he slid a shiny dagger from the inside of his jacket pocket. Oona recognized it at once as an exact replica of the one used on the Wizard. "Don't worry, Mr. Bird," said Red Martin. "I don't need to touch her." He looked admiringly at the dagger. "I believe this little beauty is thrown with the mind." He gripped the handle tight in his hand and grinned at Oona. "And believe me, Miss Crate, when I say that this one won't send you to the Black Tower. It won't even send you to meet your dear, dead parents. This one will wipe you clean out of existence . . . which is almost too bad. Perhaps in the afterlife you could have told your father what an absolute delight it was for me when I had him killed. Oh, don't look at me like that. It was simply a necessity. He kept getting in my way, so he had to go." Red Martin giggled darkly. "Though he doesn't know it, it was I who influenced the Street Council to give your father's old position to that bumbling idiot, Inspector White. The man is so stupid he doesn't even realize he got the job because of me. Life has been so much easier with him running the police force."

Oona's teeth clenched. Her suspicions were being proven right, yet it only made her feel angrier than ever. "You murdered my father!"

Red Martin shook his head, tossing the dagger from one hand to the other. "You should know by now that I never hurt anyone. I always get someone else to do it for me. In your father's case, it was a couple of thieves." His grin widened. "But in your case, I think I will make an exception. And how convenient that I won't even need to get my hands dirty."

Oona's heart was racing, her mind grasping for some way out. Anything. A thought occurred to her. "You wouldn't dare do it in front of all these witnesses," she said. But her voice betrayed her lack of certainty.

Red Martin appeared amused. "I am the only reason these ladies are alive today. They cannot survive longer than a few weeks without my supply of the root. They will keep their mouths shut. And besides, if they should decide to speak out against me, I can terminate the relationship and let them all wither away. It's quite true that they provide me with a minimal amount of crystals and gold, but I assure you, I do have other prospects for making up the lost income."

Oona's hands clenched into fists, her knuckles turning a bloodless white. "Other prospects?" she asked. "You mean like destroying Pendulum House and building your hideous hula-hut hotel and casino?"

Red Martin's eyes sparkled. "Just think of all those New York fools pouring through the gates to see the magical street. They'll need a luxurious place to stay, and of course a place to lose all of their money!"

"Horrible," was all Oona could think to say.

Red Martin gave a little bow.

"But what if it doesn't work?" Oona asked. "What if when you destroy Pendulum House, we no longer stay connected to New York, and Dark Street becomes isolated from New York completely? Or what if the Glass Gates should eventually fall? What then? The armies of Faerie could attack the World of Man as they please."

Red Martin shrugged. "A possibility, yes. But I really doubt that will happen."

"And yet you are willing to gamble with the lives of everyone?" Oona asked, but she already knew what his answer to that would be.

"I'm a gambling sort of man . . . and I believe the odds are in my favor. They are always in my favor, Miss Crate."

Oona's eyes slitted to the size of paper cuts. "Which one of the applicants did you persuade into attacking my uncle?" she demanded.

Red Martin smiled faintly. "You will never know, will you? Good-bye, Miss Crate. So sorry I have to kill you now, but sometimes killing is necessary. I suppose you, of all people, should know that. Really, even I never stooped so low as to kill my own mother . . . let alone a baby. Perhaps the world is better off without you."

Oona's throat constricted, the harshness of the words like a noose around her neck. Red Martin raised the dagger above his head, clearly meaning to make a show of it, and fixed her with his gaze.

Several of the girls took in a collective gasp.

"Stop!" shouted Sanora.

Deacon cried, "No!" as he leaped from Oona's shoulder and darted across the room. His great black wings fluttered in front of Red Martin's face, momentarily blocking Oona from view.

"Get away from me, bird!" he shouted, and then brought the blade swiftly down, meaning to cleave right into Deacon and knock him out of the way.

What happened next happened in the space of half a heartbeat. First there was a memory: Samuligan standing near Oona's bedroom door with Deacon wriggling in the faerie servant's gangly grip. Samuligan had uttered a single word . . . except that, in the memory, his voice seemed muffled, like someone speaking through a mouth full of cloth. In the next instant Deacon was standing on the dressing table, looking bewildered, while Samuligan remained near the door with Oona's hairbrush in his hand. The bird and the brush had magically swapped places in the blink of an eye.

"I just made it up," Samuligan had said, again his voice strangely muffled, like this was a very old memory that had lost some of its sharpness. And yet it was not an old memory, Oona knew. It was quite recent. The real event had taken place only the day before, and in that half a heartbeat, as Oona saw the dagger in Red Martin's hand swing down to knock Deacon out of the way, and quite possibly cut him in half, Oona made a decision to do what she had promised herself she would never do again on purpose.

The magic rose to her lips like a drink of water from a deep spring. It felt not only exhilarating, it also felt *right*.

"*Switch!*" she shouted, and in the same instant stomped her foot against the floor just as the blade slammed into Deacon's fluttering wing. Except that it was no longer the dagger that Red Martin swung; instead, it was the candle that Oona had been holding only a moment before. Deacon swatted at the candle with his wing before soaring toward the cave ceiling, shrieking like mad.

"What is this?" asked Red Martin, looking both startled and confused. He gazed uncomprehendingly at the white candle in his hand. "Where did it go?"

"Looking for this?" Oona asked. She held up the enchanted dagger. She could feel the fiery prickle of it in her hand—the dagger's enchantment sensing her faerie blood—and the heat was already beginning to grow. But she held the dagger nonetheless, suffering the discomfort, refusing to let it fall from her hand.

Red Martin's eyes rounded like wagon wheels. He took in a sharp breath of air, and then threw the unlit candle at Oona. The candle went wide and hit the bookshelf containing the newspapers as Deacon returned to Oona's shoulder.

"Don't just stand there!" Red Martin shouted at the enormous twins. "Kill her!"

Red Martin then turned and ran abruptly out of the room, disappearing down the tunnel.

The two enormous thugs came at her, clubs raised, the expressions on their broad faces cold, and distant, and eager to pummel. In that instant the pain in her hand was finally too much to bear. The heat had grown too intense, and Oona let the dagger drop to the floor.

CHAPTER TWENTY-SIX

Lux Lucis Admiratio

The twins descended on Oona like two hulking monsters.

Deacon launched from Oona's shoulder, attacked the twin with the mustache, batting at his head and clawing at his face. The second twin came straight at Oona, clearly intent on smashing her skull with his thick club. Oona dove out of the way and the club crashed against the floor, sending the dagger skittering across the ground.

The girls screamed as the first twin (the one Oona thought of as Mr. Mustache) began to swat at the open air, trying to whack Deacon with his club. But the bird was too fast. Deacon clamped hold of the man's mustache and soared upward. Mr. Mustache's scream was so high pitched, it might have belonged to one of the girls.

Oona jumped back as thug number two took another swipe at her. The swing missed her by mere inches, crashing instead against the side of the chair where Sanora had been cowering, and sending her flying across the room. A quavery wail escaped her lips as she slammed against the floor and then fell silent.

"You brute!" Oona shouted, snatching up a broken chair leg. "You'd strike a helpless little girl?"

The giant man raised the club, and when Oona brought up the chair leg to protect herself, she stumbled over another bit of broken chair and toppled to the floor. She clamped her eyes shut, thinking that this was it, certain the club's blow would send the life rushing out of her—but the blow never came.

There was a loud *thunk*, and the man staggered forward. His massive body spun around and collapsed against a carved-stone bookcase. It took Oona a couple of seconds to realize what had just happened. The thug's twin, Mr. Mustache, had accidentally clobbered his brother with his own flailing club.

Then came a sharp shriek of pain as Mr. Mustache caught hold of Deacon in one enormous hand and shoved the raven against the wall. He raised the club, clearly meaning to flatten the bird, even if it meant crushing his own hand in the process.

Oona knew instantly what she had to do. She sat up, aimed the chair leg at Mr. Mustache like a rifle, and the words escaped her mouth without her even having to remember them.

"Lux lucis admiratio!"

A blaze of sparkling lights erupted from the end of the broken chair leg, shooting across the room and knocking the club from Mr. Mustache's thick-fingered hand. His grip weakened, and Deacon fell to the floor with a *thump*. Mr. Mustache cried out in surprise as a second burst of lights picked him up and hurled him across the room. He slammed against a bookcase and collapsed to the floor, bringing an avalanche of books with him. The starry lights swirled around his head, lingering just long enough to singe the ends of his bushy mustache, and then they disappeared altogether. The man's eyelids fluttered briefly before sliding closed. He was out cold. Oona dropped the broken chair leg and hurriedly pushed herself to her feet.

"Deacon!" she called, and ran to him. "Deacon, are you all right?" Her voice cracked, and her eyes glistened wetly. She knelt to pick him up. Once he was in her hands, she could just make out his faint breath and the beating of his heart against her palm. His body shuddered, followed by a short cough. One eye opened, peering up at her.

"I've been better," he said, and winced as he moved his leg.

317

Oona felt all of the breath leave her body in a great sigh of relief. "Oh, Deacon. You had me frightened there for a moment. Are you badly hurt?"

Ruffling his feathers, he said: "I believe I may have injured my hip."

"Can you move it?" she asked.

"Yes."

"Then at least it's not broken."

"Can't be sure about that," he said.

"Oh, you'd know if your hip was broken," said Katona. "I broke mine once, almost a hundred years ago, and I can assure you, there's no worse—"

"That's quite enough!" Deacon shouted. He stretched out his wings before hopping to Oona's shoulder. She felt him wobble for a moment, but he managed to keep his balance. "I believe we should be more concerned about Miss Crone than my hip," he said.

Oona glanced across the room to where Sanora lay motionless. Filled with apprehension, Oona hurried to the girl's side, but even as she knelt, she could see that Sanora was beginning to stir. Oona placed her hand on the young witch's shoulder, helping her to sit up.

"Are you badly injured?" Oona asked.

Sanora gazed up, her vast eyes blinking dazedly. "I . . . I think I will be all right. The chair took most of the blow."

The crumpled remains of the chair lay in a heap near

the table, along with the broken chair leg Oona had used to cast her spell of light. What surprised Oona the most was that, when she looked at the splintered piece of wood, she didn't feel one stitch of guilt. She had used magic, and yet there was no trace of the horrible sense of betrayal she'd felt only the day before when she had unintentionally fixed the broken magnifying glass. This time there had been nothing unintentional about it. This time it had been her choice. *Lux lucis admiratio.* The Lights of Wonder: the very spell that had gone wrong nearly three years ago beneath the trembling leaves of the fig tree. This time the magic had done precisely what she'd intended. This time it had felt exactly right.

"Can you stand?" Oona asked the witch.

"Think so," said Sanora, and Oona helped her to her feet. Like Deacon, the girl wobbled slightly, but she appeared less hurt than Oona would have guessed, and the dress was remarkably undamaged.

Mr. Mustache moaned on the floor, and Oona approached him warily. His club lay near his limp hand, half buried beneath a pile of books. Oona kicked it away.

"We should tie these two up before they come to," she said, and then, remembering that she had dropped the dagger to the floor, she quickly scanned the room. For one panicky instant she did not see it anywhere . . . but the panic was short-lived and she let out a sigh. There

319

it was, lying on the floor in front of the bookcase filled with newspapers, safely out of everyone's reach. If any of the witches wanted to get to it, they would need to get past Oona, and presently all the witches were standing near the table, staring at her with a kind of openmouthed wonder.

"What is to be done now?" Deacon asked.

"We must still find my uncle's true attacker," Oona said. "Nothing else is more important. Red Martin has disappeared."

"There's a tunnel that goes all the way to the hotel," Sanora explained. "That's how we get the root. He's probably halfway back by now."

Oona frowned. "Well, he is still the legal owner of Pendulum House, and he intends on stopping the pendulum at midnight." She turned to face the witches. "As it seems that you are all now out of Red Martin's good favor, I'm afraid your only hope for procuring turlock root for your beauty cream will be from Pendulum House. So I suggest that you all help me in any way possible. We must destroy Red Martin's legal ownership."

"Turlock root at Pendulum House?" several of the girls said at once. They looked at one another in surprise.

"Yes. It grows in the inner garden," Oona said. "But you'll just have to trust me on that. I'm sure once we have restored the Wizard to his human form, I might be able to convince him to allow you all some reasonable access to the roots." She walked to the bookcase and stood over the dagger, peering down at its unblemished blade before turning back to face the girls. "But only under the condition that you return the dresses to Madame Iree's showroom, and admit to having stolen the daggers from the museum."

Oona slid one of the yellowed newspapers from the shelf—an old edition of the *Dark Street Tribune*—and knelt down. Moving as delicately as possible, she slid the edge of the paper beneath the dagger, rolled it around both handle and blade, creating a thick tube, and then picked it up. The paper was just thick enough so that Oona could hold the dagger without getting burned. She could still feel the closeness of the dagger, but the paper had reduced the fiery sensation to a kind of tingling heat in her hand.

Deacon half whispered in Oona's ear: "It's a good thing that Red Martin did not pay too close attention to the precise wording of the dagger's enchantment."

"What do you mean, Deacon?" she asked.

"Well, according to the enchantment," he whispered, "once Red Martin had brought the dagger into the room, he could have still used it, regardless of who actually held it."

"You mean that even though he no longer had the dagger on him, he could have still used it to kill me?" Oona said, her heart seeming to skip a beat.

"Yes . . . so long as you were no more than ten paces away, and he could see you, then he could still have used the enchantment to throw it with his mind," Deacon replied.

For a moment Oona didn't know what to say. It seemed that she had been very lucky indeed. She had a sudden fear that Red Martin might suddenly realize his mistake and step back into the room. But from the way he had turned and run, she suspected that Red Martin was currently far away from Witch Hill. And then a new thought struck her so forcefully she nearly dropped the paper. "Of course!" she whispered.

"What is it?" Deacon asked, his voice brimming with concern.

"It's . . . It's . . . of course, Deacon! Why did I not see it before?" The newspaper continued to tingle in her hand like fiery nerves.

"See what?" Deacon implored, but she did not answer. Instead, she retrieved Sanora's flimsy black dress from where she had tossed it to the ground and handed it to the young witch.

"Sanora, I suggest you return to your own dress quickly," she said. "We need to go."

"Where to?" Deacon asked.

"First things first," Oona replied. "We will return this dagger to the museum. And then we must find the inspector and gather all the other applicants. I know who attacked my uncle."

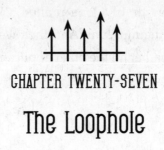

CHAPTER TWENTY-SEVEN

The Loophole

It took nearly twenty minutes for Sanora to change and for her and Oona and Deacon to find their way out of the hill by way of the enchanted entrance beneath the roots of the crooked tree. They found Inspector White kneeling down in the street, peering into one of the potholes. Samuligan sat atop the Wizard's carriage in front of the museum, watching the inspector with an amused expression on his long faerie face, the hatbox containing the toad resting safely in his lap.

It took another thirty minutes for Oona to explain all that had happened, and for the inspector to accompany them into the museum to return the stolen dagger. The inspector had been quite eager to arrest Sanora on the spot, but Oona had insisted that the young witch be allowed to return to Pendulum House, along with all of the other applicants, for a sort of "restaging" of the attack on the Wizard.

It was early evening when Oona hurried through the front doorway of Pendulum House, Deacon balancing precariously on her shoulder. Samuligan followed close behind carrying the hatbox. Sanora Crone was the next to enter, and a moment later Inspector White strode into the entryway, wearing his checkered hunting jacket. Next came Isadora and Adler Iree, along with Lamont John-Michael Arlington Fitch III, and lastly, Hector Grimsbee, his great big nostrils flaring almost to the size of his milky-white eyes.

"I hope you have a good reason for having me gather up all these fine people, Miss Crate," the inspector told Oona. "And an even better reason for pulling me away from the scene of a crime. The cobblestone case is not going to solve itself."

Oona came to an abrupt halt in the entryway, looking down at her feet. Scattered across the floor were the remnants of Isadora's tantrum from the night before: the kicked-over umbrella stand, the toppled footstool, the scattered parasols, and Hector Grimsbee's red umbrella.

"I believe we are about to solve all of these peculiar cases at once," Oona told the inspector, and when his face contorted, expressing more confusion than normal, she gestured toward the entryway coatrack. "Would you be so kind, Inspector, as to bring that black jacket? The one hanging on the coatrack. I believe it will be needed."

The inspector took in a sharp breath. "What is my jacket doing here? It is supposed to be at the tailor's getting mended."

"Just bring it!" Oona said so forcefully that the inspector took a step backward before hastily removing the jacket from the coatrack and then following Oona, along with the others, into the parlor.

Oona stopped several feet into the room. She studied the scene as if from a distance. The Wizard's robes lay empty on the floor, where he had fallen. She took in the paintings and tapestries on the walls, the ceaseless swing of the pendulum, the long bench, the two magical contracts on the table, and the large book that Adler Iree had left behind.

"Please, everyone," Oona said. "If you would resume your positions from yesterday, when my uncle was attacked, we may proceed."

"Proceed with what?" Hector Grimsbee asked, sounding characteristically peeved. "I have a monologue I could be polishing."

Isadora pointed an accusing finger at Sanora. "Why is she not under arrest? Clearly she is the one who stole my mother's dresses. Shouldn't we be more concerned with getting the dresses back before the masquerade tonight?"

Oona looked from Sanora to Isadora. "By the time we finish with this demonstration, Miss Iree, I can assure you that the dresses will be back in the showroom at your mother's boutique."

Oona raised an eyebrow at Sanora, and the girl nodded. Before leaving Witch Hill, Oona had seen to it that both of Red Martin's thugs had been tied up, and then she'd made the eight remaining witches promise to return the dresses to the shop, assuring them that if they did not, then there would be no chance of their receiving turlock root from the Pendulum House garden.

Isadora's expression brightened. She clapped her hands together excitedly and said: "Well, in that case, I should like to go immediately and begin getting ready for the masquerade."

"Me, too!" said Hector Grimsbee, scratching absently at his bloodstained bandage. "The director of the Dark Street Theater will be there, and I wish to look my best!"

"I know who attacked my uncle!" Oona shouted at them.

The shout startled Deacon into the air. He took flight and began to caw his haunting raven's cry as he swooped about the applicants, herding them toward the bench.

Once everyone was in place, Deacon returned to

Oona's shoulder, and Oona turned to Samuligan. "Now, if you would please place my uncle there, on his robes, I think we can begin."

Samuligan obligingly did as he was told, removing the toad from the box and placing him on top of the Wizard's crumpled purple robe.

"Inspector White," Oona said, "if you would be so kind as to put on that jacket and then stand out of the way, over there, beneath that portrait."

She was pleased to see the inspector do as she asked without launching into a fit of irrelevant questions. He removed his hunting jacket, tossing it over the back of a chair, before slipping his arms into the black jacket from the entryway.

"Hey, what has happened to my jacket?" the inspector asked. "I'll need to have a word with that tailor. He was supposed to fix a hole in the sleeve, not make the entire jacket bigger." In truth, the jacket appeared quite baggy as it hung from the inspector's narrow shoulders.

"Please, Inspector," Oona said. "Stand over there, and we may begin."

As Oona had instructed, the inspector took his position beneath the portrait of Oswald the Great, puffing up his chest in an attempt to fill out the jacket.

Oona scanned the room, making sure everyone was in place.

"If there is one thing I have learned throughout all of this," she said, "it is that rumors can sometimes be true. It was rumored that Red Martin was hundreds of years old. And now I know that this is true. It was also rumored that Natural Magicians, such as myself, have active faerie blood in their veins, and this has also been proven true to me." She pointed to the rolled-up documents on the table. "Had I known this fact before yesterday, then I might have recognized what was happening when I placed my hand near the second document in order to sign my name. I had no idea that the uncomfortably hot, tingling sensation that I felt in my hand was due not to my nervousness but solely to the fact that rolled up inside that oversize document was a dagger created to burn the hand of any faerie." Oona turned in a dramatic swish of skirts to face the inspector. "It was you, sir, who brought the dagger into the room concealed inside that contract."

She arrowed her finger at the rolled-up document on the table.

The inspector took in a sharp breath. "Me? But . . . I don't remember even being in the room at the time."

Oona shook her head. "Not you, Inspector. I'm referring to the lawyer, Mr. Ravensmith, of whom you are playing the role. That is why I had you put on his jacket."

"Ravensmith's jacket?" the inspector said. "But how do you know that it is his?"

"I believe, if you reach into the inside pocket," Oona said, "you will find an envelope containing an invoice for services rendered to the Wizard over the past two years."

The inspector reached into the pocket and removed a single envelope. He pulled the invoice from inside, and after a brief glance, he said: "But how did you know it would be there?"

Oona glanced at Deacon, and it was he who answered. "She knew because we both saw Mr. Ravensmith present that invoice to the Wizard yesterday. When the Wizard did not take it, Ravensmith returned the envelope to his own pocket. The jacket most certainly belongs to the lawyer."

Isadora Iree peered at Oona, one perfect eyebrow arched over a patronizing eye. "Yes. So the man left his jacket here. What is the crime in that?"

"And if you are saying that the lawyer attacked your uncle," added Lamont John-Michael Arlington Fitch III, pensively pushing his eyeglasses against his chubby face, "then might I remind you, Miss Crate, that the attacker had to have been in the room to commit the crime. Isn't that what your bird explained?"

"Hmm, yes indeed," Oona said. "It is true that Mr. Ravensmith had already left the room when my uncle was attacked. Deacon, would you please repeat what you told us yesterday? The magical laws regarding the two daggers."

Deacon looked at her, a sympathetic softness about his eyes. "I'm afraid that the magical scripture states very clearly: 'For purposes of accuracy, the throwing of either dagger must take place within a confined space, such as a room. The dagger must be carried into the room by the attacker, who in turn must visually see the victim from a distance of no more than ten paces away.' There is no way around it. The Magicians of Old were very specific."

Deacon shrugged his wings as if to say, *You asked.*

Oona, however, appeared unconcerned and even braved a thin smile. "From my understanding of it, Deacon, nowhere does it state that the attacker must be in the room in order to strike the victim."

Adler Iree took in a sharp breath, his tattoos stretching as his face flushed with excitement. And then just as quickly he frowned. "For sure, you've spotted a loophole in the enchantment, Miss Crate," he said in his lilting Irish accent. "Or, what I mean to say is, you've spotted a flaw . . . and yet I still can't see how someone could've seen the Wizard and not have been inside the room. There's nary a window to be found in here."

"Yes!" the inspector shouted, startling everyone in the room. "No windows, Miss Crate. Let's see you explain your way out of this one."

Oona decided that a more comprehensive explanation was needed. "I believe that everyone can testify to the fact that Ravensmith was wearing his jacket during the signing of the contracts. So why would he remove the jacket and hang it on the coatrack before leaving the house? It makes very little sense . . . that is, unless he was attempting to squeeze into a very tight and dusty space and did not wish to get the jacket dirty. If there is one thing we learned from Ravensmith's secretary, Mr. Quick, it is that the lawyer despises dust. I myself observed the lawyer repeatedly brushing away some invisible bit of dust from his sleeve or lapel."

Oona pointed to Oswald's portrait.

"You see, Inspector, behind that portrait is a very small and seldom-used broom closet. A very dirty closet, which I learned for myself only yesterday. The eyes of both Oswald and his companion, Lulu, may be slid aside, and whoever stands in the closet can see everything that happens inside this room. I, myself, used it just yesterday . . . but since I am not very tall, I needed to stand on a footstool in order to see through the holes. But last night, when everyone was leaving the house, there was a footstool sitting beside the closet door. I would not have noticed it if Isadora hadn't lost her temper and kicked it at me. And even then it did not occur to me that it was the same stool that I had stood upon in the closet."

"Well, if someone hadn't placed their jacket on top of my shawl," Isadora said reasonably, "then I wouldn't have been so upset, and I wouldn't have needed to kick it."

Adler squinched up his face, giving his sister a reproachful look, and then turned to Oona. "But why was the stool outside of the closet?"

The pendulum swung silently through the room behind Oona as she steepled her hands together. "Here is how it happened. Once the contract was signed, and all of us were in the room with the Wizard, Mr. Ravensmith made his way to the broom closet in the entryway. But upon seeing the deplorable condition of the confined space, he removed his jacket and hung it on the coatrack that stood conveniently beside the closet. Since Ravensmith is taller than I am, he then set the stool outside the door before squeezing himself inside. And this is where the loophole came into effect . . . one that only a clever lawyer could ever have thought up. He left the dagger inside the room while he himself made visual contact with the Wizard through the eyes of Oswald the Great."

"But how did Mr. Ravensmith know of the spy holes in the closet in the first place?" Deacon asked.

Oona cocked her head conspiratorially to one side. "Tell me, Deacon. Do you remember the lawyer's chiding remark to my uncle about the condition of Pendulum House? How Ravensmith himself had hired our old thief of a cleaning maid, Miss Colbert, and how wonderfully she had been keeping his own office and household?"

"Certainly," Deacon said. "I remember thinking the remark rather unprofessional."

"Yes, as did I, Deacon," Oona said. "And let me ask you this. Of all the people who live on Dark Street, how many can you name that would have knowledge of the broom closet in the entryway . . . and its spy holes?"

Deacon began to nod more decisively. "You believe that Miss Colbert told him about it?"

Oona rubbed thoughtfully at one cheek. "Perhaps he overheard her telling one of his other servants about it, or maybe she told him directly. Whether the cleaning maid was knowingly involved in his scheme is something we will need to ask the lawyer himself."

She fell silent for a very long moment, the swing of the pendulum keeping soundless time as it sliced through the room.

After a while the inspector thrust one gangly finger into the air. "But if this jacket was so important to Ravensmith that he would take it off to keep it clean, then why would he leave it behind after he had committed the crime?"

Oona blinked in surprise. "Very good, Inspector. Very, very good! I believe that deserves a bit of candy."

She reached into the pocket of her dress and extracted the piece of candy she had rescued from beneath the street. She tossed it at the inspector, who snatched it out of the air, beaming at her.

"The reason for the jacket remaining on the coatrack," Oona explained, "is the same reason that he failed to show up at his office today. His secretary informed us that Ravensmith is always at his office by nine o'clock sharp, without fail. But he was not there when we arrived today at nine thirty. And that is because Mr. Ravensmith never left Pendulum House."

"He what?" The inspector nearly dropped the candy as he fumbled with the wrapper.

"He is still there," Oona said. "Inside the closet."

Lamont John-Michael Arlington Fitch III took in a sharp breath. "Preposterous! Why would he remain in the closet?"

Oona strode nine paces across the room and stood beside Oswald the Great's painting. The inspector stepped aside as she stood on her tiptoes, raising her hand to Oswald's face, and snapped her fingers. The eyes blinked.

Several gasps filled the room.

"Is that you, Mr. Ravensmith?" Oona asked.

A voice emanated from the portrait. "I don't know what you are talking . . . ah . . . um . . ."

"Ravensmith?" the inspector said through a mouthful of candy. "What are you still doing in there?"

"It's simple," Oona said. "The latch on the inside of the door is old and rusted. It sticks. The closet is far too small for a full-grown man such as Mr. Ravensmith to be able to turn around and work it open, such as I was forced to do yesterday."

"Yes, yes, I did it!" Ravensmith called from behind the portrait. "I'll admit to all of it. Just someone get me out of here!"

"First you must speak the magical phrase," Oona said.

"Please!" cried Ravensmith.

"No, no, no," Oona said. "The *other* magical phrase, Mr. Ravensmith. The one that will return my uncle to his human form."

"Just let me go. You don't understand!" Mr. Ravensmith cried.

"No," Oona said calmly. "It's you who do not understand. First recite the phrase that will reverse the dagger's spell, or you can stay in there until the Glass Gates reopen."

Ravensmith gave a shuddering moan, and then uttered: "All right. The phrase is . . . is . . . 'Toadstool Pie.'"

There came a loud popping sound, and Oona whirled around to see her uncle lying on the ground, once again filling his Wizard's robes and fully restored to his human form.

He sat up, his eyes round and toadlike, but they were *his* eyes, Oona could tell, and relief flooded through her like a river.

"Well, well," the Wizard said after Samuligan had helped him to his feet. He poked his finger through the hole in his robe where the dagger had sliced through. "That was certainly interesting."

Oona ran to him, throwing her arms around him and squeezing him around the middle, feeling immensely grateful that he had actually used words and had not croaked like a toad.

"There, I did it!" Ravensmith cried through the portrait. "Now, someone please get me out of here. There is dust everywhere. And I have to go to the bathroom!"

CHAPTER TWENTY-EIGHT

Open for Business

They stood at the gate to Pendulum House: the Wizard, Samuligan, Deacon, and Oona, who felt as if her legs were about to give out on her.

Several clock towers tolled in the distance.

"Well, it's midnight," Oona said.

"He didn't show," Deacon said. "He may be a crook, but he's a smart man, that Red Martin."

The Wizard grinned. "Word spread rather quickly when Ravensmith was hauled off to jail, cursing Red Martin all the way to the police station for making no attempt to rescue him. Considering that the house was planned for demolition, I'm surprised Ravensmith remained silent in there so long. He put too much faith in Red Martin to save him. Clearly they were working together on the whole thing. Unfortunately, this is mostly my fault. When I began to run low on money several years ago, it was Ravensmith who suggested that I borrow from a private moneylender. I did not like the idea, but Ravensmith told me it was my only option, since the banks would not loan me any money . . . and I suppose I trusted the lawyer far more than he deserved. I sort of closed my eyes to it and just let it happen. I never read a single word of the legal contracts myself. I simply signed them blindly. All I knew was that it was through a company called Dupington. Ravensmith took care of the details. But I should have seen that he was a complete hypocrite. It was Ravensmith who encouraged me to take the loans . . . and then he would criticize me for spending the money as I wished. Of course he knew how much I disliked the subject of money. He set me up perfectly."

"What will happen now?" Deacon asked.

"Well, there will be a trial, of course," the Wizard said, "and Miss Sanora Crone will have to testify that Red Martin blackmailed the witches into stealing the daggers from the museum. Trials are tricky things, and Red Martin is clearly a clever man. How it will all turn out is anyone's guess."

"What about Red Martin's confession that he had

my father killed?" Oona asked. She felt a sharp twinge of anger at the memory. "The witches were all there. They all heard him say it."

"Let's hope that they all remember as clearly as you do," the Wizard said. "As I said, Red Martin is quite a tricky man. As you learned for yourself, Oona, he has the resources and know-how to slip through the Glass Gates to the Land of Faerie. No one else has ever managed to do that. I have a feeling he will be quite a difficult man to capture." The wrinkles about the Wizard's eyes sagged, and his face drew out in an expression of deep regret. "Had I known that I was borrowing money from the very scoundrel behind my brother's death, I would never have allowed myself to be convinced to borrow the money in the first place; no matter how much I trusted Ravensmith. I hope you know that, Oona dear."

Oona nodded. She could not blame her uncle for being duped. He was a trusting sort of person, and that was one of the things about him she loved. But she could not help herself from saying: "Perhaps you should be more careful about what you sign, Uncle."

The Wizard gave her a knowing grin. "Oh, I will. I hope you will be careful as well, Oona dear."

Oona smiled back, remembering the document on the table and how her hand had tingled when she'd placed the pen to the bottom of the page.

Samuligan said: "But now that the Wizard has returned, Red Martin certainly won't be able to get his hands on Pendulum House. At least I won't be needing to polish that scoundrel's boots."

"That is definitely a relief," Deacon said rather dryly. Samuligan gave him a wicked smile, and Deacon shivered on Oona's shoulder.

The Wizard clapped his hands together. "What would you all say to joining the festivities at the park? It is only midnight, and the masquerade is just getting started. I believe a little frivolity is in order."

Oona's heart fumbled at the mention of the park. She wasn't so sure she was ready for that. She was just about to tell her uncle how she felt when a boy stepped into the light of the nearby streetlamp, removing his masquerade mask as he did so.

"I came to see if there's anything I could do," said Adler Iree. Dressed in a fine, formal tuxedo, he stood beside the streetlamp, the multicolored tattoos on his face glinting in the light.

Oona smiled at him, her heart quickening in her chest. The boy cleaned up nicely, and even with his insistence on wearing that ratty old top hat, Oona felt sure that the contrast made him all the more handsome.

She considered him for a moment before saying: "There *is* something you can do, Mr. Iree."

Adler smiled, the tattoos crinkling above his cheeks.

"And what would that be, Miss Crate?" he asked.

Oona frowned, though the frown did not reach her eyes. "Why . . . Adler . . . I should think it quite obvious."

When Adler's eyebrows pinched together, betraying his confusion, Oona shook her head and was quite surprised by her own words.

"You may escort me to the masquerade, silly," she said. "You really must work on your powers of deduction."

Samuligan tipped his hat back on his head and examined Oona with his sharp faerie eyes. "Surely you cannot attend the ball in that dress."

Oona looked down at the green dress she had changed into earlier. The color matched her eyes perfectly, yet truth be told, Samuligan was right. It was a rather simple dress for the likes of a masquerade.

Samuligan grabbed hold of the skirt in his long fingers. For half a moment she thought he was going to tear it, but instead, the faerie servant clucked his tongue against the side of his mouth and clicked his teeth. An instant later Samuligan stepped back, and Oona's dress seemed to glow. It was still the same shade of green, but now the color of the dress seemed somehow alive, pulsing and moving, glittering hypnotically at the simplest movement.

Adler Iree gasped when he looked at her.

"You've enchanted the dress, Samuligan," Oona said, running her hand along the silky fabric. She whirled around, and the feeling against her skin was like that of falling rain. "Glinting cloth," she said.

"You may want this as well," the Wizard said, and produced from his robes a mask that perfectly matched the dress.

Oona held the mask for a long moment as if lost.

"What's the matter?" the Wizard asked. "Don't you like it?"

Oona sighed. It wasn't that she didn't like it. It was just that, now, more than ever, she wondered if she had made the right decision to give up the apprenticeship. She wished she could just let it go, which, after all, seemed the sensible thing to do, but ever since using the magic again, she'd begun to feel quite doubtful that she would ever be able to do so. Never before had she understood what a significant part of her the magic was. It was dangerous, true, but it was also extraordinary and could, in the end, prove quite helpful.

The Wizard seemed to know precisely what she was thinking. He placed a hand on her shoulder and said: "You know . . . if you want to give the apprenticeship one more go around, the position is still available."

Oona swallowed a stone-size lump in her throat.

She remembered her uncle's words from the day before: *You have backbone, my dear. A spirit I can only admire. It is a spirit that would serve this seat well. The things you could do.*

She thought she understood better what he had meant. There was much she could do that no one else could. Perhaps it would be different now that she understood herself a little better. And yet, another part of her was just not interested in that old life. That other part of her had its own plans. She bit at her lip, wondering why she could not simply make up her mind. It was entirely illogical.

Finally, she asked: "Could I start my detective business *and* be the apprentice at the same time?"

The Wizard scratched thoughtfully at his beard and then grinned wider than Oona had seen him do in years. "I don't see why not. It could all be worked out, I'm sure . . . but perhaps you should think on it for a while. You don't have to make a decision this instant."

Oona nodded. "I think I already have." She peered up at Pendulum House and the sign that had been erected there in the front yard.

FUTURE SITE OF INDULGENCE ISLAND HOTEL AND CASINO

She removed her magnifying glass from her pocket and aimed it at the sign. *"Deleo!"* she said.

A line of mist shot from the lens, swooping across the front of the sign and wiping it clean of letters and image. Deacon ruffled his feathers on her shoulder.

"That's going to take some getting used to," he said. "The whole magic thing."

But Oona appeared not to have heard him. She stood silently, considering the sign for a long moment. Finally, her eyes brightened, and once again she aimed the magnifying glass, and uttered: *"Advertisum correcto!"* A second burst of mist sprayed the sign, and when it had cleared, she stood back to appraise her work.

"Very good," said Adler.

"Yes," agreed Samuligan. He tipped back his cowboy hat so that he might take the sign in better.

The Wizard beamed, and read aloud:

PENDULUM HOUSE

HOME OF THE WIZARD OF DARK STREET

AND

THE DARK STREET DETECTIVE AGENCY

OPEN FOR BUSINESS

"I still think it's a rather plain name," said Deacon. "Perhaps something with a bit more pizzazz?"

"Don't be ridiculous, Deacon," Oona said. "It's perfectly sensible."

She placed her arm in the crook of Adler Iree's, and the five of them began to make their way down the street in the direction of Oswald Park and the festivities of the masquerade. Oona's pulse quickened at the thought of setting foot inside the park. She wondered if she was making a mistake. Perhaps they would get there and she would be unable to enter the gates. Perhaps she would turn and run back up the street to Pendulum House and hide in her room. Or maybe, just maybe, she would enter the park . . . and enjoy herself.

It was a mystery worth solving.

ACKNOWLEDGMENTS

It takes a lot of people to make something like this happen. Firstly, I would like to thank my editor, Greg Ferguson, whose exceptional insight and guidance were key in helping this mysterious book come fully to life, and Nico Medina, for his marvelous attention to detail. Thank you to all of the amazing folks at Egmont USA—from Elizabeth Law and Doug Pocock to Regina Griffin, Alison Weiss, Rob Guzman, Mary Albi, and all the editing staff and sales and marketing team—for helping me put Oona's story into book form. Thank you to my wonderful agent, Catherine Drayton, for her marvelous perspectives and unfailing support. Also, much thanks and love to my mother, who is nearly always my first reader, and the first to tell me if it works or not. Thanks to all of the early readers for their invaluable feedback, and last, but certainly not least, I thank my wife, Shari, who has taken such good care of me. It is because of that love and care that this story is where it is today. I know that. I feel truly blessed.

Continue the magic and mystery of Dark Street
as Oona Crate tries to solve a new case in

THE MAGICAN'S TOWER!

PROLOGUE

On the sixth of March, 1852, historian
Arthur Blackstone gave the following speech to the Historical
Society in New York City.

> "Like the hour hand on a clock, Dark Street spins through
> the Drift. It spirals endlessly within the space between two
> worlds. At the north end of the street stands an enormous
> gateway, the famed Iron Gates, which open for precisely
> one minute every night, upon the stroke of midnight,
> exposing the street to New York City. At the opposite
> end of the street stand the equally massive Glass Gates,
> the gateway to the Land of Faerie, which have remained
> locked for hundreds of human years, and are the only
> things keeping the Queen of the Fay and her unspeak-
> able army of faerie warriors from murdering us all; the
> gates . . . and the Wizard."

In June of 1853, Blackstone released his book *The Last Faerie Road: An Incomplete History of Dark Street*. It sold fewer than one hundred copies, and, unfortunately for Mr. Blackstone's New York publishers, no one took the book very seriously.

Fellow historians mocked the idea that such a fantastical place as Dark Street might exist at all: a place with candlestick trees and joke-telling clocks, not to mention a Museum of Magical History and a graveyard where spirits come awake in the night. The notion of a magical world so close to New York—one with a Wizard living in an enchanted manor house in the middle of the street—seemed nothing short of ridiculous to the serious scholars and scientific minds of the mid-1800s. And though Blackstone claimed that the street was filled primarily with ordinary people of no magical abilities at all, the premise was too far-fetched to be believed. The book was quickly forgotten by the academics, and would be remembered only by a handful of poets and artists, who themselves viewed the book, for the most part, as the ramblings of an overactive imagination.

On Dark Street, however, the book remained an acclaimed best seller for years to come.

CHAPTER ONE

The Party

(Sunday, August 19, 1877)

The contest is about to begin," said the Wizard. He pointed a wrinkled finger toward the far end of the outdoor party.

A short man in a top hat slowly ascended the steps to a makeshift stage, at the rear of which stood an oddly shaped tower. Round in some sections and square in others, the tower rose like a misshapen shadow from the center of Oswald Park. The pointy pyramid at the top of the tower was scarcely visible through the misty clouds several hundred feet above. At the edge of the stage, dozens of evenly spaced tables flickered in the evening lamplight, each surrounded by flawlessly dressed party-goers.

Murmurs of polite conversation filled the night air, and thirteen-year-old Oona Crate leaned back in her seat, arms folded, lost in thought. She hardly heard her uncle's words, nor did she pay much attention to the man ascending the steps.

Of all the attendees at the party, Oona was certain that it was she alone who felt uncomfortable with the evening's festivities being located in Oswald Park. Named after Oswald the Great—the most powerful of the long-dead Magicians of Old—the enormous park was where the tragedy had happened over three years ago: the accident that had taken the lives of both Oona's mother and baby sister, leaving Oona with the grievous knowledge that it was her own misguided spell that had killed them. Ever since, the park had been a dreaded place for her. A place to avoid at all costs.

But three months ago something extraordinary had happened . . .

Fresh from the excitement of solving the most difficult case of her life—a baffling mystery involving the disappearance of her uncle, the Wizard—Oona had decided to face her fear and attend the Dark Street Annual Midnight Masquerade. It had been the first time she'd set foot on the park's grassy grounds since the day the magic had flown out of her control. It had also been the first time Oona had danced with a boy.

The night of the dance had been magical, the boy gentlemanly and handsome, and afterward, as they took their leave, she had thought that she was finally finished with her guilt over her mother's and sister's deaths once and for all. Three months later, however, she realized that she had been dreadfully wrong.

Tonight was Oona's second visit to the park since the accident, and unfortunately for her, she had no dance and no boy to distract her from her thoughts.

Images of the tragedy buzzed in and out of her mind like pestering flies: the sparks shooting from her improvised magic wand, the Lights of Wonder upending the tree and slamming it to the ground, her own panicked cry as the impact hurtled her through the air while Mother and Flora were crushed beneath the tree's massive trunk.

She did her best to shoo the thoughts away, concentrating instead on the contest that was about to begin—the famous Magician's Tower Contest that took place once every five years—but even Oona's excitement about the upcoming competition failed to ease her heart completely. She shook her head, casting around for something solid to hold her attention.

Give me facts! she thought, and pulled her focus to her surroundings.

The tables were set with the finest of crystal and china, the food and drink of the highest caliber. Oona had been to high-society gatherings before—her uncle was extremely fond of parties—but she had not seen so many of the street's wealthy residents in one place since the night of the masquerade three months ago.

She fidgeted with the sleeve of her dress, a high-collared gray-and-white gown, more formal than she was used to wearing. The dress was by no means as extravagant as the dresses worn by the girls from the Academy of Fine Young Ladies, nor was her jewelry as stylish or shiny, but Oona had an idea that it was more than her attire that caused the party guests to glance discreetly in her direction. Oona was something of a celebrity on the street, after all: the youngest Wizard's apprentice in over a hundred years, and it was no secret that she was a Natural Magician: the rarest and most powerful form of magician there was.

As Oona had discovered for herself, it was because of the ancient faerie blood that ran through her veins that her own magic was so incredibly powerful. The deaths of her mother and sister were common knowledge, and rumors of her ability to perform extraordinary magical tasks— most of which were simply untrue—traveled up and down the street like leaves blown from doorstep to doorstep.

The latest rumor Oona had heard was that she had turned her uncle into a toad when he had told her to brush her teeth. Simply absurd.

First of all, she thought, *Uncle Alexander has never needed to remind me to brush my teeth, because brushing one's teeth is simply the logical way of keeping them from rotting out of one's head.* Thus, it followed that Oona needed no reminders. *And secondly,* she thought, *Uncle Alexander may have indeed been turned into a toad, but that was nearly three months ago, and it was not my doing!* This was also true. It had been her uncle's lawyer, Mr. Ravensmith—in cahoots with Dark Street's most notorious criminal mastermind, Red Martin—who had done the abhorrent deed. *And thirdly,* she thought, *I never use magic if I can help it.* Despite her recent return to the position of Wizard's apprentice, the truth was that, in Oona's opinion, magic remained highly unpredictable.

And if all of this wasn't enough to justify the uncomfortable stares, then there was the fact that Oona was the only person with a raven on her shoulder—and a talking raven at that. But of this, Oona did not care what people thought. Deacon was not only Oona's closest companion, but also a wealth of facts and highly useful information.

"Welcome, welcome, welcome!" cried the man on the stage. The chatter of party guests tapered off, and all eyes turned to observe the squat man at the front of the stage. He wore a tight-fitting suit and a top hat nearly as tall as he was. His small eyes took in the well-to-do onlookers. "Welcome to the Magician's Tower. I am Nathaniel Tempest, the tower architect."

A round of applause began. Oona did not join in.

"I don't know if I'd be so proud of that," she whispered to Deacon.

The tower swayed precariously in the breeze, giving the impression it might topple at any moment. The middle portion leaned south, rising slantwise for nearly thirty feet before overcorrecting and tilting north. A set of rickety steps corkscrewed around the outside, and near the seventh floor the entire structure bulged out like a great serpent swallowing an egg. The sound of creaking wood could be heard from as far away as the Iron Gates.

"Look at that monstrosity of a building," Oona half whispered.

Deacon stifled a laugh as the Wizard gave her a disapproving glance from his seat beside her. Dressed in his traditional hood and robe, the Wizard made an imposing figure, as was befitting the head of all magical activity on Dark Street. Oona considered him for a moment. Despite the fact that the only living magicians on the street were the Wizard himself and Oona, the position was still highly respected in the community, and one day, Oona knew, it would belong to her.

"Once every five years," the man in the top hat continued, "a new tower is constructed, and a new contest begun. It is a contest that stretches back hundreds of years. Anyone brave enough to enter"—the man paused to gesture toward a slanted door at the base of the tower— "will have a chance at solving the first day's challenges . . . but only the first four contestants to make it through the trials will move on to the second day's challenge. After that, two more challenges a day will be offered: a test of the mind and a test of the physical kind. Each day the last contestant to finish will be eliminated, until there are only two left. On the fourth and last day of the contest, both finalists will have an opportunity to solve the final challenge, at the tower's pinnacle; a task so difficult that, in its entire history, it has never been accomplished."

The crowd was silent. Heads tilted back, and all eyes stared up at the pyramid at the very top of the tower. It swayed dauntingly in the night air, barely visible against the night sky. It reminded Oona of the Goblin Tower in the Dark Street Cemetery, at the top of which she had rescued her uncle from imprisonment, except that the Magician's Tower in front of her appeared as if it might crumble at any moment, and the Goblin Tower had stood for nearly five hundred years.

"The contest begins tomorrow at noon!" the man cried. "I am the only one who knows its secrets, and the challenges that lay inside." He held up a leather satchel. "Only I hold the plans and the answers to the puzzles that await those brave few."

Again a round of applause filled the park, and this time Oona clapped along. Indeed, of everyone at the gathering, it was Oona who clapped the most enthusiastically. Here at last was a challenge she could embrace. As much as she disliked admitting it, her new detective business had been rather slow to catch on. She'd had only two cases in the last three months, one of them involving a missing nail file, and the other, a six-year-old girl who had hired Oona to discover the truth surrounding the existence of something called the Easter Bunny. It was most embarrassing.

But now, finally, here was a worthy challenge. The famous Magician's Tower Contest.

"Please enjoy the rest of the party," the architect said over the applause before descending the stage steps and mingling with the partygoers.

The Wizard turned to Oona. "I take it that you plan to participate in this fiasco."

"I do indeed, Uncle," Oona said. "Not only participate, but win."

"And what is the point?" Deacon asked from her shoulder.

Oona shook her head. "The point, my dearest Deacon, is to be the first. To solve the game. To overcome the mystery. What further point is needed?"

"Well, I suppose I can relieve you of your apprentice

duties for the four days of the contest," the Wizard said. "I can get Samuligan to cover for you."

Oona grinned appreciatively. Samuligan, the Pendulum House faerie servant, would be more than equal to the task.

The Wizard glanced in the direction of the table closest to their own, his face sticking out of his hood and exposing a bumpy nose and a long gray beard. Oona turned as well, drawn in by a loud voice at the neighboring table. The voice was that of Sir Baltimore Rutherford, one of the most well-known men of Dark Street high society. A handsome man in his mid-fifties, with thick sideburns and prominent brow, Sir Baltimore waved a pungent cigar in the air, and was laughing heartily at his own joke. The occupants at his table were riveted.

"As I was saying," Sir Baltimore boomed, "when I was a boy, a few years older than my son Roderick is— where is Roderick, anyway? Probably off with that new girlfriend of his. That boy's got more girls pining for him than I'd care to count. But when I was about his age, I, too, participated in the tower contest, and I made it to the top. There were just two of us left: myself and Bradford Crate."

Oona's heart lurched. She of course knew that her father—the former head inspector of the Dark Street Police Department—had participated in the tower contest, but she had not learned this fact from the man himself. Or if she had, then she had been too young to remember. The fact remained that her full knowledge of her father's youthful adventures in the contest had come from research in books. The thought saddened her. Indeed, there was so much about her father that she did not know, and would most likely never know; the bullet fired from the barrel of a thief's gun had made sure of that nearly three years ago. The loss of her father, only months before losing her mother and sister, had been like a terrible earthquake, shaking Oona's world down to its foundations.